Rhif/No. _____ Dosb./Class _____ F

Dylid dychwelyd neu adnewyddu'r eitem erbyn neu cyn y dyddiad a nodir uchod.
Oni wneir hyn gellir codi tal.

This book is to be returned or renewed on or before the last date stamped above,
otherwise a charge may be made.

GW 600240

D0364556

Glockenspiel

Also by Pauline Bell

The Dead Do Not Praise
Feast into Mourning
No Pleasure in Death
The Way of a Serpent
Downhill to Death
Sleeping Partners
A Multitude of Sins
Blood Ties
Stalker
Reasonable Death
Swansong
Nothing but the Truth
Funeral Expenses
Under Fire

GLOCKENSPIEL

Pauline Bell

Constable • London

Constable & Robinson Ltd
3 The Lanchesters
162 Fulham Palace Road
London W6 9ER
www.constablerobinson.com

First published in the UK by Constable,
an imprint of Constable & Robinson, 2009

A copy of the British Library Cataloguing in Publication
Data is available from the British Library

ISBN: 978-1-84529-869-2

Printed and bound in the EU

PEFC/16-33-111
CATG-PEFC-052
www.pefc.org

For M.E.S

with love

Prologue

Apart from on market day, it is difficult to distinguish the seasons in Brick Lane. Summer and winter, spring and autumn, paint peels from the same doors behind which the same fast food vendors serve the same curries. Perhaps the quality of the air varies slightly. In the wet season, it slides into the lungs more easily. In dry weather, the dust tickles, making young men sneeze and old men cough. Now it was May and a fickle sun glinted, at least on the bodywork and windows of the cars that were merely passing through.

This morning, two vehicles obscured the frontage of Aladdin's Restaurant. The computer salesman occupying the larger and smarter of them was pleased with life. His last bonus had contributed significantly to the cost of this new Volvo he was sitting in. With any luck, the deal he had concluded yesterday would buy his fiancée-to-be the ring she deserved – well, the one she expected, anyway.

Even better, his business here in London had been concluded a day earlier than expected and he was booked into his comfortable hotel for one more night. No one would begrudge him a day's sightseeing before he returned to the hassles of his office in the Midlands. The fat mogul who had signed away a mini-fortune yesterday had also introduced him to some of the capital's more splendid sights. He had had his fill of Westminster. Now, he would have a look at the East End. And, if this street was typical, it appealed to him. All around him were black faces and bustle. Four-storey buildings on either side of him were exotic eating houses at ground level. The myriad businesses on the levels above advertised their presence with illuminated signs and bright banners. Further along, where the shop windows came to an end, stretches of bare wall had been adorned with primitive art, carelessly executed, chiefly with a spray can, but with a keen eye for colour and balance. It overwhelmed him. Everything screamed for his attention.

He blinked, then took out and skim-read the pamphlet his mogul had given him. Running off Brick Lane, where he was parked, was Chicksand Street where Bram Stoker was supposed to have stayed on his way back to Transylvania. And then, these were the streets where most of Jack the Ripper's victims had lived. Somewhere here, too, was the famous Beigel Bakery that opened twenty-four hours a day . . .

The young man reached for his map to pinpoint the street names he had been given. What a pity that he would have to go back to Leicester before the Sunday market.

It was a vain regret. He would not be leaving London for a considerable time.

In front of the Volvo, PC Chris Buchan reached into the glove compartment of the six-year-old Mondeo that had been issued to him, took out a Mars bar and decided that you could have too much of a good thing. Not of Mars bars, of course. It was Whitechapel that he had had enough of and, in particular, Brick Lane.

Normally, he liked the place. You could get a good cheap meal here and they'd let you take in your own beer to wash it down. He'd read somewhere, recently, that there were twenty-four curry houses in Brick Lane. According to the article, this particular bit of east London had been renamed Bangla Town by the local community. Well, that was nothing compared with what he had heard some of his colleagues call it. Someone had told him that the Bangladeshis had first come here as seamen. They'd practised their cooking skills on the boats, then opened lodging houses here that had become the first Asian restaurants in Britain.

PC Buchan specially liked the ones around the junction with Hanbury Street. That's where he'd celebrate when Tariq Aziz was safely behind bars. Meanwhile, he screwed up his chocolate wrapper and continued his surveillance. The curries – and the Mars bars – had added to his present discomfort. The Mondeo's worn leather driving seat was soft and yielding but not wide enough to leave his ample buttocks room to wriggle.

During the full hour he had been sitting here, his state of mind had progressed from resentment, through boredom, to a rising anxiety. The resentment had been on his son's account. Until the call from his operations leader had come, he had planned to watch the lad play his first game for their local cricket team – first of the season for the team too. A message from an informant had changed all that. Tariq was making a trip to Birmingham. At a hurried briefing, PC Buchan had been instructed to follow him, find out who his quarry was meeting and where. That he would enjoy. It was the present inactivity that was getting to him.

He looked up and met the suspicious eye of an Asian youth, just a couple of yards from the car. The boy leaned on a railing. Its peeling paint was the same vile green as the slime that collected on the surface of stagnant ponds. Seeing that he had managed to disconcert him, the youth moved along with the glimmer of a satisfied smile. PC Buchan's resentment was back in full force. His leader had an Asian team at his disposal. Any member of it would look and feel less conspicuous than a chubby white constable who had even been issued with a huge earpiece as his only means of contacting the rest of his team. Anybody with half a mind would know him for what he was. He wasn't allowed any body armour but he was thankful for his gun. He took it out of its safe now and placed it beside him on the passenger seat, draping his spare sweater over it. They'd all been told in training that they could self-arm if they felt compromised, and he did.

He was not ashamed of feeling scared. In PC Buchan's opinion, any policeman who said he was never afraid was either a fool or a liar. He well knew that he had not been picked out for surveillance training because of his fearless-ness. He'd been picked for his driving – and possibly for his public school education. Even if Tariq suddenly appeared out of the door his crew mate Sheldon was guarding, it would be Buck and not Shelly who'd be at the wheel when the journey began. His crew mates said that on the road he had the luck of the devil, but they were wrong. It was skill and quick reactions that enabled him to tail any customer on the road. His operations leader called it his motorway misbehaviour. PC Buchan liked that description better.

He'd feel better for a chat to Shelly right now but there was nothing to say. He could hardly ask him whether he could possibly have missed seeing Tariq leaving through the back door. He groped in the glove compartment again and took out a second Mars bar. His teeth were bored! He'd be fine when the tailing started and he could keep his mind on the road.

Up a small side street Buchan saw a derelict house, half shielded by a wall daubed in white graffiti. His attention had been drawn to it by a movement in one of the win-dowless holes on the first floor. It was unlikely that Tariq could have got himself across there but might he have set someone to watch out for his watchers?

PC Buchan shook his head and concentrated afresh on the New Shalamar Restaurant that Tariq had entered over an hour ago. He liked the building. With its blue lettering on its orange signboard above the red sun canopy, it was garish but cheerful. It was a pity about the greasy paper wrappers blowing across the shop front. After a minute the door opened. In a burst of the wailing Eastern music that half irritated and half fascinated him, two Asian women appeared, in bright silks, gold-trimmed. They too stared suspiciously at him before turning away and walking behind him. He watched them through his mirror for a few seconds but they didn't turn. When he looked back to the Shalamar the door had closed.

He turned quickly, the stiffened muscles of his buttocks protesting, startled by a tap on the driver's side window. Another Asian youth stood in the middle of the road, peering at him through the glass. He held a folded map in the hand that was not tapping. The lad looked harmless enough. Besides, refusing to acknowledge him would look strange, draw attention and possibly compromise the operation. A little reluctantly, Buchan depressed the window button. Immediately, the map was thrust through, followed by the boy's other hand which now wielded a mini club. It struck Buchan on the temple.

Their eyes met for a moment, each of them knowing that the site of the blow was well chosen. Darkness began to swirl behind Buchan's eyes, but the force had been misjudged. Buchan was stunned and disorientated but certainly still conscious. The boy seemed to be deciding how to proceed and what to steal. Buchan was expecting no assistance from Joe Public, but his clouded mind wondered whether he could get the car into gear and moving. He decided against it. He would have to risk injuring an innocent passer-by. His blurred vision and dizziness would not allow him to steer safely.

He felt the youth's hands searching his pockets. When he heard a gasp and an expletive, he knew he was lost. The youth had found his warrant card. A moment later he had also found the gun. Buchan shut his eyes, waited and heard not a shot but a shout. He had misjudged Joe Public. He was grateful but dismayed, seeing the outcome a split second before it arrived. The youth turned and delivered the bullet that put an end to his would-be rescuer.

Buchan waited calmly for the second deafening report. He never heard it. The assault on his own chest put an end to his fading consciousness before his ears could register it.

11

Chapter One

On the same day, in the town of Cloughton in West Yorkshire, Detective Chief Inspector Benedict Mitchell heaved a sigh of relief as he eventually drew away from the house. His wife, four children and what seemed like half of their combined possessions had been packed fairly comfortably into the new Volkswagen Caravelle. This journey would convince Ginny that the cost of the vehicle would be well justified by the convenience. The baggage now included Michael's painting 'for Grandad', remembered at the last minute and retrieved by Caitlin, their second child and their family's minder. Who else would have known where to find it?

Caitlin was glad to have done her younger brother this service but was unimpressed by his artwork. She displayed the garish splodges of red, green and purple and demanded, 'What's it supposed to be?'

Placid Michael accepted this as a polite and interested question. 'It's a car . . . nivorous underwater spiky tadpole.' He surveyed his achievement critically. 'It was a dragon to begin with but it got a bit long for a dragon.'

His mother said, 'Yes, I can see that.' She took the vital piece of paper into safekeeping. As she turned she caught sight of her elder son, sitting, silent and gloomy, in the rear seat. 'All right, Declan?'

Declan shrugged. 'There would have been room for my glockenspiel in this car.'

'True, but not in Grandad's flat once the six of us have invaded it.'

'We won't fit in even without the glock now that we've all grown.'

Sinead pulled a face at Michael. 'Silly! You know Grandad's got a new flat and it's huge.'

'He's not silly. It's not silly to forget something.' Sinead should know better by now than to insult Michael in Caitlin's presence. 'Anyway, none of us has seen it so you don't know how big it is.'

As they entered the slip road on to the motorway Declan began to organize a game. This was not particularly good news. His games were of his own devising and rules were invented as they were needed. As Mitchell had expected, a quarrel soon broke out and everyone waited for nine-year-old Caitlin to smooth things over. When the recriminations continued unchecked, Virginia saw, through the central mirror, that the child was oblivious to them. She had been sitting hunched forward in an attempt to hear her parents' muted conversation and seemed to have picked up at least some impression of it. 'Is Daddy going to work with Grandad in the Met?'

Virginia was thankful for the form that the question had taken. It could be answered truthfully with a no.

'So, why did you say . . .?'

'We were having a private talk. You know it's rude to listen in.'

'Actually, you listen in to ours.' This reasonable objection from the rear was acknowledged and apologized for.

Virginia and Mitchell grinned at each other. At least Declan had temporarily forgotten about the glock. They abandoned their discussion and switched on the radio. Radio 4 came on. Declan requested Radio 3. Virginia sighed, compromised with Classic FM and wondered where this changeling musician they had produced had come by his genes.

A request programme was in progress. A listener asked to hear a Bach minuet which they all recognized as a piece that Declan had recently been given to practise on the piano. He bore well his siblings' unflattering comparisons of his performance with the one they were hearing now. The Mitchell parents were glad when the programme broke off on the half-hour to give the news. The weather was currently cool and bright but the forecast promised high winds. At their present rate of progress, the family should be off the road before the rough weather arrived.

The headlines followed and everyone listened as the newsreader described a shooting in east London in which a computer salesman had been killed as he was going to the aid of a fellow motorist. The other victim, a police constable, was in a critical condition, suffering from a bullet wound to the chest. Mitchell let the report continue. It was impossible to keep their children from knowing the kind of work he did. As tiny children, they'd accepted their family situation as normal, but now even the six-year-old twins were developing some idea of the danger their father faced. The children were proud both of it and of him and, with the exception of Declan, seemed not to brood too much on the situation. Perhaps they thought he was invincible.

It was, of course, Declan who asked, 'Is that where Grandad's flat is?'

Again Virginia was glad to give a truthful answer. 'No. It's miles and miles away.' Declan knew his relations were not immune to danger but she thought that his anxiety had little to do with their circumstances. It was in his nature to worry. At this moment he was probably equally concerned about the safety of his grandfather and the possibility that being deprived of his glockenspiel for a week would render him unable to play the piece he had been practising for the past month in order to play it as 'guest performer' at their local senior citizens' orchestra concert.

Safe or in danger, it occurred to Virginia that the children would see little enough of their grandfather on this visit.

Holidays for detective superintendents in the Metropolitan Police Force would be swept aside in the event of a colleague's murder.

PC Buchan was struggling to force his mind to take over his wounded matter. He shouldn't be slumped here feeling sorry for himself. He had to get out of the car and find help. The Asian tourist who couldn't find Covent Garden had smashed his earpiece and stuck something in his chest – and someone who had tried to come to his assistance was lying in the street, bleeding. But it had got so dark and foggy that he couldn't see through the windscreen or even find the car door handle. What was he doing in this car anyway? He'd promised young Callum that he'd watch his match, the first of the season and his trial for the first team. Not that there would be much cricket played in this fog. He shook his head to clear it but, strangely, it seemed to make the fog thicker.

Suddenly a black face was thrust in front of his own. Well, he'd be damned! The arrogant beggar was still hanging about, deciding whether to finish him off. Could he summon up the strength to grab him, to detain him, injure him, keep him here till help came . . .?

His superhuman effort certainly achieved a strangled yelp. Mr Wasim Shah, who an hour or so ago had skilfully removed a bullet from Buchan's chest and had come to check on his patient's present condition, had been rewarded for his concern with a painful blow between the eyes from Buchan's fist.

It had been arranged that the Mitchells' first night in London should not be spent as Browne's guests. They had justified the extravagance of the night's accommodation in various ways. Virginia's father's leave would not begin until the following day. They had been surprised by the

15

enthusiasm with which he had described to them in emails and telephone calls the details of his search for a bigger, more convenient flat. It seemed churlish to settle themselves into his new home whilst he was working and deprive him of the pleasure of showing them round it. Then Mitchell had decided that a night spent in the plush surroundings of a good London hotel would be an educational experience for the children, as well as a treat for his wife.

Virginia had laughed and protested that the plan would give the youngsters ideas above their station, then had unaccountably announced, 'If we're going to do it, then it's the Ritz or nothing.' Mitchell had blinked and retorted that what it had given her was ideas beyond his income. Virginia, having verified the cost of her proposal for the six of them, had hurriedly withdrawn her demand and a more modest option had been peaceably settled on.

The news of the east London shootings had led to their arrangements being further modified. The crime had been committed in Hotel Tango – Met-speak for the area around Brick Lane. Detective Superintendent Tom Browne, Virginia's father, would be heading the investigation. They feared that his evening would not include any socializing and that he would ring to cancel their invitation to share a family meal in the hotel restaurant. The expected call came with slightly better news. If his daughter and son-in-law could postpone their supper until ten, he would be there.

The children were not pleased, but allowed themselves to be consoled with chicken nuggets and chocolate ice cream. The splendour of the dining room awed them and the quaint costumes and manners of the waiters' old-fashioned service so amused Sinead that Caitlin admonished her. 'It's a good job Grandad Tom's not here. He'd be ashamed of you.' Sinead had immediately stopped laughing and Virginia had smiled to herself. Her elder daughter had for some time taken it on herself to be responsible for the twins. Her three siblings had never seemed to resent her interference and Virginia was grateful to be saved from the role of nagging mother.

Browne arrived promptly at ten, telling them that his leave was cancelled. They would have to make the most of his company tonight and find their own way around the capital for the rest of the week. They were glad to do so, relieved to see how much happier he looked since his last visit to them the previous Christmas. The uncharacteristic depressed expression he had worn since the tragic, early and long-drawn-out death of Virginia's mother some time ago had disappeared. As he talked his face expressed a mixture of delight in their company, enthusiasm over the plans for his new home and a suppressed excitement about his new case.

At this hour, the dining room was almost empty, though the bar was full. Family news was exchanged as food was speedily produced and gratefully consumed since none of the three had eaten since lunchtime. As Mitchell asked the waiter for drinks for the rest of the evening to be sent up to their room, Virginia resigned herself to an exhaustive analysis of the shooting incident. When they were settled in the fat armchairs arranged in a semicircle, their backs to the huge bay window of their bed-sitting room, she signalled her acquiescence by asking, 'Do you get a night's sleep before you start on your new case?'

Her father grinned. 'It nearly wasn't my case.'

Mitchell frowned. 'But it's right in the middle of your ground.'

'Yes, but the live victim was sitting in a soft skin car – a Mondeo – surveilling for Special Branch.' He turned to his daughter. 'Surveilling means –'

'Yes, I know. Keeping tabs on a suspect, probably a terrorist.'

Mitchell interrupted. 'The live victim? So, you've got the officer as a witness?'

'Well, he's breathing. The bullet's out of his chest and he's strong enough to have given his surgeon a swollen

17

nose.' Browne grinned at Mitchell's puzzled expression. 'I don't know all the story yet but the doctors have no idea how soon we can question him or whether we'll be able to make any sense out of what he says.'

'So who was he after?'

'A Muslim, Tariq Aziz, living in Luton. He's a recruiter and facilitator for the movement of arms, people, intelligence – you name it. We've had our eye on him for more than a year now. The Met got a whisper that he wants to meet a man in Birmingham. We passed it on to Special Branch and Buchan's ops leader told him to follow Tariq there and find out who he was going to meet. He was to take an extra team to follow the contact . . .'

'So where were they – these extras?' Virginia was finding the conversation more interesting than she had expected.

'Round the back of the building that they'd all seen Tariq enter. They saw nothing. They heard the shots, of course, but couldn't leave their post. The noise might just have been a diversion to distract both cars.'

Mitchell rejoined the conversation after refilling glasses. 'So Buchan is . . . what?'

'He was a lid, recruited into Special Branch for surveillance. They say he was arrogant but good.'

'So, the tip couldn't be used and this Tariq has gone underground? You've lost him?' Virginia sounded disappointed.

Her father shook his head. 'Not completely. The team has quite a substantial file on him now. They know what he looks like and his address but there's no point in picking him up. He's more use to them on the loose until they've enough evidence to establish an allegation. The team is particularly interested in a list of mail-drop locations.'

'You mean a sort of terrorist poste restante?'

Browne grinned. 'Exactly. Buchan's brief was just to come back with as much information as he could get but this centre for messages could lead the team to the terrorists' drop orders for equipment or instructions for operations or cells or codes to be used. He was to find out what and where the mail drops are. He was supposed to let the procedure carry on but intercept what went out.'

Virginia was now out of her depth. 'How was he supposed to do all that?'

Browne shrugged. 'They weren't going to tell me that. I'm just a Met detective. You can imagine how useful it would be to be able to crack their codes though.'

'So, they don't want you queering their pitch.' Mitchell was disappointed. Since his father-in-law's account had begun he had been looking forward to a bird's-eye view of how terrorist gunmen were hunted down. He added, hopefully, 'But you said it nearly wasn't your case? So they are letting you in?'

Browne shook his head. 'They're pulling out. They've spent the day trawling the street for video cameras and watching miles of film. Some of it shows very clearly what happened. For reasons that appear convincing to them, they've decided that the killer is not the man they're after. What he did rescued Tariq from Special Branch's clutches but what we have is a simple robbery and murder investigation. That, of course, is my pigeon.'

'Simple is the operative word if you've got clear film of your villain committing his crimes.'

'Well, clear film of his jeans and hooded jacket. He'd have to dress like that, of course. You get stared at if you're not a hoodie in Brick Lane.'

'So, why are they so sure that it's not Tariq?'

'They said, if it was, he must have had access to a quick-acting growth hormone . . .'

The bantering stopped as the door opened to admit an uninvited visitor with staring, unseeing eyes. Virginia rose and went to him, taking him by the hand and leading him back into the adjoining room. Browne frowned. 'Still sleepwalking then?'

'Only when something's upset him.'

'You don't think he's been listening . . .?'

'He wasn't awake enough to understand if he was. He's in a strange place. There's been a shooting in London and that's where his grandfather lives. When we heard the news on the car radio he asked how near Brick Lane was to your flat. Then there's his glockenspiel . . .'

'His what?'

As Mitchell explained, they could hear Virginia calmly settling her elder son back into his bed. Bed seemed a good idea to both men. When his daughter came back to join them, Browne offered his thanks for supper, handed over a flat key and made ready to leave.

Mitchell, unusually hesitant, began, 'You will . . .'

'Pass all the evidence I'm given on to you so that you can show me where it's pointing? I'll think about it, Benny. I suppose it would be one way to clear up within the week.' Mitchell could hear him chuckling as he walked to the lift and disappeared.

Waking up the following morning, Browne resented the cancellation of his long-awaited holiday less than he had expected. He was never quite sure how to fill in his time when he was not in the middle of a case. He missed his daughter and her family, but only as the background to his professional life. He couldn't honestly say that he was sorry not to be able to show them the sights, or spend whole days in their company. He loved them dearly but had often found their actual presence more than a little trying. Only after Hannah had died had he realized how often she had soothed the tension between himself and his daughter.

Today they would all be settling into his flat and making themselves available whenever he could snatch a break between his multifarious tasks. He would not see enough of Ginny to become more than mildly irritated by her scattered possessions marring the good order he maintained and required in his home. The children, thank goodness, whether by inheritance or by training, were almost as meticulously tidy as Benny.

Arriving at his office, he began to plan his day. He would make time to take the youngsters out to lunch. Once he had overseen the preliminary briefing his DCI was quite capable of checking on the routine beginning of a murder enquiry. He'd better use his cellphone to arrange it. Benny might well have organized his troops and checked out of the hotel already.

Ginny answered him, readily approving his plan, only pleading, 'Don't let them drag you into McDonald's. This is supposed to be a mind-broadening few days.' He grinned, gathered up his papers and ran down the stairs to the incident room in the basement.

He found a hive of activity there. Two men from BT were still busy installing direct lines and answering machines. Several officers stood in front of the huge whiteboard to which were pinned a few stills from the video films he and the Special Branch officers had examined the previous day. Proven facts would soon appear on it, indicating to all concerned an instant picture of the current state of the case. At present these were pitifully few. The victims' full names – Christopher James Buchan and Timothy Ellis – their dates of birth and occupations constituted the total. As the superintendent came into the room the buzz of chatter died away and his men took their places at the tables arranged in a horseshoe in front of his own.

Browne waved a hand towards the board. 'That's what we know, plus the fact that Mr Ellis is dead and PC Buchan is in the ICU at the Royal London Hospital. He was taken there by helicopter and operated on yesterday afternoon. No more news of him than that so far.

'I don't think a lot of personal details about the victims will be useful if this investigation is into an opportunist robbery followed by murder to assist our villain's escape. However, we shall go through the motions just in case we're wrong. I have PC Buchan's service record here. I shall leave it in the file. Anyone here ever worked with him?'

Two hands were raised. Browne nodded at the men. 'Speak to the DCI before you leave.' Mindful of the telephone engineers at the back of the room, he paused to choose his words carefully.

One of the men, realizing his dilemma, grinned at him. 'We'll be away in less than five, mate.' He was better than his word.

Browne regathered his audience. 'On the surface, this looks like an easy ride. Several officers arrived at the scene just twenty-four minutes after the crimes were committed, we have the whole show on video and one of the victims of the attack is still alive, though not yet fit enough for us to question him. The videos give us fairly clear pictures, not only of the villain and his victims but also a host of witnesses. The public will hear all this and expect the perp to be named and shamed in tomorrow's papers. Not having X-ray eyes we can't see through the hood but we won't be forgiven for that. Now, the bullet –'

'Not much point in wasting money having that tested.' Browne glared at the brash young uniformed constable who continued unabashed. 'We know only too well which weapon it came from.'

'And you'll be able to prove to us, when the gun's used again, that its bullet matches the one we have. Good.'

The young man muttered, 'Sorry, sir.' Browne forgave him and continued. 'Although the video films failed to show us more than the general build of the man we're looking for, they were useful. We can see that some considerable and hostile attention from a number of people is paid to the white man in his Mondeo. The tall, hooded youth is lingering at the end of an alleyway, also watching him. Enough of his face is on view to see that he's black and has Asian features but he's too far away to ID him personally.'

'How do we know this hooded person is either a man or young?'

Browne's nod acknowledged this as a fair question. 'You'll all be seeing some of the film later this morning. Watch him when he runs away. So, if you will allow me, this young man takes a map from the pouch-pocket on the front of his jacket and pats his pockets. He then approaches the Mondeo. His manner is quite pleasant and he frowns over the map, seeming to be lost.'

Browne's DCI asked, 'Was he looking at the map before he approached PC Buchan, when he was still in the alley?'

'No. As soon as the window is lowered, the youth pulls a cosh of some kind, quite short, no more than eight inches or so. He hits his victim on the temple. As Buchan slumps over the wheel he shifts whatever he'd used to cover the gun on the front passenger seat. The youth sees and grabs it, probably now suspecting who Buchan is. He stops to consider for a minute, during which the man in the car behind decides to have a go. Ellis – not officially identified yet but we have his driving licence – gets out of his Volvo and shouts.'

'How do we know that?' The pushy constable again. Browne controlled his irritation.

'His mouth moves. The Asian lad turns to look at him. When Ellis is almost at point blank range the lad fires into the middle of his chest. Quite a few people are watching but no one else interferes. There's a small boy, standing very close, paying rapt attention. I want him found, for his own protection as much as for anything he can tell us.'

The pushy constable nodded his approval. Browne was beginning to find him amusing. He said solemnly, 'I'm glad we see eye to eye. So, after a quick look round, our man now ransacks Ellis's pockets and stuffs the small stuff into his hoodie. He'll know that someone's ringing us, but he'll also know that it's going to be twenty minutes or so before we can get there. With Ellis lying bleeding on the ground, for reasons known only to himself, he puts a bullet into Buchan before running. No one follows him, though several folk try to help both victims as soon as he's gone.'

Browne turned to the chatty constable. 'What's your name?'

'Watson, sir.'

'And have you any theories about why this man shot PC Buchan, who was unlikely to be able either to identify or detain him?'

Nervously, Watson stood his ground. 'I have, sir, but I think I'll wait for some evidence before saying.'

Browne roared with laughter. 'We'll get on then. You all know practically as much as I do now. I've done all the talking this morning because I had facts you needed to know. Now go and find some to share with me. Your action sheets are in alphabetical order. Don't snatch and muddle them. Those stills on the board have been duplicated. If your action requires pictures of particular witnesses, you'll find them clipped to your sheet. No slacking. Remember that this character has both a gun and a police warrant.'

Watson played his last shot. 'Sir, a tall young black lad won't be able to pass himself off as a fat middle-aged white cop.'

Browne nodded solemnly. 'I should have thought of that, Watson. Wait a minute, though. He might have a fat white friend or even be a clever photographer who –'

'Yes, sir. I'm with you.' Clutching his sheet and beaming happily, Watson trotted off to distinguish himself. Browne climbed the stairs back to his office, trying to work out why the filmed record of what had been classified as an aggravated robbery made him feel so uneasy.

The children, when Mitchell delivered them to the small restaurant Browne had chosen, were full of enthusiasm about their morning spent in Hyde Park. Browne hushed them long enough to invite their father to share the meal but was glad when he declined. The children were more fun and less discreet without a parent's restraining presence. Once they had described the delights of their morning of pony riding, watching the boats, feeding the squirrels and climbing and swinging in playgrounds far superior to those in Cloughton, their conversation did not disappoint him. The park might have met with their approval but not so his flat. Michael, having handed over his picture of the elongated dragon that had mutated into a giant tadpole, announced, 'I drew you another one when we got to your flat.'

Browne was giving effusive thanks for both offerings until Sinead, with a glance from under her lashes, remarked, 'He did it on your white wall.'

Caitlin glared at her sister before assuring her grandfather, 'It's all right. Daddy got it all off.'

Sinead, intent on mischief, ignored the glare. 'When Mummy saw it she said at least it made the place look as if somebody lived in it.'

'And not like a film set,' Declan added, for good measure.

Browne bit his lip. 'And what did your father say?'

Caitlin cut in quickly to minimize the damage. 'He said if Mum could be so tidy here, so as not to annoy you, then why couldn't she do it at home.'

Browne's lips twitched again. Michael regarded him placidly. 'You're trying not to laugh, aren't you? I don't know what's funny but we don't mind if you laugh.'

Browne decided the last laugh was his. He had obediently entertained the children away from McDonald's but they had still eaten chicken nuggets followed by mountains of ice cream.

Returning to his office, Browne felt his heart sink when he found PC Watson hovering outside the door. He grinned at him. 'Solved the case already, have you, constable?'

'No, sir, just followed instructions. You wanted to see the little lad on the video. He's downstairs. His brother's come along as well.'

Browne dropped his bantering tone. 'Well done you. Where did you find him?'

'Trying to duck under the police tape at the scene and shouting at the SOCOs that he could tell them just what happened. He was quite happy to come with me when I said my boss would be grateful for his help.'

'What about the brother?'

'He's twelve and the little kid's nine. The older one said he had to keep an eye on Kyle. Wouldn't give his own name and was none too pleased I'd got a name out of his brother.'

'So where are they?'

'In the foyer with the desk sergeant. I was going to take them home so their mum could sit in while I questioned them. They said she was in bed with her customer and she'd have the hide off them if they went into the house. I didn't think that I . . . well . . .'

'That you should interrupt them? Well, it wouldn't have been very polite, would it? And it suits us to have the mother unavailable. Do you know which school should be privileged by their attendance at this hour of the afternoon?' Watson shook his head. 'Find out and get on to them. If they haven't got a spare body to lend us they can at least give us the name of the boys' social worker. I reckon they're likely to have one.'

As Watson scurried off, Browne reached for his phone and punched the button for the desk sergeant. He arranged for a WPC to feed the boys Coke and crisps in the canteen, prayed briefly for a chaperone with some common sense, then settled to some mind-numbing paperwork until these instructions were carried out. Too late, it occurred to him, as he shuffled the despised forms, that, if his grandchildren were on half-term holiday, it was likely that the Brick Lane pair were too.

The next interruption was a phone call from his DCI who was spending the rest of his morning in court. The summing up was taking time. Things were progressing slowly. He doubted that he would be available to his superintendent before mid-afternoon. Browne was pleased. That left him with the opportunity to talk to the two boys himself. Half an hour later, the desk sergeant's call made a welcome break in his report writing – doubly welcome when he heard his message. Terry Fletcher was asking for him. Here was just the man he would have picked. 'Send him up here, would you? Give us ten minutes, then we'll have the boys and some coffee.'

Browne welcomed Fletcher warmly. The man had a sympathy and often a respect for his young clients, but no illusions about them and no sentimentality in his dealings with them. He was probably one of the few social workers who actually had rescued the odd adolescent from a life of crime. The two lads currently offering themselves as witnesses he knew intimately. 'Danny and Kyle Bird. They've been on my list for three years. There's been one incident of shoplifting and a good many of vandalism but I have them under my wing because they're considered to be in moral danger. Some of Mum's customers are known to swing quite a few ways.'

He grinned and wound his long legs round the rails of the chair he had taken. 'I've come to defend your rights, not theirs. The boys are quite capable of standing up for themselves. They understand the system perfectly – at least Danny does and he plays it with skill. He's engagingly open about it, as you'll see. They'll play games with you but, if you get them on your side, you'll find them sharp and observant.'

'Would you talk to them together or separately?'

Fletcher considered for a moment then decided: 'Together, I think. Sidelong glances might tell you more than they'll say.'

Against his better judgement, Browne had rewarded Watson by allowing him to be present. 'You can stay if you don't interfere.' It was the constable, therefore, who brought the boys in, then retreated to a chair by the door. They were unabashed by the office and the introductions. Danny turned back to Watson to enquire, 'This your boss-man then?'

Browne smiled as the constable looked at him for permission to answer and, even then, restricted himself to a nod. He took the children in detail through the events he had seen on film. 'Where were you and what were you doing before all this business started?'

'I was –' A none too gentle nudge from Danny removed the cheeky grin from Kyle's face and changed the direction of his answer. 'Er . . . just messing about.'

'I'm more interested today in what you saw than in what you were doing.' Both boys looked relieved. 'So, where were you messing about and could you see the young man who did the shooting before he went over to the Mondeo?'

'We was kicking at some –'

Danny forgot where he was. 'Can it, Kyle! Can't you get it into your thick skull that you'll be ten in five more weeks? You'll have to watch out for yourself after your birthday and you have to start practising now!' He turned back to Browne. 'We was standing outside the balti house, looking at the Volvo.'

'And the man?'

'We was watching him as well. He was looking at the other car, the scruffy Mondeo. We saw him take the map out, but we knew he wasn't lost. He was casing some joint. We was surprised when he went to the scruffy car. There'd be better pickings in the new one with the cool dude sitting in it.'

'Tell me exactly what you saw him do next.'

'He went across the road, stood in the middle, outside the driver's door.'

'Did he knock on the window?' Danny shrugged and Browne turned to the younger boy. 'Kyle, you went nearer, didn't you? Did he knock?

'Yep.'

'Then what?'

'The driver bloke buzzed the window down. As soon as it moved the black bloke pulled a torch out of his hoodie. He shoved the map in the geezer's face and whacked him on the forehead with the torch – I think it was a torch.'

'All right. Now, think carefully. What did he do next?'

'I thought he'd go through the bloke's pockets, quick as he could, but he reached right across for something. 'Spect it was the gun. He didn't have no gun when he went across there. I didn't see one anyway.'

'Did he go through the victim's pockets after that?'

Kyle shook his head. 'He just stood there. I'd have got on with it fast if it'd been me –'

'That man . . .'

Danny's remark petered out and at first Browne thought his interruption was a diversion from his brother's boasting about his own superior thieving ability. Then he saw the boy's face and realized that he had become absorbed in this reconstruction and was about to make a comment on something he had observed. 'Go on, Danny.'

'Well, he might have pinched the Mondeo man's gun or he might not. I didn't see that bit, but he knew how to use it. Soon as he realized the bloke from the Volvo was going to stick his nose in, he whipped round, had his gun cocked an' let him have it.'

Brown's misgivings about the case were increasing. It was not a simple robbery that had gone wrong because the robber panicked. It had taken these two embryo villains to bring to the surface of his mind the worries that the video film had caused him subconsciously. But the decision had not been his to make. And this might be the last big case he would oversee before he retired at the end of the summer. He desperately wanted to work it.

29

Danny was not impressed by Ellis's courage, nor sympathetic about his fate. 'He was a fool. What did the stupid nerd expect?'

Browne pushed his speculations to the back of his mind and returned to his immediate task. 'You're a very intelligent observer, Danny. Can you finish the story? What did the hoodie man do next?'

'He took stuff out of the dead man's pockets but not much.'

'How did you know he was dead?'

'It was point-blank range – and he looked pretty dead to me. Most of his blood was all over the road.'

Sadly, Browne realized that such grim sights were more commonplace to this child than they were to himself. Danny reported the condition of the corpse quite dispassionately. There would be no bad dreams to wake him tonight. He asked, 'Did anyone try to stop the man?'

'Nah! Everybody came running into the street when the gun went off but they all just stood staring. Nobody moved at all for a bit, then they all started jabbering into their mobiles. The hoodie ran off up the alley, nearly knocked Kyle over.'

Browne turned to the younger boy. 'Did you get a good look at his face?' He half hoped for a negative answer. The last thing he needed was this child's murder on his hands. He saw the same thought was in Danny's mind. Kyle received a second nudge and a shake of his head.

'No,' Kyle replied obediently. 'But I heard somebody say they thought the hoodie was Tariq's cousin.'

When Mitchell had collected the children after the lunch with their grandfather, he found Virginia still exploring the new flat. Concern for Browne rather than prurient curiosity was the reason for her close appraisal. She totally understood that, after her mother had died such a painfully lingering death, he wanted a fresh start, away from everything that reminded him of it. She knew he had missed herself and her brother, not to mention his grandchildren, once he settled in London, and they had worried about his falling into a depression. They had been delighted, therefore, by the enthusiastic emails and telephone calls about the new flat and had listened patiently as he described his plans to decorate and furnish it. This, though, was rather grander than she had expected.

She paused in the doorway of the huge sitting room, shaking her head at her husband. 'He must be practically destitute after this.'

Mitchell agreed. 'It must have cost him an arm and a leg and a few other bits of vital equipment.'

'Double reception room, four bedrooms, huge breakfast room, two bathrooms, twenty-four-hour parking. And it's practically on the Edgware Road, only a short walk to Hyde Park, Oxford –'

Mitchell had had enough. 'Give it a rest, Ginny. You sound like an estate agent.'

She was not offended, merely asking, 'Have I kept it tidy enough?' She was well aware that her housekeeping, which verged sometimes on fecklessness, upset her father. Now she began to consider the evening meal. It was some years since she had ceased to find her own atrocious cooking skills amusing. She had taken lessons and had improved to the point where her children trusted her sufficiently to bring their friends home for tea, but the flat's enormous and lavishly equipped kitchen was intimidating her. 'I don't know how half these things work, or even what they're supposed to be for.'

Mitchell's attempt to encourage her was not flattering. 'Stop worrying. He'll be so full of the case when he comes in that he won't taste what he's eating.' This prediction proved correct, for, when Browne eventually arrived home, the children, even Declan, had been asleep for hours. There was therefore no polite conversation over dinner beyond Browne's effusive praise for Virginia's casserole. Virginia

31

was content but neither fooled nor flattered. The conversation amused her.

Her father described his day in some detail, partly to humour his son-in-law but chiefly to use him as a sounding board and as a release for his concerns about keeping control of his case. Mitchell was careful not to interrupt the flow and give his father-in-law time to reconsider the wisdom of passing on so much classified information to the officer who had once been his bumptious and impulsive DC.

When the recital finally came to an end, Mitchell asked merely, 'Any chance that I could see the CCTV videos?'

Now Browne was relaxed and his laugh genuine. 'I observe that you've finally learned a bit of self-control. I was waiting for you to ask me that last night.'

Mitchell took this as a yes and decided not to press the request further. He waited for Browne's direct question before offering his advice. He knew it was what his father-in-law had hoped for and expected. 'Even I take orders when they tell me to do what I want to do. Yours are to find the bloke who shot Buchan – and then to prove it.'

'It's not as simple as that.'

'Why isn't it?'

'Because I don't have your gift of looking all your own worst faults in the face and being not only tolerant of them but smug! Still, Tariq is one of the commonest Asian names we come across and most Asians do seem to have enough cousins to populate a small town.' So, this Tariq who was cousin of their hooded friend might well not be the same one that Buchan had been surveilling.

Virginia smiled tolerantly at the two heads, bent towards each other. She slipped out quietly to the kitchen and replaced the elaborate pudding, with which she had intended to impress them, in the cavernous refrigerator. She came back to the dining room carrying cheese and biscuits. She would save her masterpiece until they could give it the attention it deserved.

* * *

The following Monday, with their holiday at an end, the Mitchell family drove back to Cloughton in cheerful mood. They had enjoyed the break, being delighted to see Grandad Tom again and to find him in such good spirits. Mitchell himself was quite ready to be back on the job. Virginia had hardly laid hers aside since she had half written a piece intended for one of what used to be called the broadsheets on a child's view of the London sights. The twins and Caitlin were enthusiastic about their return to school and Declan was ecstatic at the thought of being reunited with his beloved glockenspiel. He clutched in his hand Grandad Tom's parting gift to him. It was a CD of the percussion playing of Evelyn Glennie.

Listening to it had both delighted and dismayed him. 'I'll never be as good as that.' His grandfather was sympathetic, his mother more pragmatic. 'You will be,' she told him, 'when you've practised as much as she has.'

Uncomforted by either, Declan had pointed out the difficulties of adequate practice when parents refuse to transport your instrument. 'And, if you'd asked him, Grandad Tom would have told you that there was plenty of room for it.'

They made good time on an uneventful journey so now the evening would go as they had planned it. Mitchell would cut the grass whilst Virginia cooked supper so that the twins could be put to bed at a reasonable hour. Virginia had driven the final lap, barefoot as she preferred when circumstances permitted. Having parked outside the front door, she fished under the seat for her shoes. Mitchell sighed and muttered to himself. 'I knew it was too good to be true.

Virginia straightened, slipping her feet into sandals. 'You mean you didn't realize that the weeds would have the temerity to show their faces when you weren't there to frighten them?' Then she saw what he meant. Their neighbour was standing by the wall that separated their gardens, beckoning enthusiastically. Both knew that, short of being unmistakably rude to her, their timetable for the evening would need some amendment. Then, Virginia saw that Mrs Gledhill held some brightly coloured cards in her heavily veined hands. She brightened. 'She's got play tickets. I'll buy them to sweeten the snub.' She opened Caitlin's door and handed her a key to the house. 'Put the kettle on, Kat. Declan, help the twins out of their belts and take them in.'

Mitchell was already hauling luggage from behind the back seat. He could hear his wife's placating tone as she thanked the old lady, whose daughter was heavily involved in Cloughton's semi-professional repertory company. 'What's the play?' He failed to hear and dreaded to imagine the reply. Virginia's voice continued. 'That's an interesting choice. Yes, I'll certainly come to it. I like Rattigan and I've never seen a production of *Harlequinade*.'

Mitchell grunted as he hauled the largest suitcase up to the front porch. He'd never heard of Ratty-whoever and had no wish to be enlightened. He was surprised. Virginia was good at pleasing old ladies but she didn't usually lie to them. He chuckled as he remembered her privately expressed opinion of the Cloughton Players' last production. He dumped his case and grinned at Declan who had delivered the twins to his sister and had come out again to help him. 'Leave this big one to me, but you can dump the rest of the stuff under the stairs.' He nodded his head in the direction of Mrs Gledhill. 'Your mother's planning a cultural evening for us all.'

Declan cast up his eyes, picked up a couple of bags and disappeared. When Virginia came back inside, the huge case had joined the rest of the luggage. Mitchell realized that his wife had, in fact, told no lies. *The Browning Version* was, she told him, in her opinion at least, one of the best one-act plays ever written.

'Version of what?' Mitchell asked suspiciously.

Virginia attempted to explain both the answer to his question and the plot of the play but Mitchell had stopped listening. She noticed Declan looking apprehensive and

34

assured him that it was not a play for children. In the manner of most pre-adolescent children, after being warned off something he had not wanted to do, he immediately pleaded to be allowed to do it.

Mitchell waited for his own reprieve. When it failed to come, he remained silent. He had no intention of attending the performance but nor did he want the ticket returned. He quite approved of there being a theatre group in his home town so long as no one expected him to patronize it.

Virginia knew when she was beaten. 'You'd better go and mow the lawn then. I told Susie Gledhill that you'd cut hers for her when you've a spare minute.'

'Fine. I'll do it the night that you go to see this poncy play.'

'Poncy isn't the only word you can use to describe a play – though I can see the attraction of the alliteration. Anyway, I don't suppose Rattigan would mind you using it. I seem to remember you referring to *A Midsummer Night's Dream* with the same phrase.'

Mitchell appealed to his son. 'Did you understand any of that?'

Declan smiled at his mother before he answered. 'I think so, and I think you do too. You're just teasing Mum.'

'Well, maybe I am. Just so long as she knows I'm quite serious about not going to see a play about a version of something Greek that's set in a poncy – sorry, I mean a superior – public school where you get crammed with useless notions from books in languages that nobody speaks any more. I'm off. Might be time to cut both lots of grass before your mother's got round to cooking supper.' He beamed at his wife and ruffled his son's hair, noting that it would have to be cut again very soon if Declan's friends were not to discover the shaming fact that it curled like his mother's. He whistled as he made for the garden shed, happily unaware that within the week he would very much regret his forcefully expressed decision.

He had been hoping for a spectacular sunset tonight, both to welcome him home and as a reward for his efforts in the garden. It was not to be. Clouds gathered, as he guided his machine in steady lines, and began to empty themselves over him as he submitted it to its usual meticulous cleaning. The horizon, when he raised his eyes, appeared as a line where greyish green below met pearly grey above. The grey progressed quickly through leaden to black as the downpour plastered his garments and his hair to his body. Never mind. It was Yorkshire rain.

Chapter Two

On Tuesday morning, the police station foyer accepted Mitchell as if he had never been away. There was maybe just slightly more of a spring in his step as he approached Mark – inevitably Magic – Powers, the laconic desk sergeant, to ask, 'What have I missed, then?'

'Not much. A car was stolen. A wall fell down.'

Mitchell turned to PC Smithson who had walked in behind him to appeal for more details. Smithson too was dismissive. 'That was my pigeon. Whoever helped it on its way to the ground wasted his effort. It was a single-brick affair, round a jungle of weeds, and half the mortar had fallen out of its own accord. I wish whatever ran into it had demolished the house and garden too. The whole property's an eyesore. Spoils Lower Edge Road.'

'Isn't that where Shakila lives?'

Smithson nodded. 'About ten doors away.'

'Right. And that's all that's happened while I've been away? I might as well extend my leave and finish putting the garden to rights . . .'

'Heath Lees School's lost all its computers again,' Magic interrupted. He looked smug, as though his remark had prevented his DCI's return home.

Mitchell tutted. 'Such excitements. It's a wonder you're all bearing up so well. I'd better get busy before my desk collapses under the paperwork that's waiting for me. Oh happy day!'

Smithson beamed. 'I used to sing that in Sunday School. *Oh happy day that fixed my choice On thee my Saviour and my God . . .'*

Smithson's joyous bass roar followed Mitchell up to the first floor but faded into the general noise as he tackled the further flight up to his office. He was glad that another officer in the place was pleased to be here as well as himself. Even so, paperwork had so dampened his enthusiasm for the place by midday that he felt called to the Fleece for an early lunch. Closing his office door, he saw his sergeant emerging from the general office further down the corridor. Good. He could make his meal feel like a virtuous continuation of his morning's work. She would have her finger on the station pulse and could bring him up to speed with everything that was important.

The two officers descended the stairs to the foyer, pausing at the last turn to observe with interest the customer at Magic's desk. Tall, and thin rather than slim, the man's appearance demanded interest and speculation. Out of the side of his mouth, Mitchell asked, 'A poser, or what?'

Jennifer Taylor grinned. 'Definitely not a what.'

'Must be a poser then – the longest, thinnest one I've seen and I've seen a few.'

'It's the suit, partly.' Seeing Mitchell's baffled expression, she went on. 'Single-breasted jacket, buttons low, deep V, narrow trousers. All elongating.'

Mitchell sniffed. 'If you say so.'

'And look at the shirt. No tie, but buttoned up to the neck . . . Well, it's a free country, I suppose. The government hasn't forced the bloke in the street to wear a uniform yet. He's definitely out to make an impression though.'

Mitchell began to move forward again, lowering his voice further. 'He's made one on me. Some poncy barber arranged that bird's nest on his head.'

Jennifer laughed. 'I don't think whoever created that would call himself a mere barber. You're right though. I even wonder if that beard might be by benefit of curling tong . . .'

She stopped muttering as the man turned and glanced at them, eyes hooded, a generous moustache spreading over his top lip. Embarrassed by their display of bad manners she set off hurriedly for the outer door. Mitchell nodded to the man and, seeing that he too was about to depart, stopped and held the door for him. The man smiled, showing teeth that spoiled whatever impression he had aimed at.

Mitchell displayed his own, which had been more carefully preserved. 'Magic sorted you out, did he?'

Sergeant Powers' name was displayed on his desk and Mitchell saw that his latest customer appreciated the nickname. 'Yes. He used it to get my car back, minus its petrol but otherwise as I left it. Does he use a standard police wand or provide his own? Whichever, I'm grateful and came in to thank him.'

Mitchell raised an eyebrow. 'Unusual though that is, I'll attribute it to your good manners and not the police issue wand.' The two men saluted each other and Mitchell joined his hungry and impatient colleague.

The bar at the Fleece was beginning to fill up with lunchtime drinkers, but, through the door at the far end of it, Mitchell could see that the restaurant area was still almost empty. Two women sat at a corner table at which there were two more chairs. More company was obviously expected. They looked very familiar. DC Caroline Jackson raised a hand holding a pint tankard. DC Shakila Nazir beckoned her sergeant and her DCI to join them. Mitchell turned to his sergeant. 'You rang them whilst I was talking to the grateful car owner.'

She was unrepentant. 'What if I did? They've got the drinks in and, with any luck, they'll have ordered the pies.'

'Someone had better try to raise Adrian then or he'll have a persecution complex for the rest of the week.'

The two DCs answered Mitchell in chorus. 'In court.'

'Oh well, I suppose I can cope with this monstrous regiment of women.'

'Where does that come from?' Caroline asked.

'You mean my accurate description of you folk?' Mitchell shrugged. 'I've no idea.'

The pies arrived in short order. Caroline and Jennifer applied themselves to the food. Shakila paused to make a note in her book. Mitchell smiled to himself.

Such was the day's lack of excitement that Mitchell arrived home on Tuesday evening in time to join his children at the supper table. However, the twins were still running round the garden when he parked in front of the house. He saw that Susie Gledhill was shepherding some visitors from the front door of her house to their car. A further glance showed him that his wife was of their party.

He had looked too long. A frenzied waving followed by an imperious beckoning commanded him to join the group next door. 'How fortunate,' Mrs Gledhill called. 'You're in time to meet my daughter.'

His mind still numb from a day of form filling and report writing, Mitchell failed to produce an excuse. He joined the little group and regarded the daughter, who seemed as little enthusiastic as himself to begin the acquaintance. The woman reminded him of pictures of 1940s screen actresses that his great-aunt had cut out of her film magazines when he was a small child. Clumps of crimped, strawberry blonde hair hung round her shoulders, drawing attention to the inappropriately undewy complexion and thickened waist. The mouth was full-lipped but small and the expression slightly peevish. She offered a hand languidly. Mitchell shook it and told her, quite truthfully, that her mother had told the Mitchells a great deal about her.

'This is Margot and this . . .' Mrs Gledhill paused to pull forward a reluctant boy in his early teens. '. . . is my grandson Robin. You'll see Margot again in a few days. She's playing Millie Crocker-Harris in the play.' Mrs Gledhill gave the last two words oral inverted commas. 'She wasn't a very nice lady. Still, Crocker-Harris wasn't altogether a very nice man – though you do feel sorry for him as the story unfolds. '

Mitchell was suddenly inspired. 'Mrs G, I'm going indoors before you tell us any more of the plot and spoil the performance for us.'

Susie Gledhill giggled delightedly and the Mitchells hastily made their escape, pursued by effusive thanks 'for my lovely smooth and stripy lawn'.

Safe in the kitchen, Mitchell asked, 'How long had you been trapped there?'

'Long enough to be grateful for my rescue. Susie was singing the praises of the new director – on the strength of having watched one rehearsal. This is only his third production. I had noticed they were attempting rather more demanding plays over the last weeks. Susie says even a brilliant actress like Margot has improved a bit since he took over and she claimed that he was the one who discovered that the boy could act. Robin put her right there – reminded her that he was Buttons in his school pantomime and Peter Quince when his comp did scenes from Shakespeare. By the way, have you been having PR coaching today? That's the most tactful exit line I've ever heard from you.'

Mitchell simpered. 'Sometimes my underlying good nature can't help but show itself.' In a more normal tone, he added, 'That's a nasty shiner her boy's got. Did you find out who gave it to him?'

'I don't think his mother knows. Robin's story is that a bigger boy just came up to him and hit him. He won't give a name – says he doesn't know. Apparently Robin is in *The Browning Version* too. Quite a big part. One of the characters is a boy of about his age who's having coaching . . .'

Mitchell held up his hands. 'Not that again. Just tell me about the real boy.'

'His mother seems just as concerned about whether they can disguise the bruise with make-up when the play opens as she is about whether the older boy is likely to black her son's other eye . . .'

A burst of percussion music from Declan's bedroom drowned her next sentence. Grinning at Mitchell, she raised her voice. 'I'm becoming less and less grateful for my father's generosity.' The cascades of notes, played at lightning speed, made a veil of sound. Virginia closed the door but continued to listen to the muffled music. She frowned. 'Just a sec. I'm getting very familiar with that CD. This piece isn't on it.'

Conspiratorially, they crept upstairs. The door was ajar and Virginia pushed it further open. Their son, oblivious to them, wielded hammers at a speed that made them just a faint haze of white. Impressed, they returned downstairs. 'Sounds to me as though he hasn't been held back by a few days without practice.' Virginia went back to preparing supper.

On Tuesday morning, PC Smithson had had a public relations task to fulfil. He had the knack, an invaluable asset to his colleagues in all departments and at every level, to persuade the man in the Cloughton street, at least temporarily, to see an event from the police's point of view. His solid build, benign expression and avuncular manner reassured and comforted complainants. They believed that Smithson at least would do his very best for them. Their confidence was not unfounded, because Smithson, as far as it lay in his power, would do just that.

When, therefore, the telephone line to the desk in the station foyer had become jammed with calls from the irate owner of the collapsed wall, Smithson was the obvious choice of officer to soothe him and explain to what lengths the force was going to find the driver who had had the temerity to knock it down. He walked along the pleasant road where he knew that DC Shakila Nazir also lived, and tutted once again at the weed-choked garden and the grubby, chewed-looking curtains.

Having demanded the personal attention of a Cloughton police officer, the owner of the offending house was not at home to receive him, but help was at hand. From across the road, where he had been attending to an already perfect flower bed, an elderly man hurried over. He introduced himself. 'Name o' Smithson, same as you, but I'm Wilfred. Don't suppose you are.'

PC Smithson agreed that they did not share given names and asked about his intended quarry.

'Gone to take his dog for a run. At least he isn't too idle to do that – though he won't have taken no pooper scoop with him to clean up its mess. You might have a word with him about that.'

Smithson nodded sagely and agreed, without committing himself, that that sounded like a good idea. 'I don't suppose you noticed any incident that might have caused this damage?'

The man gave a throaty chuckle. 'I might have, at that. T'other day, I saw a sparrer land on it. Weren't the sort o'wall to stand up to treatment like that, and they're vandals, them little buggers.'

Smithson laughed dutifully. 'I reckon we both appreciate the difference between this wilderness and that patch of perfection in front of your house, but we coppers can't pick and choose. We have to do our best for all . . .'

Smithson's new friend was not fooled. 'True. Not to mention that he's probably ringing you lot day and night, demanding a nicely built, double brick affair as compensation for this bit o' shoddy!'

Smithson said, conspiratorially, 'I wish I was allowed to agree with you but you probably understand . . .'

'Oh aye, I can see as you have to treat all alike.'

'And you're sure you didn't see or hear anything to help us?'

The man shook his head. 'Day it happened we none of us heard anything much. There was a wedding going on down the road.' He waved a hand in the direction of Shakila's house. 'A lot of Asians live hereabouts. One of your lot's one of 'em. Nice young lass. Any road, the Asians like to get 'emselves well and truly married, all the crowds of relations there for days and their crash-banging sort o' fireworks. A little tinny crash and a few seconds o' bricks falling into them weeds would've been drowned. Them sort o' fireworks'd be illegal if it was us lot setting 'em off.'

Quickly Smithson turned to a safer topic and the two Smithsons enjoyed a few moments' general conversation. The policeman was genuinely grateful for advice on how to get a good autumn showing of dahlias and his name-sake went back home in the sort of pleasant glow that follows having given some good advice to a fellow man.

In spite of his black eye Robin Ridgeway was feeling rather pleased with life at teatime on Tuesday. David Page, his mother's partner, was at a meeting with some of his polit-ical friends. His mother was across the road, attending to a friend and neighbour who was ill, and his friend Janil had brought *Stormbreaker* for them both to watch. In Janil's case it was for the umpteenth time but for Robin it was the long-awaited first, though he was not going to admit that to Janil. And, even now, the film would have to be stopped if either of the grown-ups returned – which might give him away to Janil.

He had heard his relations comment on how much more carefully he had been brought up since Mum had met David. They seemed to think it was a good thing but he didn't see it that way himself. The new rules and regula-tions had cut him off from his friends so that their lives were more interesting and exciting than his own.

For now, though, he was happy, thrilled even to hold the DVD case in his hand and read the tempting descriptions of the action on the front. *Death-defying car chases! Jaw-dropping gadgets and enough adrenalin to boot James Bond into a bin liner!!* Robin wondered what adrenalin was. He thought he would ask his mother later, then changed his mind. She would want to know where he had read it and, not knowing what it was, he would be unable to make up a suitable lie. Not that Mum herself was specially against his watching violent films, but she was certainly against doing anything to annoy or upset David.

This particular DVD wasn't new. Robin didn't understand why, suddenly, there was so much interest in it at school. That new boy who'd gone straight into the school's first XI when he'd only been there three weeks was said to be keen on it. Maybe that had started all the fuss. Robin hadn't even heard an outline of the plot. If he had asked at school, they would all realize that he had not seen it – and it wouldn't do to ask at home.

As he watched now, all the snippets of conversation he had heard in the playground slipped into place. Alex Rider in the film lived with someone who wasn't his dad. Till the old chap got bumped off, everyone thought he was a boring bank manager, but he was really a spy. He wondered how many boring old people that he, Robin Ridgeway, had met were really living exciting lives that no one knew about.

What about David Page, Mum's boyfriend? He was a stodgy old schoolteacher. Maybe all the fuss he made about hating guns and violence and war was to cover up his gun smuggling or drug dealing or . . .

He pressed the pause button to try out this theory on Janil who was unimpressed by it. 'My mum thinks he's like that because his grandfather used to march with CND and spend his life at union meetings or sticking up for people in the Third World. She says he was brought up to it and never learned to think for himself. She thinks he needs to get a life and live in the real world.'

After considering this for a few moments, Robin decided that his own theory and Janil's mother's were both wrong. David would never have what it must take to be a spy, but he did stand up to people who laughed at his opinions. He wondered what CND stood for and what the Third World might be. There wouldn't be any mileage in asking Janil. His mother offered her opinions on everything and everybody non-stop. Janil would have learned what she said parrot fashion without even realizing it was sticking in his mind.

Anyway, if there was a hidden side to David, it wouldn't lead to an exciting career for Robin. David hadn't prepared him for a spy's life. Apart from the lack of crack shooting, they hadn't done any of the necessary things together, no scuba diving, no mountaineering, no learning a dozen different languages.

There was a gunfight on the screen now. Robin paused the film again as Alex Rider aimed his weapon. Janil turned indignantly but Robin forestalled his friend's protest. 'That gun . . .' Janil continued to glare. Robin perfectly judged his pregnant pause before repeating, sententiously, 'That gun . . .' His tone suddenly changed to one of nonchalance. Not for nothing was he currently the juvenile lead in the local repertory company. '. . . is a bit like mine.'

Janil was puzzled. 'Yours? Don't be stupid. Your dad even made you throw away that one you won at Harry's party.'

'He isn't my dad.'

'Well, he's the bloke who lives here and tells you what to do. What's that if it isn't a dad?'

Robin considered. It didn't seem to him to be a very accurate description of Janil's own silent and strange father. He dismissed the thought and returned to his friend's question. 'He tells me things *not* to do anyway – and playing with guns is one of a whole list of them.'

Nonchalance gave way to gravity. 'That's why I had to get myself one secretly. And mine's a real one.'

There was stunned silence from Janil, followed by a roar of laughter. 'Nice one, Rob. You had me believing you for a minute.' He grabbed the remote control. 'Now let's see the rest of this before your dad gets back.'

They watched to the end, missing only the long list of acknowledgements. Janil whipped his DVD out of the player and into his pocket as David Page's voice was heard in the hall downstairs. Robin parted with Janil amicably, not offended by his disbelief in his own unlikely claim. He ought really to be grateful to him. At least he had made it possible to see *Stormbreaker*. Now, he, Robin Ridgeway, would be one of the crowd in the playground who discussed it constantly. He would let Janil go on thinking his gun was a joke. Anyway, Janil was not his best friend. He was round here because his elder brother was home for a holiday from uni in Cairo or some such place. Youssef was the centre of attention at home and Janil's nose was out of joint. If he decided to share his secret with anyone, there were various reasons why this particular friend wasn't the most suitable candidate.

On Tuesday evening, when the twins were in bed, Declan and Caitlin busy with homework and his wife immersed in the final revision of her article for the *Guardian*'s women's page, Mitchell could no longer resist telephoning his father-in-law. If there was no excitement in his own job for the immediate present he would get a vicarious thrill from hearing the next instalment of Browne's investigation. He would try his number at the flat. If things were sufficiently hectic for him to be still at the station at eight thirty at night, then he'd just have to entertain himself with what the television had to offer.

Browne answered immediately. 'I hoped it would be you. My DI's spent the day in court and is now celebrating his wedding anniversary with his wife so I've been without a sounding board.' Mitchell was delighted. He was now doing Tom a favour by listening to his day's progress.

His father-in-law was not happy. 'The local rag has come out with exactly what we expected – pointed out that the whole crime is on video and that there were scores of witnesses and you can imagine the rest. Ended up with . . .' Mitchell heard a rustle as the offending paper was picked up. 'Here it is. *They'd better not take Agatha Christie for bedtime reading. That would really confuse them.* It would really disappoint them if we nailed the villain tomorrow morning.'

Mitchell chuckled. 'If I wasn't an honest man, I'd tell you that they'll be printing an apology in their next edition. I can't understand why Buchan was shot. The computer bloke, yes. He was coming up behind him and might have had something in his hand that he could use as a cosh. It was madness to shoot a copper though. He'd got his warrant and his gun. He'd put him out of action. He'd know we'd pull out all the stops for offing a PC.'

'Just in a panic, maybe, or perhaps he thought it would increase his street cred. Fortunately we only have to worry about finding him, not supplying him with a motive.'

'You were going to have a look at PC Buchan's service record. Any joy?'

'Some possibilities. Before he went into Special Branch he seems to have been involved several times in dealing with racial attacks. Hoodie might have had a personal axe to grind. As far as my own involvement is concerned, that would be convenient. It wouldn't be aggravated robbery as it's classified at the moment but it would be simple murder and therefore still my pigeon.'

'Right – and it wouldn't matter then whether Hoodie's cousin Tariq was the one Buchan was after or not, at least as far as your inconvenient conscience is concerned. Anything from the two men who'd worked with Buchan?'

'Nothing very specific but one of them said that, before his elders and betters taught him to keep his mouth shut, Buchan was known for his view that most Asians provoked the attacks made on them deliberately. The doc's letting us talk to Buchan in the morning. He may have some ideas of his own.'

'Anything from ballistics yet?'

'Only bad news. Could be three weeks before they can give us anything.'

'Why?'

'That's what we're asking them. Meanwhile I've been taking another look at what those two sharp youngsters had to say – the Bird brothers. Not just their official statements, I went back to the transcript of the shorthand version a PC did at the interviews. Kyle said that Hoodie wasn't casing the new Volvo but was definitely observing Buchan's scruffy Mondeo. I'd forgotten that. Buchan was his object. Then there's young Danny's comment about Hoodie's familiarity with his gun. Where would he have learned to use it so confidently, safely and effectively?'

'He'd only have to have a father or an older brother involved in a gun club, or maybe he's been an army cadet. Besides, if the video's all you've got as evidence of his age, he could be as old as mid-twenties.'

'I don't think so. I've watched it at least half a dozen times. There's something childlike about the agility he has as he spins round and dodges through the crowd. I think he's still in his teens. By the way, the photo lab has produced an enhanced picture of the cosh. Young Kyle was right. It was a torch, expensive affair. Looks to me exactly the same as one an ex-sergeant had. That was a LED Lenser Police Tech Focus, heavy and in a black rubber casing. I'm missing that sergeant, looking for a replacement among the current troops. Watching a young DC on the job is a better way to find a likely customer than making him answer questions from a panel of folk who aren't going to have to work with him when he's appointed.'

'True. Going back to getting an ID on Hoodie, would Special Branch tell you anything they know about Tariq's relations?' There was a long silence. 'Well, I can see that you don't want to do that if you can find any other way.'

'Benny, you're scaring me. You're finally growing up and seeing some point in obeying rules, but the effect of having you work for me all those years is turning me into a maverick.'

'So, what's your problem? Welcome to your second childhood. May it last you through your retirement, Chief Super, sir.' Laughing, he replaced the receiver.

Chapter Three

The Mitchells had misjudged Margot Ridgeway's concern about her son's injured eye. On Wednesday morning, to Robin's dismay, she announced her intention of accompanying him to school and speaking to his teachers about its policy on bullying. The boy had been surprised but pleased when David had taken his part and tried to dissuade his mother from her plan. Their conversation had taken place in the kitchen but Robin's hearing was sharp and, as he sat on the floor in the hall, packing his books into his satchel, he had heard enough to follow the gist of it.

'I don't think we should interfere at this stage. I want to get the real story out of him before we say our piece.'

'I know he fantasizes a bit but that injury is real enough. It could have been very serious.'

'I know, but we don't know that it happened on school premises. Even if it did, the school might make the sort of fuss that would make life harder for Robin.'

'He copes very –'

'I didn't mean to disparage him but he's not the physical, sporty type who finds school easy . . .'

Robin thought he'd find school a lot easier if he was allowed to watch the ordinary television programmes the other boys took for granted, argued about and re-enacted in the playground. As he buckled the leather straps of his bag over his books, he realized that, for once, his mother was winning this politely conducted argument. His heart sank lower as he understood that David had not only given in to his mother's persuasion but that he now intended to accompany them to the school himself. If only David's school were not just outside the Cloughton authority where the holiday dates were slightly different. Then he would have had to be teaching maths at his own school in Bradford and not interfering in Robin's life at the South Cloughton High.

Dragging his feet, Robin trailed out to the car and climbed into the back seat. This was the morning he had been intending to surprise everyone with his views on how they might all prepare themselves for exploits like Alex Rider's. They would hardly be prepared to accept the ideas of someone who entered the playground with Mummy and Daddy, one each side of him. He looked around for Janil, saw him in the centre of a crowd and made to join them.

Janil's voice, squeakily incredulous, floated across the tarmac to him. 'He must think we're stupid or something. He told me last night that he'd got himself a real gun. Is he a fruitcake or what?' A gale of laughter was stifled as someone saw the family arriving. Scarlet-faced, Robin followed David and his mother into the building. How was he going to face this situation? Was he going to have to produce the gun to stop them making fun of him?

Robin's head of year made her visitors welcome, ushering them into easy chairs in her office but not going to the length of offering tea. 'You've anticipated my letter.' She picked up from her desk a white envelope addressed to Margot Ridgeway but not yet stamped. 'We're a bit worried about Robin ourselves. Not that he's in trouble of any kind but there are a couple of things – the black eye, a falling off in his work ...' A plump hand was raised to indicate the intangible nature of her concern. 'We thought there might be something happening in the family, or a health problem perhaps, that it would help for us to know about.' Miss Hardy sat back and waited for their response.

Margot caught David's eye and wished that she had listened to him earlier. She should have waited, made time to agree with him how much they wanted to reveal. She wanted this motherly woman's help for her son. She saw that she would be tying Miss Hardy's well-manicured, beringed hands if she failed to give her the information she needed to understand Robin's social problems and to find out who had hurt him – but how many personal details was David happy to reveal? For now she had better play safe and just deal with the immediate problem.

Miss Hardy seemed to understand something of her dilemma and offered what was meant to be a helpful question. 'Can you tell me exactly what happened and what was said when Robin first came home with this injury?'

Margot refused to look at David but felt his warning glance in the ether. She stared at the wall over Miss Hardy's left shoulder and recited the bare facts. 'We'd got tea ready early because Robin was being picked up by his father and taken to the theatre for a play rehearsal. He's got an important role in the . . .'

Gems flashed as Miss Hardy's hands waved again. Margot wondered if she talked with them to show off her valuable jewellery. 'Yes, we know all about the play and Robin's part in it. We've got a group from school going to the Friday evening performance – just Years 11 to 13, of course, what we used to call the fifth and sixth forms. Do go on.'

Margot breathed a huge sigh of relief when David joined the conversation. Now she could take her lead from him. 'We heard the door open and Robin called that he was just going to wash his hands. He would usually have done that in the kitchen but we know now that he wanted to examine his face to see whether we would notice the damage to his eye. The pain of it ought to have told him that that was a vain hope. He stayed upstairs until we got impatient and called him down. He refused at first to explain what happened. When we pressed him he produced a story about an older boy who hit him, almost knocked him over and walked off before he could get his balance.'

Feeling on safer ground, Margot added, 'Then he turned to David and said he hadn't been fighting.'

'I abhor violence and he knows that I would take him to task for it if he tried to settle his disagreements with his fists.'

'He doesn't seem to us to be an aggressive boy. I doubt whether he would have struck the first blow – in fact, I doubt whether he would raise his fists to defend himself. If he's been forbidden to do that, we may have identified his chief problem.'

David's lips narrowed and he withdrew from the conversation. Miss Hardy, perhaps wanting to give him time to consider her accusation, turned back to Margot. 'I assume that you've come to school partly because you think this putative older boy attends here. Quite honestly, I can't think of any boy on roll who would inflict a potentially serious injury on a thirteen-year-old for no reason. That doesn't mean I won't investigate the matter very carefully.'

'Putative boy? That means you don't believe in him, I suppose.' Now David was angry.

Margot sighed and attempted to ease the situation. 'Robin was nervous about not being believed.' She paused. Should she finish the story here or share with the school their own ideas about the situation? If she spoke up in front of this sympathetic teacher there would be no going back. She consulted her partner by means of a quick glance and received a small shake of the head in reply.

David attempted to distract Miss Hardy by taking up his tale again. 'Robin said he didn't feel like going to the rehearsal and we didn't feel we should make him. That's all really. We wrote a note to get him excused from his homework and he went to bed soon after tea.'

'But there aren't any health problems – apart from his being understandably upset about being attacked and in pain from the injury?'

Margot needed to confide in this woman, as a release for her own mounting worries. She decided to go a stage further. 'Robin isn't sleeping well – and so, of course, neither are we. He has nightmares quite often, wakes up crying and asking someone to let him go. When we've soothed and fully wakened him, he can never remember what the dream was about.'

Miss Hardy had taken out a notebook and was writing in it. 'How long has this been going on?'

Probably feeling that they were now being taken seriously, David spoke up again. 'For at least some months. Perhaps we ought to explain a bit more. I believe Margot informed the school that Robin's father left home two years ago. You may not have realized that I am now Margot's partner. Robin and I get on well and I have been careful to take an interest in his hobbies and his general welfare. I came to your last parents' meeting with Margot to hear how he was getting on. He got a very good report . . .'

Sensing Miss Hardy's impatience, Margot slipped her hand into David's to encourage him to reach his point. He became expansive. 'Just over four months ago, Margot discovered she was pregnant. I wanted to be a proper father to our child and promptly moved in with her. We intend to marry before the birth.

'Foolishly, we expected Robin to be as pleased as we are. He's just thirteen. Not the right age to watch strange physical changes happening to your mother, nor to welcome a sibling who will always be too young to be a friend or playmate. On top of that, going for a walk with me or for a meal at a restaurant was quite different from knowing that I was in his mother's bed when he woke up every morning and still around when he went to bed at night.'

Miss Hardy's pencil flew and Margot wondered just what she was writing. It suddenly occurred to her that

Robin might have inflicted his injury on himself in a bid for attention. If so, his plan had worked too well. He had certainly misjudged the amount of force to use. Had he thought David would refuse to believe that he had not been fighting himself? That David would be angry with him and that she would take his part, changing the balance in the relationship in which the three of them were involved?

She shook her head. She was fantasizing. Suddenly, she wanted to go home. They had exposed themselves sufficiently to this efficient teacher. She was sure that the possible attack would be properly investigated and that Robin's temporary lapses of concentration in lessons would be dealt with sympathetically. They should keep the rest of their fears to themselves until they had examined and possibly justified them.

She began to gather her belongings and to thank Miss Hardy for her concern and patience. David, looking both surprised and relieved, held the door for her and followed her out to the car park. She noted his set expression but made her apology anyway. 'You were right. We shouldn't have started anything without being sure of our facts.'

He appreciated this capitulation. 'Well, in the meantime we might have made life a shade easier for the poor little beggar. Something's wrong with the kid. I don't think it's just having me around. He knew it was coming and seemed all right about it. Why did he refuse to go to the rehearsal with Paul?'

'Perhaps he felt too rough to go anywhere with anybody.' She turned the key in the ignition, put the car into gear and signalled left out of the school car park, then added quietly, 'During the night, he asked me if, when we're married, we could change his name to Page as well.'

'Does he think he won't belong here after the wedding? That he won't be part of the new family? That he'll have to go and live with Paul?'

'If he does, we can sort that one out as soon as he gets back from school tonight.'

David returned to the question they had been discussing for some weeks. 'If that sod is buggering him I'll make him swing for it!'

As Margot Ridgeway's car passed the Cloughton police headquarters a man was entering the building, almost losing his battle with the stiff revolving door. Emerging triumphantly, he gazed with interest around the foyer. Then, remembering his mission, he strode importantly to the desk where the sergeant on duty gazed at him impassively.

When this failed to elicit the man's purpose, Magic spared him a word. 'Yes?'

His visitor was not impressed. 'And good morning to you too. I want to speak to PC Smithson.'

'And your name, sir?'

'Smithson.'

'Your own name, please?'

The man sighed. 'Smithson, same as his. And, before you ask, he's not my brother or my dad or my son. We're just blessed with the same name. Now, can I speak to him?'

'About?'

Wilfred Smithson was becoming seriously annoyed. 'Nowt to do with you. Just give him my name and he'll come.'

Which, having nothing more urgent to do, PC Smithson did. He conducted his visitor to the least inhospitable of the interview rooms, which, at this time of day, smelt only of the disinfectant that, at some ungodly hour of the morning, had been used to make it fit for human habitation.

He had placed two cups of station tea between them and Mr Wilfred Smithson drank deeply from his own, sighing between gulps of the scalding liquid. The constable, unruffled, allowed the histrionics and waited for his current companion to state his business. If his visitor wanted to take the skin off his tonsils it was all the same to him. He watched the man feel in his pocket and bring out an object wrapped in a paper tissue.

He could see, as his eager witness shook the object out on to the table, that he expected to make a great impression with it and PC Smithson was certainly impressed. The object hardly seemed worthy of such excitement or such close scrutiny. The little metal cylinder was scarcely more than an inch long, blackened and burnt-looking.

'That there is a cartridge case,' Mr Smithson explained kindly. 'And that there cartridge case has had a bullet in it, which I have not found yet. No doubt I shall come across it when I eventually get that damned ugly yucca out of my border. Pricked my young grandson something cruel on Sat'day when he ran into it, an' I never liked the thing anyway. I suppose I could o' waited till I'd found both on 'em but then I thought again. You'd be wantin' to see this case, soon as possible . . .'

PC Smithson held up a hand to stem the flow. A smell of cordite rose from the cartridge case and its enclosing tissue so that he knew the bullet had been fired recently. 'You did exactly right, sir. Thank you for being so prompt – but we'd like to do the searching for the bullet ourselves if you don't mind.' He sought frantically for some pretext to keep the old man away from his own property until someone could be sent there, then saw that his efforts were not needed. His namesake seemed delighted by the idea.

'You mean I'm goin' to have a whole tribe of your white-coated folk, searching? Actually in my garden?'

The constable shook his head. 'We needn't trouble them. I reckon the force knows how to find something without disturbing possible evidence – which I'm sure you've been careful about, seeing that you realized so quickly what you'd found.'

His witness nodded, only half mollified. 'They will be in uniform though, your chaps?'

'Your neighbours will certainly know you've found something that interests us.'

'You'll be wanting my fingerprints, I reckon, for elimination like?' PC Smithson bit his lip. So, he'd handled the case. Pity. His witness's cup however was full. 'I suppose they'll be wanting cups o' tea an' suchlike.'

'They might if the bullet takes a lot of finding.'

'I'd best get back and put the kettle on then. I'll go in the back way so's not to trample over the soil any more.' The man got up to attend to his social duties to the force, but stopped at the door. 'I've got an apology to mek to a sparrer.' When the constable looked mystified, he tutted. 'Yer not very quick on the uptake for a policeman. That wall of old fleabag's, I bet it were shot down. That little bird had nowt to do with it.'

At morning break on Wednesday, Elsa Hardy put one of her scarlet-edged cards on the staffroom noticeboard. *I have some concerns about Robin James Ridgeway, Form 8B. Would staff who teach that form please try to attend a 10 minute (I promise!) meeting in my office at 12.45 p.m.*

It seemed to her that her concern was shared when, with less than two hours' notice, and during a busy midweek lunch break, eight members of staff responded to her appeal. Very briefly, she reported the information she had been given by Robin's family. 'I really am keeping you for as short a time as I said. We're probably agreed that Robin is a bright lad whose standard of work and general demeanour have deteriorated over the last term to a point where we ought to be taking some action. I need to know more about the situation than the parents are prepared to tell me. Does anyone here have something useful to contribute?'

Robin's teachers had obviously been considering the matter. To save their own and Miss Hardy's time, comments followed quickly.

'From what I've overheard, his home situation's a bit volatile just now.'

'It's two years since his father left. He seemed to survive that with very few problems.'

'But then he was left in an unhealthy twosome with Mum.' Mrs Parry, who taught religious studies, took herself to task before anyone else could. 'I don't know why I said that. I've just taken against her because she looks like a 1940s starlet, which can't help Robin much.'

Someone broke in and rescued her. 'And now, Mum's pregnant – most uncool – and maybe he thinks the infant will replace him as the boyfriend has replaced Dad.'

The English and drama specialist added her view. Ignoring her colleagues' sighs, she spoke at length, managing only to convey that Robin was a sensitive boy, with talents not only unappreciated by his peers – but actually made fun of. 'I intend to get tickets for this production he's in. I haven't seen him act except in little classroom sketches, but I've seen his face light up when he talks about the Cloughton Players – always to adults, of course. I am not saying, by the way, that any fall off in his work is the result of the time he's spending at the theatre. It seems to be the only time he's happy.'

Further comments seemed merely to be supporting what had been said. Miss Hardy glanced at her watch. 'Thank you for that. If those of you who have spoken could let me have something in writing – and watch this space. All right. It's five to one. You can go.' Seven of the eight filed out hurriedly giving her no opportunity to mention that there was 'just one more thing'. Robin's form tutor had remained behind.

She waited for the door to close then spoke abruptly, as though afraid that she might change her mind. 'I'm beginning to suspect that the lad is being abused in some way, possibly by the mother's partner who moved into the home four months ago.' She relaxed when Elsa Hardy nodded, apparently unsurprised. 'I may be quite wrong and I know, if we're overheard talking about it I could get the school into serious legal trouble.'

'You're a sensible girl. I imagine you have something specific to support what you've said.'

The girl shrugged. 'Not much, though. I saw Geoff Hollins explaining a maths problem to him. He leaned over to point to a diagram and just touched Robin's shoulder. Robin flinched quite noticeably. I was hoping Geoff would tell you himself just now.' Her hand went to her mouth. 'Oh hell, I didn't mean . . .'

Miss Hardy smiled. 'Don't worry. I don't think any of us have any doubts about Geoff's orientation. What makes you think it's Mr Page?'

'I only said possibly. Robin's just been so subdued since he moved into their house, and – well, he is a bit creepy. That's all really.' The girl got up to leave. Reaching the door, she stopped. 'There's something else. I've heard some of the boys in my form laughing because Robin's claiming to have a gun – a real one.'

'Have you spoken to Robin about it?' The girl shook her head. 'Then I think that I shall have to.'

DCI Mitchell was entertaining his sergeant and his only available constable to coffee when PC Smithson's apologetic call came through. The constable described his morning's interview diffidently. 'There's probably not much in it, sir, but that cartridge case still smelt of cordite so I thought I'd let you know. Shall I send a couple of men round?'

Mitchell considered, then decided. 'We'll have the works, I think. I don't like the idea of guns on my ground. Get the pulsar team into the old chap's garden, organize a house-to-house, do a check on your namesake. Any chance of any CCTV? No reports on CAD? Right. Get back to me with any problems – and, of course, any results.' He replaced the handset and grinned at DS Taylor. 'Good job we haven't been supplied with videophones up here. He seems to think I'm too busy to be interrupted. Well, now we have work to do. Hallelujah! Where there's a cartridge case, there's always a bullet.'

Jennifer turned to DC Nazir and shook her head. 'Shakila, did you see what he slipped into his coffee? He might have shared it with us.' Shakila, solemn-faced, suggested that a gun would be a good place to start looking for a bullet.

They settled to treating the incident seriously and Mitchell felt comfortable again. At least something was now happening on his ground. He had left his team to its paperwork until its members refused to look him in the face. If business hadn't begun to look up today he might have been reduced to catching up completely on his own.

Both senior officers turned to Shakila. The shell had been found in a garden only a hundred yards or so from her own and she knew all the people who might have information to offer. Many of her neighbours were Asian and if she were the one collecting their observations there would be little point in their retreating into Hindi or Urdu as a way of avoiding questions.

She considered, then shook her head. 'I'll do it if you send me, of course . . .'

'But you, as always, have other ideas. Let's hear them.'

'Well, they all know that I'm a police officer but they think of me more as a neighbour and friend and fellow Pakistani. If two large male constables called when the men are at work, the women might well ask me . . .'

'How to hide what they don't want to tell? Wouldn't you feel you'd been dishonest?' Jennifer asked.

Shakila shook her head. 'They're not stupid. They wouldn't tell me that one of them had stolen a gun to shoot his brother's white girlfriend. They might be scared, though, because their English isn't wonderful in some cases or because they don't understand how our systems work. They don't mix much outside the local community and they aren't sure what gets them into trouble and what doesn't. They can use me as a sort of filter. They have done before.'

Jennifer looked at her curiously. 'You didn't speak any English before you came over here as a teenager, did you?' Shakila shook her head. 'And when you lived with your brother's family, before you got your flat, you all spoke Urdu at home?'

'Yes.'

'So, how is it that your English is perfect, no foreign accent, no mistakes . . . you even get Benny's jokes before Adrian does. How come?'

'I worked at it,' Shakila replied shortly and turned back to Mitchell. 'So, what do you want me to do?'

'You'll do as you think, as usual. Send Smithson and Chalmers to play good cop, bad cop, but get the right answers between you. You're the one for the high jump if they're wrong.'

Satisfied, Shakila rinsed her cup, dried it, replaced it on the tray and departed. Jennifer said, 'We'd miss her. She never leaves anyone to clear up after her in any sense.'

'If ever she went, yes, we certainly would.' He gave his sergeant a hard look.

'So, what have you got for me to do?'

'Can you check with Shakila in case there's a little corner shop in the area? If it's run by a Pakistani family it'll probably have a video camera to protect it. They're paranoid about attacks on their small businesses – with good reason. We might strike lucky although it's a long shot.'

'I'll pardon the pun.'

'Yes, do that. Oh, and follow the good example you've been set. Wash your cup and leave it on the tray. Don't leave someone else to clear up after you.'

Jennifer grinned. 'Gladly, but don't think I'm doing yours.'

* * *

The computers missing from Heath Lees School occupied Mitchell for most of the rest of the day and he gave the tea party in Wilfred Smithson's garden no more thought until he arrived home. Over the preparation of supper, which pleasant task he and Virginia shared between them whenever possible, they also shared the main events of their day, each with the other. Mitchell made much of PC Smithson's description of his ebullient namesake.

'Yes, I know about that,' Virginia told him. She put down her chopping knife and fetched their copy of the *Cloughton Courier*, delivered each Wednesday afternoon. She pointed to the *Late news! Stop press!* section at the bottom of the back page.

To his dismay, Mitchell read, *Cartridges found in local garden. Police seek bullets. Who has the missing gun?* Through gritted teeth he growled, 'This had better be from the idiot who, unluckily for us, found the thing.'

Virginia asked, 'How seriously are you taking it?'

'We weren't as concerned about it as we'll have to be now. Can you just imagine tomorrow morning? Parents driving their kids to school and demanding that they aren't sent out to play, the station phones ringing with frantic questions, crackpot sightings of suspicious-looking characters with pistols poking out of their pockets . . . ouch!!'

He glared at the blood running from the end of his finger as the knife he was wielding came to the end of the onion and attacked his flesh. Virginia calmly offered first aid and the good advice to save his agitation at least until these annoying things actually happened.

Mitchell decided that he would not trouble his father-in-law that night but, when the telephone rang just after supper, Virginia announced, 'My father, for you.'

Browne had made what he considered to be a significant advance which he was eager to describe. 'There's a PC allocated to this enquiry who's a pain in – well, various parts of my anatomy but he's a genius at turning up useful witnesses. He was the one who brought in the two Bird lads and now he's found a chap who once worked with Hoodie. It was a year ago and they were both students – the witness still is, in fact. It was casual work in a brickyard just outside Milton Keynes.'

'And he's sure it's the same man?'

'So he told his girlfriend. Just a few minutes before the incident they'd raised a hand to each other. They weren't going to cross the road to speak – it was just an acknowledgement. It does suggest though that the killing was not premeditated or Hoodie wouldn't have drawn attention to himself.'

'Why did the chap not come forward sooner?'

'He didn't want to come at all. Wouldn't have if he hadn't made the mistake of discussing it with the lady friend, who just happened to drop a hint to PC Watson. Watson's been hanging round the scene in his copious spare time, hoping for just what happened. As she said when Watson brought her in, "Old mates are one thing but topping two innocent blokes even if one of them is the bloody fuzz isn't on."'

'So now we can stop calling him Hoodie and start following him up under his real name.'

'No we can't. According to O'Reilly, the reluctant witness, his mate was wearing the hooded thing when they worked together and had the same nickname.'

'And you believe that?'

'No, but I think the name is more likely to slip out accidentally if we don't push for it. We sent someone to interview Buchan today but he's still a bit confused. The medics say it'll be better tomorrow. Fortunately they seem to think our going over what's happened is likely to be therapeutic rather than stressful.'

Mitchell had been waiting to slip in his own tale of the Cloughton gun that had demolished a wall and left a shell in a neighbouring garden but decided now that it would be an anticlimax. Besides, this was Tom's last big chance and he wouldn't try to steal his thunder.

In fact, Thursday brought less panic than Mitchell had expected and at least one useful piece of information. Yet another inhabitant of Lower Edge Road presented himself at the station desk. He had heard what he had taken to be a firework but now realized could have been a gunshot . . . Magic let him get no further before ringing his name and business through to Mitchell's office. Once he was discovered to be a man whose sanity and veracity Shakila was prepared to vouch for, Jennifer came to escort him upstairs.

John Betts was anxious that not too much importance should be attached to his revelations. 'It could still have been a firework, sergeant. The kid was really terrified but those fireworks the Asians love at their weddings are so damned loud. It might just be that that scared him.'

'Tell me about the boy. Where were you and where was he?' Jennifer hoped that her impatience with all witnesses who began in the middle of their story was not reflected in her tone.

'It was Friday – or it might have been Saturday teatime.' Jennifer managed not to sigh. 'Anyway, I was on my way to the allotment and I'd got round the corner, not in my road but just into Cain Street. Then this boy came round the corner from behind me, just after I'd heard the bang – whatever caused it. He was quite a tall lad, but you could tell he was only a kid. He was running as if seven devils were after him.'

'Did you know him?'

'I sort of recognized him. I think I'd seen him before but I'm not sure where. There's always plenty of kids around down our way. Not too many whites though.'

'So, you're here because you think this boy saw something that frightened him, possibly a person who shot a gun at someone or something.'

66

Mr Betts cheered up, glad to have made himself so easily understood. 'There's something else.' Jennifer had feared there might be. 'When I set off for the allotment, Old Fleabag's wall was still standing. When I'd done my bit of digging and walked home, it was just a pile of bricks on the pavement.' Jennifer sat less than patiently through a diatribe on the laziness of building single-brick walls, but managed to thank her witness for his parting advice. 'If I was you, I'd try and find that boy. Then he could tell you what he saw.' With the description he had given her, it would not be easy advice to follow. The boy was tall but only young. He was, however, white. In Lower Edge Road that would make him quite conspicuous.

That evening, Mitchell rang his father-in-law for the third time since their return to Cloughton. Virginia was intrigued. 'I'm glad you're getting on so well with my father but isn't a call every night bordering on the effusive?'

Mitchell grinned. 'He knows why I'm ringing and so do you.'

'You're trying to live his life because yours has stopped happening?'

'Be fair. I've spent three days being a normal family man, coming home for supper with my wife and kids at a respectable hour and hearing about everyone's day as we sit round the table – and reading bedtime stories to the twins.' He added, his tone changing from indignant to bemused, 'It is weird, though, having no urgent work to do. Things this week are quieter than I've ever known them. I've something to look into though. Have you seen anything of Shakila this week?' Virginia shook her head. 'I think there's something bothering her. Most of the team had lunch with me on Tuesday and she took very little part in the conversation – and she's not meeting my eye in briefings.'

'She'll have been out on a limb again, maybe fallen off the branch this time. She'll be waiting for you to find out.'

Mitchell shook his head. 'I don't think so. If she was in bother I'd have heard something. She'd probably have told me herself.'

'Oh well, if it's serious you'll hear soon enough. Go and ring Dad for your own bedtime story from him. What's happening about his villain?

'Tom's found someone who appeared, on one of the videos, to have spoken to the hoodie just before he approached PC Buchan's car. The witness, O'Reilly, is a student at Birkbeck. He's sure that Hoodie was a chap he'd worked with labouring on a building site last summer. He refused to be parted from the hooded top even then, so it became his nickname. O'Reilly didn't have any other name for him but said Hoodie was a grafter and gave value for money. Apparently he didn't talk much but at one point he mentioned that he had relatives "up north". O'Reilly thought that might mean Leicester. Down there, anywhere further north seems on a par with outer Mongolia.'

Virginia wrinkled her nose. 'And that's as far as he's got?'

'Seems so. The PC, Buchan, is making a good recovery. He's pretty sure he would know his attacker again and it quite definitely is not Tariq Aziz, the man Buchan was supposed to be tailing. Your father's much more forthcoming with the details now that I'm well off his ground.'

Virginia grinned. 'Well then, you'd better get the next thrilling instalment.'

Chapter Four

Friday arrived without Virginia's having found anyone who wanted to use the tickets that had bought her escape from Susie Gledhill on the family's arrival home from London. She was quite pleased by the prospect of attending the double bill of plays alone. She respected Rattigan's work and it suited her to concentrate on the performances, free from any social responsibilities.

She had been surprised when Susie Gledhill had told her which plays had been chosen as the first few productions of the company's new manager and director, Stephen Thompson, and wondered what the local rep would make of *The Browning Version*. She was unfamiliar with *Harlequinade*, the equally short piece that would precede it and make up the programme. It sounded as though it might be some kind of pantomime and she imagined it not to be a suitable companion piece for the story of the psychological disintegration of an ailing and ageing public school classics master.

The company's forte being slick comedy, the first half of the programme should go well. *The Browning Version* she knew to be a deftly and tightly written classic. Virginia was not expecting that this performance would sensitively convey its message nor demonstrate Rattigan's major achievement in winning audience sympathy for an initially not-very-likeable character. She doubted that Margot Ridgeway's ex-husband, whom she had met only once, would do the part of Andrew Crocker-Harris anything approaching justice.

Harlequinade proved to be fun. The cast kept the atmosphere light and the action fast and Virginia enjoyed the results. She saw the arts correspondent from the *Cloughton Courier* scribbling enthusiastically. She knew him well but went in search of the G&T she had ordered, leaving him to finish his accolade in peace.

The stage curtains were open and the stage well lit as the audience reassembled after the interval. The lights in the auditorium dimmed and the chattering died away. The stage remained empty just long enough for the audience to become curious but not impatient to find out who was about to enter this hotch-potch of a post-war academic's living room. Virginia began to be impressed by the new director's finesse and settled down to give his production a chance to absorb her. John Taplow, in the person of Robin Ridgeway, appeared round the edge of the screen. Virginia had met him for the first time in his grandmother's garden earlier in the week. She had been surprised to learn from a later conversation with her neighbour that the boy was just thirteen years old. He was tall, with a mature manner, and had seemed rather older.

Now she recognized immediately that the boy was in his element. He was John Taplow, reluctant to report to his teacher for extra work out of school hours but unfazed by entering his living room as instructed and finding no one to meet him. He wore the dated school uniform and old-fashioned wire-rimmed spectacles quite unselfconsciously, though the latter must have pressed uncomfortably against his sore eye. He had no lines to speak yet but he was absorbed into his stage character. She could see that he was totally aware of the eyes of the audience on him and comfortable with them.

His 'Sir!' was enquiring, puzzled. He shrugged, enjoyed this opportunity to satisfy his curiosity about a schoolmaster's private milieu. He put his books on the table in front of the chair set out for him opposite to the master's own. Then he sat, still without speaking, surveying and assessing the room. He noticed a small box of chocolates on a sideboard to his right. After a furtive glance at the inner door he turned, opened the box, counted the sweets inside, removed two, ate one. His movements were infinitesimal, yet he showed the audience his struggle with his conscience and his assessment of risk before putting the other one back.

When the young man playing the junior science master came on to the stage to join Robin, Virginia realized that she had been holding her breath. This actor's name meant nothing to her. His part was not demanding and he played it adequately. Virginia waited for the lines where Taplow had to mimic the classics master making his academic 'jokes'. The boy repeated them, using a gentle, throaty voice which amused her. The scene continued with the entrance of Crocker-Harris's wife, Millie. Taplow was sent on an errand so that the two could reveal their extramarital relationship. She and the reluctant science master, Hunter, discussed the cuckolded husband and Virginia decided that Robin was a far better actor than his mother. Fortunately, she only had to play a shallow and neglected wife, hungry for sex, and she proved adequate in that role.

Suddenly shocked at her own judgemental attitude, Virginia stopped being patronizing and settled down to enjoy a much better rendering of this play she admired than she had been expecting. When Crocker-Harris finally made his appearance, she almost laughed aloud as he spoke in just exactly the gentle, throaty voice that Taplow had imitated. Suddenly, she realized that Andrew Crocker-Harris, his wife Millie and Taplow the pupil had, in real life and as recently as two years ago, been husband, wife and son. Robin had most likely been practising mimicking his father's voice for most of his life.

Paul Ridgeway proved to be yet another talented actor. Skilfully he made his character grow in stature.

Crocker-Harris's huge contribution to the successful running of the school became apparent even as all the more forceful people around him hurt and betrayed him in turn, his wife, his headmaster, his successor in the classics department. Then came the crux of the play. Taplow, who had been dismissed after his coaching, returned to offer his teacher genuine good wishes for his future and tentatively to hand over the gift of a book, Robert Browning's verse translation of the *Agamemnon*, bought second-hand with his own pocket money. He had inscribed it in Greek with a phrase Crocker-Harris has used in a recent lesson, 'God, from afar, looks graciously upon a gentle master.' Virginia sat entranced as the delightful scene unfolded, with the master's embarrassed tears and the boy's uncomfortable sympathy. She settled herself again. Just a quick run through to the end now.

Millie's seducer, the science master, had been invited to dinner and arrived before Taplow left. He was shown the little book and showed himself genuinely pleased that his colleague had received such pleasure from this pupil's tribute. Taplow departed and Millie herself came in to greet their guest. Out of sheer ill nature, she revealed that Taplow had been mocking him in front of Hunter. The book, she said, is his sweetener, to make sure that, in spite of his peccadillo, he would still get a good report.

His emotional state had aggravated his heart condition and Crocker-Harris retired to take extra medication. Hunter, who was becoming increasingly disillusioned with Millie, finally decided, in view of this display of gratuitous spite, that his relationship was at an end. He refused to listen to her excuses. For the first time, Virginia began to feel a morsel of sympathy for Millie as she burst out, 'Why should he be allowed his comforting little illusions? I'm not.'

The quarrel would have continued but an explosion from somewhere close to the theatre startled everyone, for a few seconds, into silence. Virginia was angry. Another

Asian wedding! Now the rest of the performance would be continually interrupted and the carefully built-up atmosphere had been shattered. But there was no follow-up. The young man playing Frank recovered first. 'Listen, you're to go to his room now and tell him that was a lie.'

Millie refused and the quarrel grew more bitter. Eventually, Hunter refused even to stay for dinner. Millie grew more distressed and beseeching. Now for Crocker-Harris's change of heart. Virginia wondered whether Paul Ridgeway would manage to carry it off. He had let the other characters destroy his so magnificently. Would he be able to dominate his two persecutors and leave the stage with his dignity intact? She waited for his cue as anxiously as the cast. 'I'm not coming to Bradford, Millie.' Both players turned to the door which would open slowly and bring the main character back. It didn't. Millie and Hunter looked at each other. Hunter spoke his cue again, this time raising his voice. Nothing happened.

Virginia was desolated. Some minor crisis backstage had killed a magnificent production. However soon the dialogue continued now, the play was ruined. It couldn't sustain two interruptions. She ground her teeth as, from the upper balcony, came the faint suggestion of a slow handclap. As if in answer to that signal, the recalcitrant door now opened. Through it came a bearded man, an academic gown covering his clothes, a copy of the script in one hand, Crocker-Harris's bottle of medicine in the other. He handed the bottle to Millie as he moved down left. In a daze, she held it up to the light as she had been instructed in rehearsal.

In a fair imitation of Paul Ridgeway's throaty voice he gave the line. 'You should know me well enough now, my dear, to realize how unlikely it is that I should ever take an overdose . . .'

Woodenly, the three players spoke the lines of the play through to its close. The audience sat, rapt. The play itself had been fascinating but they could dine out for weeks on what was happening now.

After Crocker-Harris's bathetic last line, 'Come along, my dear. We mustn't let our dinner get cold,' the bearded man closed his copy and held up a hand as if to stop the applause. There was no applause. The audience sat absolutely still, in perfect silence. The man stepped forward and addressed them with a strained smile. 'As you'll have gathered, we've had a slight mishap backstage. I apologize for falling far below the standard of Mr Ridgeway's – of Paul's performance, but at least I made sure that you knew how the story ended.' The three players on stage took a quick bow. No one else appeared. The three stepped back and the curtains closed. For some seconds, the audience sat on, still in silence.

Virginia used the vital seconds to get out of her seat and down the aisle to the door that led backstage. Being both a police daughter and a police wife, she seemed to have developed a nose for such things. That mini-explosion had been no firework. Pulling out her mobile phone as she ran, she punched in Benny's number, thanking providence that she had decreed this play unsuitable for Declan and remained adamant in the face of his pleas. This was the second time that she had attended a social engagement without her husband and had felt impelled to call him to it as the scene of a possible crime. This time, she hoped that there wouldn't be a body – and, if there was, that she would not be the person to find it.

The door opened on to a narrowish corridor. It seemed to be full of people, milling round, bumping into one another and shouting, the women's high-pitched questions and surmises underpinned by the bass bellows of one of the cast of *Harlequinade*, advising everyone to calm down. To one side, his back to the wall, Virginia saw Robin, looking bewildered and holding a hand to his right eye. Margot stood in the centre of a group who were hurling questions at her. Was her ex-husband feeling ill before the performance began? Had he passed any kind of message to her as he made his exit?

Gradually, the company became aware of Virginia standing in the doorway. To most of them, she was a stranger and the hubbub died as they tried to work out why she had appeared. It occurred to her now that she had no right to be there. It was quite possible that Paul Ridgeway would be found, maybe even had been found, and that help had been summoned. He had not acted as though he were ill but she supposed that such afflictions as heart attacks could happen very suddenly.

The long-haired, bearded man who had read Crocker-Harris's part and announced his 'slight mishap' took advantage of the lull to gain control. The assembled company was apparently used to his taking charge. When he asked them to stand still and listen, they did so. 'Did anyone backstage see him come off?'

The consensus was that Ridgeway had exited centre-back and should have waited there, having only six minutes before his re-entry. The furthest he could safely have gone was to the small cloakroom at the bottom of a short flight of stairs that led down behind the back corner of the stage, actors' left. 'And he'd have to have been sharpish at that!'

Now the company had forgotten Virginia. The bearded man, presumably the manager Stephen Thompson, asked, 'Is that outside door still locked?'

The actors and their retinue looked at each other, waiting for an answer, and Thompson ran down the stairs to check for himself. The rest followed, but quietly, watching over the banister rail. Virginia joined them. Thompson tried the door and it opened soundlessly. Mouths dropped open. There was a concerted movement towards it but Thompson held up his hand and the movement stilled. As Virginia watched, he deputed the young man, who had played the science master and cuckolded Crocker-Harris, to go and look around outside. 'Have a look in the shrubs, just as far as the wall. Don't go up into the car park. It's unlikely that he'd go there and, if he did, someone will soon find him. There'll be crowds out there. Who's checked the dressing rooms?' Most people seemed to have tried this.

After a moment, Thompson nodded towards the Harlequin who had done the calming, indicating that he should join the search. He reserved for himself the task of keeping the remainder of his company in order. As the two selected men went out he left the door behind them ajar but no one followed. The noise level had risen a little but the voices were subdued. Someone asked, 'Where did Paul park his car?' No one answered.

Virginia struggled to picture the scene outside. As far as she remembered, there was, beyond the door, only a narrow stretch of scrubby wasteland and then an ivy-covered wall some six feet high. No light could be seen from where they all stood watching so that the two searchers had only that spilling through the doorway from inside. Stephen Thompson was thinking aloud. 'There's nothing to go out there for. I suppose, if Paul felt ill, he might have needed a breath of air. It's hot in here, particularly backstage. But – that door's been locked for weeks. How did he know it would open and why didn't it creak?'

His speculations were cut short by the return of the science master, who swallowed before announcing, 'We've found him. He's lying on the ground. He seems to have hurt his head.' The man swallowed again, making the assembled company aware that this was a euphemism. 'Tony's putting my coat over him but we haven't tried to move him. Can someone . . .' Presumably about to ask for an ambulance to be summoned, he saw that this was being done. Instead, he asked, 'Has anyone got a torch?'

No one either answered or produced one but a voice from behind Virginia called out, 'Dr Vaughan was in the audience. I bet he's still in the bar.'

Now there was a rush for the door into the auditorium but, again, a hand raised by the charismatic Thompson put an end to the disorder. He nodded to another young man. 'Neil, you go.'

Virginia turned to look for the injured man's ex-wife. Did she not want to go to him? Apparently not. Over in a corner Margot Ridgeway was bending over her son, using cotton wool and baby lotion to remove make-up from around his sore eye. They all turned as the inner door swung open again to admit Dr Vaughan – with Neil, at a run, in his wake. In the time since he was summoned, the doctor could certainly not have come all the way from the bar. He swept through the mêlée, asking only, 'Through here?' and disappeared outside. Neil trotted after him, fiddling with the array of buttons on the huge torch he had managed to acquire.

As the company waited in silence for news, Thompson realized that he was still wearing the academic gown in which he had impersonated Crocker-Harris. He wriggled out of it and tossed it over a mysterious wooden construction that might have been embryo scenery for the next production.

Virginia had been sure, since the 'science master' had returned to the building, face set and lips tight, that Paul Ridgeway was no longer alive. Still no one had questioned her presence. She had been here for less than ten minutes, which had felt like several hours. Now she approached Stephen Thompson and spoke to him quietly. He listened, then nodded and gave the now-familiar hand signal to gain the company's attention. Before he could begin on his list of instructions, Dr Vaughan reappeared, but remained standing in the doorway. A minute shake of his head told all of them his verdict before he spoke. 'I'm afraid Mr Ridgeway is dead.'

Stephen Thompson gave everyone a few moments to absorb the news and to speculate about the situation, then he strode over to stand beside Dr Vaughan. The assembly

77

quietened to listen to him. 'Officially, this is a sudden death, possibly even a suspicious one. Thanks to Mrs Mitchell,' he acknowledged Virginia with a wave of his hand, 'whose husband is a detective chief inspector in the Cloughton force, we know that there are certain procedures to be followed in these circumstances.' Swiftly and with no opposition, he left Dr Vaughan and his Harlequin player, Tony, in charge of the body outside and shepherded the whole company into the nearer and larger dressing room.

Virginia was satisfied that she had done her best to preserve the scene. Thompson had control here. He had listened to her and co-operated. She knew that her husband would want to stop the audience going home but she had overstepped her own authority already. Since there was so much to gossip and speculate about, probably only a few would have departed by the time that Benny arrived. Now, she wanted to get home to her family and release the friend who had been commandeered to look after them until she arrived. It was fortunate that Cavill had been visiting when she had made her call to Benny, and Declan would be delighted to be left with him. However, minding her children would not have been the way he had planned his evening. As she drove away, she felt ashamed that her regret for the death of Paul Ridgeway was no greater than her regret that she would never feel the same again about a very clever and moving play.

The theatre's women's dressing room was not an inviting place in which to await the impending police invasion. Large and draughty, it was lined on two sides by panels of timber-framed hardboard, much paint-splashed, leaning against the wall and waiting to be adorned with whatever setting was required for the next production. Along a third wall ran a wide shelf beneath which, at intervals, stools were tucked. Above these, mirrors were propped against the wall. Other mirrors, full-length and in wheeled frames, were littered about, left wherever they had last been peered into. There was an assortment of seating, mostly mismatched and shabby but clean armchairs. Harsh light from fluorescent strips across the ceiling made tired faces ghastly in spite of the make-up that most of them still wore.

Adam Lessing ignored the armchairs. If he bagged one he would only have to relinquish it to one of the women. Instead, he carried a dusty floor cushion to a corner where he could lean against the wall. Settling himself, he became aware of the general frustration that no one liked to give voice to. The whole company, players, stage crew, scene painters et al, had worked hard for weeks to make tonight a success and not the least part of their sorrow now was for the loss of the good reviews they had expected – perhaps, if they'd been lucky, in a couple of national papers. They were exhausted and not even the members of the Harlequin cast who had been able to complete the performance of their play felt any of the euphoria that usually carried them through the jollifications after a first night.

They talked in two subdued groups, separated by the casting which had temporarily turned the company into two 'families'. In the Harlequin group the chatter became gradually less subdued until one unfortunate woman laughed aloud. A horrified silence followed, broken by a black constable who enquired for Stephen Thompson and bore him away.

Lessing was not shocked. Every play made the members of its cast intimate with each other as they sympathized with those who had been found fault with, advised each other helpfully, quarrelled bitterly and found out about each other much that would not have emerged in any other way. The Harlequin lot had had a lot of fun and were high on the comedy still. The single laugh had not meant any disrespect to Paul or his family. From his corner he could see no one actually weeping but he did not feel that the company was uncaring. Paul was a good actor and had been reasonably popular with most of his colleagues in the company. Dependable too, though he had got into the habit of a few too many drinks over the two years since he and Margot had separated.

Lessing tried to assess what he had felt when he had gone outside and found what he had taken at once to be a body and not an injured man. He hadn't been certain, of course. So far, even the medics weren't committing themselves to any official statement – not to the company, anyway. When had he realized what he was seeing? What questions had he asked himself? He couldn't remember. He would forget it for now, calm down and think of something else. At least nobody could suspect him of any responsibility for what had happened. He had been in full view of dozens of people since before Paul had left the stage. He had been the first to go outside but Tony had been hard on his heels and they had come up to Paul's body together. For just the same reasons, the police could be sure that Margot too was in no way responsible for what had happened. Not directly at least.

Thank goodness Stephen had had the presence of mind to take over so quickly. Of course, he always had the book to hand. In fact he usually knew the text so well that he could shout missing lines from the auditorium if the official prompt was busy doing something else at a particular rehearsal. And, since he was the one who had demanded all the movements, he knew what they were. He probably didn't trust Lessing and Margot to stall and play along for a minute till Paul got himself where he should be. Lessing had felt a little slighted by that – but he was fairly new to the company. Stephen was still assessing him and, anyway, if he had tried to improvise, he wouldn't have got much back-up from Margot. She'd have stood and gaped at him. He didn't think she was very bright.

He twisted round to look for Margot now. There she was, as he had expected, mopping at dry eyes with tissues supplied by a retinue of men. She wasn't a good enough actress to simulate grief, on stage or off, or to pretend anything convincingly. She had been nicely cast in this piece – nicely in its original sense – as a shallow, spiteful woman . . . Was that fair? Well, she was petulant and selfish anyway. And she should know better than to wear that hair like a cloak round her shoulders at her age – even though it was thick and that nice reddish gold that she liked to call strawberry blonde.

He supposed his own reaction to tonight's tragedy was as selfish as anything Margot had done. He was sorry about Paul's death chiefly because he wouldn't be able to act with him again. He'd been damned good. Lessing himself had been disappointed to be cast this time in a part that was so undemanding, whatever Stephen said about it to the contrary. What Stephen called his 'telling' scenes were the ones with Margot, who thought that acting meant fluttering her eyelashes – though, if he was right about that, then she was acting for all of her waking life.

He sighed, wriggled himself into a more comfortable position on the lumpy cushion and wished that the two plays could have had their expected two-week run. He could have made the part grow. He could have traced his gradual disillusion with Millie Crocker-Harris in a subtly changed attitude towards her in each succeeding exchange. Then, by its final night he would have made something of his performance that he could remember with pride and that Stephen would consider when he was casting for their next new production.

He pulled himself up short. Whatever kind of priorities did he have? Suddenly, he remembered Robin. Poor kid, where was he and who was with him? Looking round he was glad to see it was Lucille. She was a part-time nurse, wasn't she? She'd have to be a part-time something. The wardrobe-mistress money wouldn't keep body and soul together. If she was as good a nurse as she was a wardrobe mistress, Robin was in good hands. Lucille was a sensible, sympathetic woman who should have had a string of kids of her own.

On the other side of the stage, in the smaller room normally allotted to the men, Mitchell was organizing his forces. For the first time since leaving London, he felt that he was home again – professionally he meant, of course. He knew that his friend, Cavill Jackson, husband of his DC Caroline, was perfectly happy to be left playing piano duets with Declan. The boy had been equally delighted. Ginny should be back by now so that their commandeered child minder could go home. Mitchell grinned to himself. Whatever Cavill now planned to do with his evening, it would not be some pleasant dallying with his wife. Mitchell himself had plans for her.

He had radioed the town centre beat bobby as soon as he received Ginny's call and, with appropriate reinforcements, the man had corralled a large proportion of the evening's audience in the theatre bar. He had even thought to have the bar closed after a short period, so that, 'You should have reasonably sober witnesses telling their all, sir, when you're ready for them.'

Dr Holland, the pathologist, had arrived but seemed not to be on his usual form. He had attended the plays, left without visiting the bar, and arrived home only to find a summons to return. He was currently examining Paul Ridgeway's remains. When a few moments with the deceased had restored him to his usual good humour, Mitchell would go out to see what he could tell. For now he was sharing with his assembled team the few facts he had so far been offered.

They were interrupted by a knock at the door and, at a nod from Mitchell, Shakila went to admit their visitor. Mitchell recognized him at once as the man he had met in the station foyer whose attire had startled him and whose appreciation of police efficiency had impressed him. The man offered Mitchell his hand and introduced himself. 'Stephen Thompson. I'm the owner, manager of this place and director of the players.' He made no reference to their previous meeting. 'I need to know what's to happen to my immediate plans for the theatre. Presumably we won't have our official first night tomorrow. I have no problem with that. Without Paul we wouldn't make much of a showing. How do I let people know and how much am I allowed to tell them?' He met Caroline's stare but still addressed himself to Mitchell. 'Sorry to be pragmatic rather than sentimental, but that's how I am.'

At least, Mitchell allowed, he had not claimed that this brave and practical approach was cloaking his grief. He promised him some kind of guidance by the end of the evening. 'But that may well be much later than you're expecting.' Having dismissed Thompson, he turned back to his team. 'Right. We have two urgent tasks. We have to find a gun, possibly two guns, and we have to find a killer. That should keep us busy for most of the weekend. Two shooting incidents have left us with a collapsed wall and a man with a bullet in his brain.' He nodded to Shakila. 'At least I hope it's still in his head because the other one that the pulsar team found in your road was a pancake-shaped piece of lead alloy that tells us zilch. So, your preliminary thoughts, please.'

'This one's a record breaker,' Jennifer observed. 'Once before we were on an enquiry where we knew the time of death within half an hour. This time, it's within six minutes.'

'The killer needn't be a player. We're going to have to find out if anyone in the audience didn't stay in for the duration – and almost anyone could have been hanging around on that rough ground during the whole evening.'

'It needn't be anyone to do with the company or the audience or the building.'

'Yes it must, surely. He or she would have to know

when Ridgeway was coming offstage and how he could get outside . . .'

'We'll have to get a plan of the whole building early on or we shan't be able to follow what they tell us about where they all were.'

Suggestions came thick and fast. Mitchell lost track of who was speaking but managed a quick note on each point. The door opened again and PC Smithson's head appeared. 'There's a chap at the outside door. Says he's the live-in partner of the woman who's the former wife of the victim.'

Mitchell sighed. Smithson had suggested half a dozen motives for this killing in one succinct sentence. He shook his head and retuned to what his PC was saying. 'Wants to know what's going on. At first he just wanted to congratulate everyone and see why Paul didn't finish his lines but now . . . Well, do I let him in?'

Mitchell considered. 'Yes, but don't let him join the others yet. Find a corner somewhere and do your Dutch uncle act. Find out where he's been all evening, how he got on with the victim after he had replaced him, how the boy got on with both of them. You know the drill.' Smithson nodded and disappeared.

A muffled volley of car doors slamming drew Mitchell to the window. Through the fast-gathering darkness he made out the SOCOs' car and a redundant police surgeon. He glanced at his watch and stowed away his notebook in his case before turning back to his team. 'I'll consult my list of your comments when I'm sorting out the actions for tomorrow but we need some information before we do any more theorizing. I'm going out to see what Dr Holland can tell me. It won't be much – they've hardly had time to set up the lights yet. Jen, see if you can find somewhere quiet to have a word with the ex-wife and the young son. I suggest you try the green room. Find a female PC and be all sweetness and sympathy but keep your eyes and ears open. Shakila, you find Smithson. Either join in the discussion they're having or let Smithson go and see if Margot Ridgeway's partner will tell a female detective more than he'll share with a male PC. Adrian, can you find a uniform to get names and addresses from all the folk in the other dressing room. Except for Thompson, Margot Ridgeway and the boy, they can all go as soon as we know where to get hold of them. Then can you go and mingle discreetly with the crowd in the bar and see what you can provoke them into telling you? First drink's on expenses. Caroline, stay here. Stephen Thompson is yours.'

The team members separated to perform their respective duties and Mitchell found a staircase that his accurate sense of direction told him led backstage. Finding the door which led to the outside, he opened the ball catch carefully with a bank card and crossed the strip of wasteland where the SOCOs were organizing themselves. Beyond the wall that bounded it were the flats the council had put up on the land that had been the churchyard before the church building had become the theatre. Now that darkness had fallen, their uncurtained windows shed a limited light on the scene, so that Dr Holland knelt by the body even as the arc lights were being erected in a wide circle round him. As Mitchell approached, the pathologist, his expression solemn, began to sing softly.

'"Who saw him die?"
"I," said the fly, "with my little eye.
I saw him die."
All the birds of the air fell a sighing and a sobbing . . .'

Mitchell growled. 'I'm damned if I'm going to join in the chorus. What are you on about, anyway?'

Holland beamed up at him

'I mean that I know my job. DCIs, even the stupid ones, can usually see for themselves that a victim had been shot or stabbed in the back or clobbered over the head. What you always ask is when did it happen – and, in this case, it seems that you can work that out for yourself too. So, what you need is someone who saw who did the shooting. And that, my friend, is down to you, so can I go back to my supper now?'

Mitchell grinned. 'You couldn't keep your nose out if I said yes.'

Dr Holland did not deign to reply but busied himself with explaining to the photographer exactly what combination of single shots and videotaping he would require to demonstrate the position of the body in relation to its location and what shots he wanted of the wound in Ridgeway's forehead.

As the lights sprang on dramatically, the pathologist was moved to declaim again, this time, mercifully, in speech. *'We fat all creatures else to fat us, and we fat ourselves for maggots. Your fat king and your lean beggar is but variable service, two dishes but to one table.'* He waited for a reaction.

One at least of the SOCOs was unimpressed. *'Hamlet,* Act 4, Scene 5,' the man muttered. Then, smiling smugly at both Holland and Mitchell, 'I'm not just an ignorant scientist.'

Mitchell laughed aloud and settled to watch the familiar procedures in high good humour. He saw that the SOCOs had begun their searching at the furthest point of the patch of ground from where the body lay. The police surgeon hovered, fearful of annoying Dr Holland, but loath to lose his fee now that he had reported to the scene. Under the arc lights, Dr Holland began a more detailed examination of the remains, working swiftly and silently, his expression now serious. After some minutes he beckoned again to the two waiting photographers and had them record various scratches and pressure marks that his further examination had revealed. After a while, he stood back to allow the photographers to work alongside the exhibits officer, recording clues *in situ* before they were collected, bagged and labelled for the lab.

Mitchell looked up at the pathologist hopefully but Dr Holland turned to overseeing the laying of the whole body, with its head, hands and feet encased in plastic bags, on a sheeted board. It could now be transported to the lab, pretty much in the position in which they had found it. As the board was carried away, the pathologist, still uncommunicative, followed it.

Mitchell did not feel he had wasted the time he had spent out here. He had watched everything carefully and would be able to run the procedures over again in his head, analysing and preparing his questions for Dr Holland. Satisfied, he went back into the theatre in search of his sergeant.

Caroline, left to herself in the men's dressing room, was amusing herself by reading the various notices pinned to a cork board on the wall. She grinned at a selection of scurrilous cartoons cut from an assortment of publications, cast an eye over the rehearsal schedules for three plays and tried to decide whether it was worth copying a list of names and telephone numbers into her notebook.

She turned as the door opened to admit her interviewee, who was escorted by a uniformed constable. The PC made himself inconspicuous in a corner whilst Caroline eyed Thompson without speaking. His hair, thick but somehow limp, straggled into his collar, his garments were bizarre but, as he posed for them in the bare room, his arms akimbo and hands on hips with studied nonchalance against a garishly painted piece of scenery, it was the constable and herself who seemed to her to be out of place. Weary now, the man was cadaverous, his eyes sunken but burning still with the euphoria of a first night, however much its success had been overshadowed by events..

She left Thompson in the position in which he had arranged himself and sank into a comfortable armchair before asking, 'How long has this building been a theatre?'

Thompson gave a slight shrug. 'I can't tell you exactly, but it was taken over about a year before I arrived here in Cloughton. The company's finances were in a dire state so it sold the original theatre to the council and that's now a bingo hall. It was a more central site and sold for enough to clear the debts and to buy this place, which is a fair distance from the shops but conveniently near the train and bus stations.'

Caroline smiled to herself as she read in the PC's face his opinion that the interview was not achieving its purpose. She nodded to Thompson to continue.

'It's serving us very well. There wasn't even much expense in adapting the internal appointments. The pews were conveniently ranked with a steep rake so at first they only had them upholstered. In front of them was the pulpit and, behind it, a raised platform for what a century ago was a huge church choir. Then there was the organ behind that. The choir's platform was the basis for the stage and the organ's still there behind it, though it's in a lamentable state of repair.' Caroline knew all about the organ. Her husband had enthusiastic plans for its restoration. She wondered whether this man could be persuaded to agree to them and whether his permission would be needed. She made a mental note to find out exactly what Thompson meant when he claimed to own the theatre. Meanwhile, his account was continuing. 'The stage is a bit cramped for us but . . .'

Now Caroline raised a hand to stem the flow and change the subject. 'Can you tell me something about the company members and how you're organized? How many of you are there?'

'There are twelve of us who are a sort of permanent staff, which restricts our choice of material a little. Sometimes we double up the parts but that makes a very heavy rehearsal commitment for the people concerned. Occasionally, suitable friends and relatives are given minor roles.'

'What do the Equity rules say about that?'

Thompson smiled, causing the deep-set eyes to disappear altogether. 'I'd rather not answer that until my lawyer gets here. Seriously, we aren't a sufficiently large dot on the map for anyone in Equity to consider our arrangements a threat. If and when we are, we'll be able to afford to be above board about such matters.'

'Fair enough. Tell me about this production.'

'What about it?'

'All about it. I've got the general gist of the plot from various sources but I can't see the point of the title. Where does Browning come into it?'

This thawed Thompson enough for him to abandon his uncomfortable pose and take the armchair next to hers. He spoke slowly and clearly for the benefit of these unlettered police officers. 'The poet, Robert Browning, translated the Greek tragedy *Agamemnon* into English verse. The book that young Taplow gave to his teacher was a copy of that translation. Actually, there was a longer version of this play made for British television in 1955 with Peter Cushing as Crocker-Harris.'

'Would you have preferred to produce that version?'

'No. I admire the piece as a one-act. It's tight and compact. Everything is in and there's nothing extraneous.'

'So, you choose the plays the company puts on without reference to the players?'

'Yes. And that's an innovation.' He grinned. 'It used to be – well, more democratic. What I do with them is all a bit more serious than what they're used to. Some of them resent it but the good people are glad of the chance to stretch themselves, prove what they can do.'

'When they're expertly coached, you mean?'

'When they've got a play they can get their teeth into is what I mean. You can't teach people to act. They can either get inside someone else's skin or they can't. Sorry. I'm rather mixing my metaphors."

'Is that so?' Caroline turned to give a smug smile to her PC. This conversation was going just the way she wanted. 'So all you're claiming credit for is choosing the right plays.'

'And the right casting. If you start with getting that wrong, nothing else will go right.'

'So, in a small company like this you'll be doing a lot of type casting. That's going to limit your choice of play to twelve types of character . . .' Caroline was enjoying being deliberately obtuse.

Thompson shook his head impatiently. 'I don't mean that at all. You just have to know the strengths and weaknesses of your people, then use the former and try not to reveal the latter.'

'Give me an example.'

Thompson sat further back in his chair, brought his right ankle up to rest on his left knee and smoothed the folds of his voluminous, electric blue trousers. Then, ready to continue his account, he said, 'The first play I put on here was Goldsmith's *She Stoops to Conquer.*' Caroline hoped they were not to be treated to a long synopsis of another play. She smiled, hoping that this would indicate that she knew it well. After all, if, later on, she needed to, she could always go to ask Ginny. 'One of the company who rejoices in the name of Peter Hall wanted to be either Hastings or Marlowe.' A sidelong glance told her that the constable's shorthand was equal to the speed at which this information was being delivered. 'In the end, he had to settle for Mr Hardcastle and he wasn't best pleased. Paul got Marlowe. The chap who got Hastings wasn't cast for the Rattigan. Bit of an egghead – doing a lecture tour in the States.'

'Did the ill feeling persist?'

'Hall's, you mean?' Thompson shook his head. 'It wasn't brought to me to deal with. That's all I can tell you. He's with the others in the dressing room, so you can ask him. He played the headmaster tonight.'

The PC's voice startled both the others. 'What have you got lined up to follow this production?'

'We're doing *Hobson's Choice* next.'

'I've seen that. That's the sort of stuff they did before you changed everything.'

Thompson swivelled his chair to face his new interrogator. 'Yes, but it's good theatre, just as well constructed as the Rattigan. And there's nothing wrong with doing light comedy. I just objected to our doing nothing else.'

Caroline reclaimed her witness. 'I read an article in the local paper about you and the difference you've made to the company. It said you often have a full house and the programmes are booked up well in advance. I think it said you've cleared the company's debt.'

Thompson smiled. 'It did, but I'm afraid we haven't quite managed that yet. Things are distinctly healthier though, financially.'

'So what's your secret?'

'Beyond a good play, well cast? There is one other small thing I do that makes a difference. I tell each of the characters, casually but privately, that, major or minor as far as length is concerned, theirs is the most important role in the play. I don't feel that I'm cheating them, because, as I explain it to them, I find I'm convincing myself. I told Paul, for instance, that he was the one that all the audience will empathize with and that the change that is the crux of any good play happens to him. Then, to young Robin, I stressed the importance of the change again and pointed out that he was the one to bring it about. He had to make himself a pupil that even this crusty old master had a soft spot for. If he could show the audience that he is the only person the old man has any feeling for, they will understand how much Millie hurts him by suggesting that the gift of the book was just a sweetener. I told Peter Hall that his headmaster must be patronizing , his insincere compliments on Crocker-Harris's scholarly publication must humiliate. The head's the one who begins the build-up of anger that finally leads to the main character's rebellion and change of heart.

91

'It wasn't a technique that worked so well with Millie. Margot hasn't got much weight. She's certainly the best actress we have, which isn't saying a great deal. And then, she wasn't helped by being cast opposite Adam Lessing – the science master chap. He's fairly new here and I'm still getting his measure. Adam sulked because he didn't get the main part. He's not cast at all in *Hobson*, though now I'll have to let him replace Paul as Jim Heeler, Hobson's drinking pal. He won't like that. He wouldn't have minded ageing up to show his versatility in a major part but it'll take some persuasion to get him to be an old soak who's just the main man's sidekick. I don't think I'll keep him long – might let him go at the end of *Hobson* – unless he quits before that. I hope he does go of his own accord, although I wouldn't be so unpopular for sacking a newcomer as for getting rid of a foundation stone like Margot. What I certainly wasn't considering was sacking Paul and I'm rather less than pleased with whoever did!'

That night, the intruder in Janil Iqbal's bedroom had Robin Ridgeway's face but his figure was man-sized – a huge man too, taller than his father and bulging with muscles. The gun was in his right hand and the long fat forefinger rested on the trigger, ready to squeeze.

A glance out of the window showed street lamps shining on bodies that were strewn haphazardly over the road. Each one had a gaping wound in the middle of its forehead, just as the late news said that Robin's father had had.

The intruder raised his arm, took careful aim with his weapon, then spoke with Robin's voice. 'Here's my gun. Maybe when you're out there with a hole in your head, you'll believe what I tell you.'

Janil opened his mouth to scream but heard no sound coming from his own lips until his actual screaming woke him. It woke his mother too. Her appearance in his bedroom doorway, outlined against the light from the landing, helped him reorientate himself. She came over to the bed, taking his hand in one of hers and feeling his forehead with the other. He gritted his teeth, submitting to her ministrations because he needed things to become normal again, even if normality irked him.

He parried her questions. No, he couldn't remember what the dream had been about. No, he wouldn't like a glass of hot milk. Yes, he thought he could go to sleep again now. Youssef appeared and came in looking shaken himself. Janil was dismayed to have incurred the teasing that would follow later, but grateful to his brother for persuading his mother to go back to bed. In fact he remembered the dream vividly, could not have swallowed any hot milk and was sure that he would remain awake till morning.

Chapter Five

On Saturday morning, Mitchell was fuelled by the mixture of energy and excitement he always felt when his men gathered for the first briefing on the new case. He was pleased to see that the uniformed section included both the wisdom and experience of PC Smithson and the youth and enthusiasm of young Bob Beardsmore. For more than one reason he planned to do all he could to get the lad transferred to CID. Smithson would have been an equally welcome addition to the team but the older man had had no such ambitions for himself and, with retirement only months away, would hardly be considering it now.

Mitchell was further cheered when he picked up the file that he had laid out ready to receive today's contributions. He had expected it to be empty, but saw now that it contained a detailed account, with her own comments, of Caroline's conversation with Stephen Thompson. This included a typed transcript of some young constable's meticulous shorthand record. Mitchell made a mental note to find and commend him. The SOCO had added to these items a detailed sketch plan of the waste ground where Ridgeway's body had been found, and some unknown person had contributed a plan of both floors of the theatre building. He displayed these treasures to the officers in front of him and apologized for delaying the start of the briefing. 'The superintendent wants a word before the investigation begins and then to sit in on today's session until he has a grasp of the situation and how we intend to deal with it.'

Ignoring the impatient murmurs, Mitchell strolled across to Shakila. She surprised him by looking both alarmed and embarrassed. He ignored this and asked what he had intended. 'I saw you busy at the computer earlier this morning. Haring after a theory about this bunch of villains already – or was it something private?'

She shook her head, looking relieved. 'I was interested in how someone in Cloughton could get hold of a gun.'

Mitchell shrugged. 'Nick it from someone who had one legally, I suppose.'

'But there's been all the fuss about the shell in the garden and the theory that the collapsed wall was shot at. Wouldn't that make all the registered owners – and I shouldn't think there are many of those locally – check that theirs were safely where they should be?'

'Our customer may be a registered owner. What did you find, anyway?'

Shakila fished in her case for a printout of what she had found. Mitchell read it and asked for a copy for the file. 'We'll discuss this in the briefing. Did you find anything else?'

Shakila grinned. 'Yes, I know who the monstrous regiment of women were.' Seeing that Mitchell remembered their exchange during lunch four days ago, she went on. 'In 1558, John Knox published a pamphlet called "The First Blast of the Trumpet Against the Monstrous etc etc".'

'What was it about?'

'It said the Bible makes it clear that women should never rule over men. I copied one sentence out.' She scrabbled again, in her pocket this time, and read from a scrap of paper. '*God, by his revealed will and manifest word, stands plain and evident on my side.*'

Mitchell raised an eyebrow. 'Who was this Mr Knox? What was his authority, his job?'

'I don't know. Sounds to me like he might have been a detective superintendent.' Mitchell laughed aloud at this sally, which was Superintendent Carroll's cue to come in.

Making no enquiry about the joke he walked to the front of the room and began on his routine address. 'I see from the file that you've made your usual efficient start.' He ended, as always, looking at Mitchell and then at the men disposed around the room, 'I leave the investigation to you with the utmost confidence.'

Mitchell smiled to himself. It was the same speech that they had heard from Superintendent Petty, appropriately named and universally hated, and Petty's successor, Superintendent Kleever, now disgraced. He was sure that they had had to learn it as part of the superintendents' training course. He gave renewed though silent thanks for Superintendent Carroll who probably meant every word he'd said to them.

He came forward now to take over the briefing, drawing his officers' attention to the few items that adorned the noticeboard so far. There was a selection of the police photographer's stills taken the previous evening and a picture of Paul Ridgeway in life, presumably contributed by a member of the company. In a role from a previous production, he wielded a sword with a vicious-looking narrow blade, though possibly it was only made of foil-covered card or hardboard. It had almost certainly been taken at a rehearsal rather than a performance since he was clad in a short-sleeved white T-shirt with a heavy rock group's logo and black knee-length shorts. The fair hair was tousled. The man's age was hard to judge. His forehead was deeply scored but the rest of the face was almost unlined. Perhaps he had frowned a lot. The man was well muscled and attractive because of his strong features and lively expression, though he was not handsome.

Mitchell supplied the information they could not guess. 'The victim is Paul Thomas Ridgeway, aged forty-four. He was one of the salaried members of the company but apparently all of them need to top their theatre earnings up to make ends meet and Mr Ridgeway's method was to give piano lessons.'

He glanced at Caroline who, before she was asked, said, 'All right. I'll see what Cavill knows about him.'

'Thank you for that – and for staying up last night to produce this.' He indicated the file with her neat report and grinned at her. 'Anything you think we should hear right now? Don't say too much or these folk will think they needn't read it.'

She considered. 'Well, I don't know if he did it deliberately but Stephen Thompson made it plain that there was plenty of resentment between certain of the actors and a fair amount against himself. At one point I almost wondered whether Ridgeway had been shot in mistake for him.'

'I take it you're not serious. There's no physical resemblance . . .'

Caroline shook her head. 'No. There's a chap called Hall who I gather took the lead in most of the flimsy comedies they did before Thompson arrived. Thompson doesn't think Hall's capable of playing in the serious stuff he wants them to put on now. He – Hall, that is – is resentful of Ridgeway for being successful in what he thinks of as his parts and holds it against Thompson that he let it happen.'

'Was Hall acting tonight?'

Caroline nodded. 'He played the headmaster.' She anticipated the next question. 'He was on stage for only a few minutes. He's not the only one to be given a small part when he expected a main one. It would be interesting to know whether Ridgeway was well regarded under the old regime or whether it took Thompson to see his potential.'

Mitchell nodded. 'Adrian? Any gems from the bar?'

Clement shrugged. 'I heard a lot of wild theories being aired. Most people still hadn't realized what had happened. I don't know if you were thinking there'd be anything to be gained by keeping things under wraps for a while, but, if so, there's no chance. Both Carter and Farrell from the *Clarion* were in the bar, plus a chap who works for Yorkshire television who beetled off to phone his people as soon as he knew a suspicious death had occurred. We'll probably feature on tonight's local news.'

'We appeared on last night's, I'm afraid,' Superintendent Carroll put in.

Clement nodded an acknowledgement of this and continued, 'I've got my report here but I don't think there's anything that's helpful at this stage.' He handed over a couple of sheets of notes and subsided.

'And Shakila? What did David Page have to tell you?'

She shrugged. 'He certainly talked a lot, but all it amounted to was that he'd supported his family by coming to see their play, he'd enjoyed it much more than he'd expected and now he wanted to collect his wife and take her home. She was pregnant and would be very tired and what was all this melodrama about anyway. Until he had an explanation he was not saying another word. Then he started saying it all over again and the double dose I got was in addition to him saying it all to Smithson before I arrived.'

'Right then, let's press on. Actions are on the desk over –'

As Mitchell had expected, it was Shakila who interrupted, glaring at him and demanding, 'What about you and the sergeant with the boy and his mother?' After a moment, she dropped her eyes and added a conciliatory 'Sir.'

With a nod, Mitchell transferred the question to Jennifer, whose expression told them she had nothing useful to tell. 'The DCI asked me to do the talking.' She bit back a smile. 'Said it was more sympathetic for a bereaved and pregnant ex-wife and a thirteen-year-old than having to talk to him.' Mitchell's face remained solemn. 'We did our best, put a sofa into a corner of the green room, offered tea. It was no use. The boy said absolutely nothing and Mrs Ridgeway didn't manage much more than yes and no.'

Beardsmore spoke up for the first time. 'I've only seen them all together as a group. Which one is she?'

The answer came from Clement. 'The one with the Alice-in-Wonderland hair, wrinkles and middle-aged spread.'

Mitchell said quietly, 'Didn't you hear Jen say she was pregnant?'

Scarlet-faced, Clement tried to disappear into his chair. Jennifer hurried on. 'We know that she was on the stage for all of the relevant time so she didn't actively have anything to do with the killing. She may just have been unwilling to talk in front of her son. And probably she was quite shocked herself. After all, divorced or not, she had been married to the poor bloke for years. We need to see her separately. The boy didn't look good. We may have to wait a while before we can talk to him.'

Straight-faced, Mitchell turned to Shakila. 'Does that answer your questions? Are you ready to take an action sheet now?'

None of the officers was sure whether their DCI was annoyed or teasing. They began to distribute the sheets in silence. Hastily, Mitchell sought a way of demonstrating his goodwill and, after a moment, borrowed a dismissal stolen from his father-in-law. 'Right, look at what I've planned for you all. Anyone who feels underworked, please remain behind.' To his relief the briefing broke up in laughter. He stopped laughing when he remembered that his next port of call was the path lab and there was only the dreaded backlog of paperwork to occupy him until it was time for that.

He was thankful to be reprieved. Superintendent Carroll had held the door open as his troops filed out. Now, he shut it and pulled up a chair for himself, facing his chief inspector across the desk. Mitchell was quite prepared to answer his questions frankly. Naturally, the man had to keep himself well informed about the state of all the cases being worked by his men. He rarely sent peremptory demands for them to bring information to his office and they were accustomed now to his friendly 'dropping in' to acquaint himself with what was going on. He made suggestions rather than giving orders though it was clear to the teams that the suggestions were to be complied with.

On occasion, Mitchell had found himself to be out of sympathy with them and had not held back from saying so. So far this had not led to his resignation being demanded.

Now, the superintendent asked, 'What do we know so far about the victim?'

Mitchell enumerated the scanty facts on stubby fingers. 'An actor, semi-pro. Wife in the same company. They've been separated for the last two years . . .'

'Divorced?'

'I didn't ask that last night. The ex-wife's pregnant and she and the baby's father hope to marry before the birth so divorce is presumably part of the plan. The new partner lives, with the ex-wife, in what was the marital home, together with the son of the marriage. Ridgeway and his ex were at least on speaking terms and co-operated over their son. The estranged couple were playing opposite one another in last night's production. That's about all so far.'

'So, what's the preliminary plan?'

Mitchell glanced at his watch. 'My own programme starts with the PM in just under an hour. I sent the troops out last night to talk to as many theatre people as possible so that we can compare their first reactions with the lies and evasions they'll have cooked up overnight. This morning I've sent Adrian to talk to Mrs Ridgeway's new partner at home. This afternoon Caroline and I are going to look at Ridgeway's flat.'

'You're not taking Jennifer?'

'The man taught piano to a few private pupils and was something of an amateur performer. Caroline's asking Cavill if he knows him . . .'

'All right. I follow your thinking. Anything from the SOCOs yet?'

'They've collected their usual lorryloads of litter. No sign of the weapon.' Mitchell waved a ham of a hand towards a scribbled note on his desk. 'They're excited about a wad of still-soft chewing gum that was under the body and stuck to the back of Ridgeway's coat. They might get a saliva sample from it.' He picked up a couple more sheets of A4 paper, this time neatly typed and clipped together. 'This is from Shakila. She's been to her friendly computer to find out if it tells people how they can buy a gun.'

'And does it? Surely not in this country.' Mitchell handed over the sheets and the superintendent began to read, forming the words silently with his lips. *'Can I really buy a gun on the internet? Absolutely, as long as you do the following . . .'* He looked up and said, activating his vocal cords again, 'This only refers to the States but you might get round that if you were determined and knew the right people. Are you going to follow it up?'

Mitchell shook his head. 'Not before I've tried to trace the gun that allegedly demolished a wall in Lower Edge Road.'

'How kosher is that business? Who've you got on it?'

'Smithson, with Shakila who's a neighbour and knows Mr Wilfred Smithson socially. They asked him how he knew he'd found a cartridge case and not something an electrician or a plumber had dropped.'

'And?'

'He's ex-army. Anyway, the thing smelt of cordite even though he'd wrapped it and handled it.'

The superintendent nodded, then put away his notebook, his usual preliminary to concluding an interview. He paused at the door before finally leaving. 'And your own immediate thoughts?'

Mitchell considered, drumming his fingers on the desk until his primary concerns separated themselves from the mass of speculations wriggling around his head. 'The most urgent task, of course, is to find and confiscate the gun – or guns. As far as the theatre business is concerned, I think the way ahead will be much clearer if we can work out why the shooting was done at such an inconvenient and risky time. In another couple of hours, Ridgeway would probably have been alone in his own place. Why

101

did the killer court so much danger by shooting him whilst dozens of people were milling around?'

The superintendent smiled. 'You've just told me that the PM isn't for another hour. That should give you plenty of time to deal with such a simple problem.' As always, he closed the door silently behind him.

Mitchell had recourse to his usual cure for all ills, mental and physical. Turning with contempt from the coffee machine with which his office was supplied, he took out his earthenware jug and the coffee he had ground as soon as he had arrived at the station that morning, and set about brewing his medicine. The telephone rang. Would the DCI, Magic enquired sweetly, like to speak to a Miss Elsa Hardy who had some information about Robin Ridgeway that she would like to discuss with him?

Mitchell sighed. A spinster without a life, who wanted to get a bit of attention and excitement from him to brighten her weekend was all he needed! 'Only on condition,' he growled, 'that she's prepared to come and drink coffee with me.' He wondered if this message would be passed on to Miss Hardy and decided not. Magic had never wasted words.

The lady appeared, escorted by a young uniformed officer who seemed already to be on familiar terms with her. Mitchell nodded to the girl to take the chair by the door and rose to shake hands with – and assess – this matronly woman who had come to do her duty and waste his time. As she eased herself into his capacious visitors' chair, Mitchell revised his opinion of her age. She had walked across his office like someone middle-aged but the high forehead was unlined and no veins were discernible on the backs of her hands. She was dressed in an unlikely fashion for a Saturday morning. The floor-length skirt clung unflatteringly to her hips and he would have thought the slightly quilted silky jacket, straining at the buttons, was more suitable wear for a cocktail party. Not, he had to admit to himself, that he had attended many of those.

He thanked her for sacrificing her Saturday morning. She cut him short, immediately stating her credentials and her business. Despite her physical shortcomings and her ignorance of what kind of clothing would flatter them, she had a dignity that came from her confident manner. Her voice was both warm and authoritative. Though he still considered her no feast for his eyes, Mitchell made her a mental apology and decided he would do well to heed what she had to say.

'I'm Robin Ridgeway's head of year at South Cloughton High School. I'm responsible for the pastoral care of a hundred and twenty twelve- and thirteen-year-olds, within the limits of school life. Also, of course, I monitor their academic progress. I'm here this morning because there is a rumour going round the school – or at least round Year 8 – that Robin has, or at least claims to have, a real gun with ammunition. You can understand why I have to make you aware of this. If there is any truth in it, it must be followed up. If there isn't, then the story has appeared at an exceedingly awkward time and we have to minimize the damage it might do.'

Mitchell checked that the young constable had settled to her shorthand then smiled at his visitor. 'You'll surprise me if you tell me you haven't tracked down the source of this rumour.' He saw she was pleased at the compliment.

'As far as I can gather, the story came from a boy in Robin's form, Janil Iqbal. I didn't know that he was a particular friend of Robin, but apparently the two of them were watching a DVD together at the Ridgeways' house when Robin made the claim. Janil didn't believe him.'

'Is Robin normally a truthful child?'

Miss Hardy sighed. 'The report that Robin's junior school sent to us when he arrived said that he came from a troubled home and lived in a self-protecting fantasy world. The trouble at home was not defined and when we enquired we were told that a divorce was in the offing. His father actually left home at the same time as Robin's transition from junior to secondary school, so his life on two counts was unstable. He doesn't live in a fantasy exactly. He hasn't given up on reality but he finds it uncomfortable. The events at home mean that he's exchanged a background of constant bickering between his parents for the influence of a rabid pacifist who, rather inconsistently, becomes quite aggressive himself if Robin so much as enjoys a friendly scuffle.'

'You're acquainted with Margot Ridgeway's new partner then?'

'He comes to school events with the mother. That means that the father has stopped coming. It's understandable but a great disappointment to Robin. To get back to whether he's truthful, he doesn't tell lies exactly. Under the new regime at home, any rough-and-tumble play is labelled violence. Robin is expected to play peaceably and quietly, preferably with just one other child at a time. The mother's partner told me that at the last parents' evening. He said he didn't want the boy going around in a gang because the gang mentality changes that of the individuals in it.'

'He's right about that.'

'Maybe. Anyway, Robin entertains himself dreaming up scenes of excitement and adventure. He tries to share them with other children. They aren't used to things happening only inside their heads and assume Robin is describing actual events. When these become too far-fetched, they label Robin a liar.' She looked up from playing with her rings and gazed at Mitchell. 'I wanted to speak to Robin himself about the gun – real or imaginary – but I suppose that would constitute interfering with a witness now. Anyway, I wanted you to understand him.'

'Can I have the Asian boy's address?'

'Oh dear.' She looked down again. 'All right. I suppose you do need to speak to Janil, and anyway you could easily get it from someone else.' She took a pen and notebook from her handbag and scribbled the required details.

Handing over the torn-off sheet, she half rose as though to leave, but then sat down again. 'There's something else.'

Mitchell had thought that there might be. 'Let's have it then.'

'Robin was late for school yesterday morning. He said he'd been for some emergency dental treatment. He looked strange, a bit shaken, but he didn't seem to have a sore mouth. I asked for his parents' note excusing him from the two lessons he had missed before break. He hesitated, as though he was trying to decide what story to tell, then said that he must have lost it.'

'So, you think he was not being truthful?'

She nodded. 'I think it was a lie. I think he was scared.'

'Did you ask him?'

'I thought I'd check with his mother first. I can't worry her with that now, of course. And then . . .'

'Then what?'

'I noticed that his fingernails were filthy.'

'I assume that in Robin's case that was unusual.'

'Yes, he's a fastidious boy – the nails were clean at the tips but dirty deeper down. He'd obviously cleaned them as far as a nail brush would reach but the dirt was further down. Mine are like that when I've been gardening. You can only get them clean by soaking in the bath.' She bowed her head, silent for a moment, then held his eye again. 'The black eye he has – you know about that?' Mitchell nodded. 'Could he have got it from the recoil of a gun?'

'Which he buried somewhere, perhaps in the waste ground behind the theatre yesterday morning, and with which, less than twelve hours later, he shot his father?'

Miss Hardy glared at the DCI. 'You're putting words into my mouth.'

Mitchell nodded. 'Yes, but only ones that were already in your head.'

She dropped her eyes and stared unseeing at the surface of the desk between them. 'I'm going now. I wish I hadn't come.'

Mitchell talked to his visitor for some minutes longer but she refused to be drawn into any further useful revelations. After she left, he made quick notes on the information he had been given, then rang for Shakila.

She appeared almost immediately, settled herself without invitation on the chair opposite him and waited to hear the reason for her summons.

'Do you know a family on your estate called Iqbal?'

'Several.'

'This one has a young teenager, name of Janil.' He handed her the slip of paper on which Miss Hardy had written her pupil's address.

She nodded. 'Got them. The boy's not in bother, is he? They're a nice family. They have the reputation of having the best garden in the area – though our friend Smithson who brought us his cartridge thinks it's a jungle compared with his. The older brother Youssef is studying abroad, but I thought I saw him the other day. The mother's very strict with both of them. Not sure what work the father does. He's rather an odd man, not exactly communicative with anyone outside his family, but he comes and goes regularly morning and evening. They're all very quiet and well behaved.'

'You know them fairly well then? That's good. Janil's just a possibly useful witness.' Mitchell gave her a brief account of Miss Hardy's visit and the information she had volunteered. 'You think the boy will talk to you freely – and without the mother interfering?'

'Probably. What do you want me to find out?'

'Anything you can pick up. I think Miss Hardy was holding some information back. She knew she'd have to tell me something but she came this morning to assess me and find out how best to combine doing her duty as a citizen with protecting her charges. If she thinks we know . . .'

Shakila grinned. '. . . more than we do we can trick her into telling all because there's nothing to lose. Do you want me to go now?'

106

'I'm feeling generous. I'll let you finish your computer search first.'

'How did you . . .?'

'Where else would you have been to have got here so quickly? Where do you always go and hide when you think my orders might clash with your agenda?'

She reached the door before telling him, 'It takes one to know one.'

Arriving at the path lab Mitchell found that the perky little pathologist, whatever had subdued him the previous evening, was his own eccentric self again. His eyes twinkled behind their bottle-bottom lenses as the chief inspector climbed into the garments he was required to wear in the lab. Mitchell thanked him for giving this post-mortem examination top priority. 'It makes our job a lot easier when we can have all the scientific and technical details you can dig out for us as soon as we start on the job.'

'I too always want to get at a corpse as soon as possible after death,' he assured the DCI. 'If it's kept in mortuary storage then pathological clues fade or change and I can't tell you so much or so soon. Delay affects my reputation too. Who was it who said that the psychiatrist knows nothing and does nothing, the surgeon knows nothing and does everything and the pathologist know everything but is always a day too late?' Mitchell neither knew nor cared. He watched the little man who was tying on the remarkable piece of headgear he chose to wear for these proceedings as he declared, 'I won't have that said about me. I've spent half an hour on this customer already this morning.'

As they entered the lab where Paul Ridgeway's body waited for them on the table, Mitchell saw that work on it had indeed already begun. He was glad that Dr Holland had stopped philosophizing and returned to the case in point. He asked him, 'Obviously, we're going to need a ballistics expert, but what kind of things might you be able to tell us this morning about the weapon that's been used – from your general experience?'

Dr Holland became expansive and Mitchell kept his sigh as silent as he could. 'You'll undoubtedly need technical assistance to reconstruct events but I'd be failing you if I couldn't at least show you how to distinguish between entrance and exit wounds, or give you a preliminary view of the range and direction or help to confirm or rule out suicide.'

The body had been unwrapped from its plastic sheet, its clothes removed and the surrounding debris collected and bagged. Mitchell assumed that the external examination was now completed since, as he continued his lecture, Dr Holland's hands were busy plucking and snipping samples of scalp, facial and pubic hair. '. . . I have to know something about common types of firearms in order to say whether a given weapon might possibly have caused specific wounds. Paul's is a bullet wound. The entry is a clean round hole which will be slightly smaller than the bullet which caused it.' Mitchell blinked, partly because this sounded illogical and partly because Dr Holland had decided to be on first-name terms with this corpse. Surely the man was not about to perform a PM on someone he had known well?

At a wave of his hand, the pathologist's assistants and acolytes stood back out of his way so that he could point as he continued Mitchell's education. 'What we have here is a contact wound. There's indentation of the skin round it where the muzzle was pressed and the wound is split and scorched because the gases from the explosion couldn't escape. However, let's get the show on the road in the usual order. We'll fish for bullets later.'

Not expecting that the routine part of Dr Holland's examination would turn up much that was germane to his investigation, Mitchell gave it only perfunctory attention. He tuned in again when the voice addressing the suspended microphone muttered, 'Hm, liver's a bit the worse for wear.'

'Do you think this man drank enough for it to be the reason for a divorce?'

The pathologist shrugged. 'How much is enough? If she's a Wee Free, then maybe. However, you can ruin your liver without being regularly inebriated so it's difficult to say. I imagine Mr Ridgeway's drinking would have shortened his life by a year or two if having his brains blown out hadn't shortened it by more than that.' He moved to the end of the table and surveyed his victim's head. 'Right. Now for the part you've paid your money to see. As we have the bullet lodged in the skull here I won't take your time up now with how we track its progress through the body.'

Mitchell gave silent thanks for this small mercy. 'So, there's no exit wound?'

Dr Holland chose to ignore this redundant question. He continued the monologue. Mitchell knew that it was designed less for the benefit of his taped record than to entertain himself or irritate whichever police officer was sent to witness his performances. 'The centre brow is a popular site with self-shooters. You can see the skin indentation where the muzzle was pressed in contact. It has pinned the force of the discharge on to the scalp, splitting the entry wound. So, could this wound have been self-inflicted, you ask me.'

Mitchell was indignant. 'No I don't, not unless our friend here had asked a mate to come and take the gun away. If he did, we shall be after him as an accessory.'

The pathologist nodded and continued his commentary. 'You see the hairs are singed. They're slightly blackened, but only the muzzle area is soiled with particles of burned powder. The tissues under the skin have been bruised by the blast and some have been blown away from their supporting structures. The cherry red tint is caused by the carbon monoxide in the gases that have been forced in.

See the soiling from the spin of the bullet. It revolves between two and three thousand times a second and wipes its surface grime as it enters the body – uses the skin as a doormat.'

Dr Holland stopped pointing and settled to work on his victim's head. 'The bullet here is lodged in the skull. I'll have to remove it with some bone attached rather than get it clear at this stage, otherwise I'll spoil the rifle marks for you.'

It came as a welcome distracting thought to Mitchell that his elder son might be interested in the workings of a revolver. There was an informative DVD in the station training section that he had watched with some interest himself. He'd borrow it again and watch it with Declan. Having averted his eyes from the gory performance in front of him, he steeled himself to watch the remainder. He saw that Dr Holland's forceps were swathed in gauze and rubber. 'Had an accident, have they?'

Their owner sighed. 'I'm trying to preserve your evidence for you. Anyway, this is my lab. I make the jokes around here.'

Eventually the procedure and the accompanying lecture came to an end and the bullet, having been safely extricated from its messy surroundings, was bagged ready to be sent to ballistics. Mitchell departed without subjecting his stomach to the further insult of the pathology lab's coffee.

Having fallen asleep only when the dawn light coming through his bedroom curtains made the room feel safe again, Janil Iqbal woke late on Saturday morning. Drawn by hunger, he dressed without washing and crept towards the kitchen, hoping that Youssef would have left to study in the town library. Hearing the voices of both his mother and his brother, he remained sitting on the bottom stair and listened.

110

'I should never have let him stay up late for the local news but it's what he usually does when there's no school the next day.'

'You weren't to know there'd be a shooting in sleepy old Cloughton. Anyway, the boy's thirteen, for goodness' sake. He knows what goes on in the world.'

'Well, at least put that newspaper somewhere else.' Janil knew that the *Bradford Telegraph and Argus* would be on the breakfast table as usual and that it would probably contain at least a reference to the events at the Playhouse the previous night. They'd probably sent a reporter to write up the new production, and the man, whoever he was, would have had a less boring night than he'd expected. Janil knew that the newspaper would be removed. Youssef usually did as his parents wanted, just as he did himself. He could imagine, though, his brother's impatient shrug at this mollycoddling of his younger brother.

His mother's next remark startled him. 'I think Janil's in some trouble at school. His head of year kept him behind after lessons earlier this week. He said it was only to ask for his version of what another boy had done. He had a cagey look, though. I'm not sure I got the right story – not the whole story, anyway.' Janil was startled. How did his mother know that he had had to see Miss Hardy? Had he really had a cagey look? There was never much possibility of fooling his mother. He decided to distract her by appearing for breakfast.

He sat at the kitchen table and heard Youssef's sigh as his mother fussed with cereal packet and milk. As soon as the bowl was put in front of him his hunger disappeared and he could not eat. Instead, he heard himself ask, ' Mum, do you think it could have been Robin who shot his dad?' Why had he said that? The words had formed in his head only as he spoke them. He had better either get a hold on himself or go back to bed.

His mother gave him a hard stare. 'Whatever sort of a question is that? Is that what your bad dream was about?

You'd better be careful what you say. You could cause a lot of trouble.'

Janil took a deep breath. 'Robin told me he had a gun. Not a toy one, a real one.'

She shook her head scornfully. 'Yes, but he's into acting, isn't he? He likes saying things that make folk pay him attention.'

Youssef gave his unasked opinion, as Janil had known he would. 'Robin Ridgeway's a nutter – even more so than the rest of your friends.' For once he had said something helpful. Now Janil could pretend to be offended. He pushed back his chair and walked to the door, slamming it behind him and so avoiding the nauseating bowl of now-soggy cereal.

Uma Iqbal glared at her remaining son. 'He's upset. Leave him alone. I'm going to keep him with me today – keep an eye on him. We can't have him talking like that with the police around to hear him.'

Youssef said, thoughtfully, 'What if the other kid did kill his father?'

His mother cast up her eyes. 'What's the world coming to? You're serious, aren't you? Where would a young schoolboy get a gun from? How would he know how to use it?'

Youssef laughed. 'Four questions in a row. I'd rather be back at uni taking exams.'

'Well, you soon will be. I hope you're going to do some studying today. This isn't just a holiday, you know.'

Youssef slipped an arm round his mother's shoulders. 'I'll go to the library this afternoon. There's rain forecast for later but it's sunny this morning. I'll dig over some of that ground next door so it's ready for Dad and me to start planning his vegetable garden. I promised him to do it while I'm home. It can be my penance for scrapping with Janil. I wouldn't do it so much if you didn't fuss over him as if he was still five years old.'

'Why don't you let Janil help you? Digging is a nice soothing activity. It would do him good.'

Youssef cast up his eyes. 'No way. We'd start sniping at each other again. If he's been awake most of the night the best plan would be to take him a cup of tea and a couple of aspirins and let him sleep till lunchtime.'

She shuddered. 'Don't say that.'

He was surprised. 'What have I said to upset you now?'

'Sniping. If you don't mind, we'll have no more talk about guns.'

Chapter Six

When Shakila arrived at the Iqbals' house later in the morning, she decided that the description she had given her DCI of the family's general good conduct had been less than accurate. Repeated ringing of the bell brought no one to the door but some family members were certainly at home. Loud voices raised in argument – and in Urdu – came, she thought, from the back garden.

She followed the noise, passing through a series of clematis-clad arches, till she reached a terrace running along the back of the house. It gave a view the length of the garden but there was no sign of the shrieking boys. It sounded as though the quarrel was getting physical and she moved forward to find the antagonists and separate them. She paused when she heard the name of Robin Ridgeway. She considered. Once the boys became aware of her presence, she would learn little if anything more about the cause of their disagreement. No one yet was screaming with pain. She'd wait for another few moments. By now, she had worked out where they were. Peering through the greenery growing up a trellis that conveniently screened her, she saw that the Iqbals had annexed to their already large garden half of the plot next door. She could see old Mr Dale, in the neighbouring house, coming out to water the pots on his own little terrace. He must have found his considerable plot too much for him and leased or sold a chunk of it to his neighbours who had neatly fenced it to be included in their own.

It must have been a recent transaction because the newly acquired section had obviously not been dug for some time. In fact, the argument seemed to be about the digging of it and, peering till her face was buried in leaves, Shakila could see that a tentative start on putting things to rights had been made in the far corner. Somehow, Robin seemed to have been involved in the digging and his interference was a problem. A shrieked demand from Janil that Youssef should let go of him decided for her that it was time to interfere. She stepped round the trellis and confronted them.

Good manners stopped their fight in front of a neighbour. Common sense stopped it in front of a police officer. Youssef, with a muttered word, half greeting, half excuse, pushed past her and disappeared through the garden and into the house. Shakila made no move to stop him. She thought it unlikely that he either could or would tell her anything useful, and Janil would be more willing to talk to her without his brother's inhibiting presence.

Free of Youssef's physical grasp, Janil seemed more puzzled than upset. She led him to a bench beside a small pond in the established part of the garden, gestured to him to sit beside her and waited for him to initiate the conversation. After some moments of silence, he said, 'We've been fighting – quarrelling, I mean – most of the time he's been home. We never used to. He used to show me things, take me out, teach me to do things.'

He had spoken in English and she followed his lead. 'What is it that you're arguing about?'

The boy shrugged. 'He says Mum spoils me, but when he got back last week I got sick of the fuss she made of him. All his favourite food on the table whether Dad and I liked it or not. And he picked all the TV programmes, loads of news programmes, not just the news itself but all the discussions about it as well.'

'Perhaps he needs to keep up with events. What's his subject?'

'Engineering. Our uncle's a partner in an oil company. Youssef's been promised a place there if he gets a good degree.'

'Well, he certainly needs to stay up to date with that. Where's he studying? It's not locally is it?'

'No, he's at Cairo University. That's where our uncle's company headquarters are.'

'It would be good for you to visit him out there some-time. I think all that's wrong between you is because of your age.'

Janil said sulkily, 'I can't help how old I am.'

'How many years between you?' He held up seven fin-gers. 'Think about it then. For the best part of the last two years he's been away, studying. Before that you were still at junior school. He's never taken you seriously before. Now you're both having to adjust to being near-equals in the family. You've stopped being Youssef's little brother, his plaything. You've grown up a bit and have your own friends and interests. Naturally you no longer want to fall in with whatever he suggests the minute he mentions it.'

'But he wants me to grow up. What he's annoyed about today is – well, when I was having breakfast, he said Mum treats me like an infant. And why should he mind that Robin dug a tiny bit of garden? He said Robin had made the job impossible. He'd chopped up the couch grass roots with a spade instead of teasing them out with a fork. Now it's impossible to find them all and each piece will root itself again.'

Shakila nodded. 'I can see Youssef's point. It must be annoying to be helped by someone who makes the job more difficult.'

'He didn't do it on purpose. It's unreasonable of him not to like Robin. He's only met him twice when he called for me. He was only here two minutes, before we both went out again.'

'Just my point. He probably has nothing at all against Robin personally but he's used to having you available, thrilled to have him take notice of you. Now you sometimes turn him down because you're with your own friends. Who's the new friend who's taking your attention from him? Now especially, because Robin's father's been killed and you're likely to spend more time trying to help him. Youssef wants Robin out of the way, at least until he goes back to university, so everything he does is wrong. Digging the garden was wrong. Not helping in the garden would have been wrong too, just because it was Robin who was doing – or not doing – it.'

'Well, I did say yesterday that I couldn't play tennis with him because I was meeting Robin.'

Shakila asked, intrigued, 'How did Robin come to be digging your garden, anyway?'

'We were going to do it together as a surprise for Dad. Youssef hadn't said anything about Dad asking him to do it. Anyway, we'd just got all the stuff out, the spades and things, when Gran's neighbour rang to say she'd fallen. We had to go over there and Robin had to go home. I didn't realize he'd actually stayed and done a bit of digging. But what was wrong with him doing that? It was kind of him and he even cleaned the spade and put his and mine back in the shed.'

Shakila grinned. 'What you've got to learn about adults is that they're not as direct as children. What they complain about is not always the thing they're really upset about.'

Janil wrinkled his nose. 'So, when Youssef shouts at me, I have to guess what he's annoyed about and not listen to what he's actually saying to me?' He shook his head at the complicated workings of adult minds. After another silence, he said, 'I wish you were my mum.'

Shakila laughed. 'Well, I certainly don't. And none of this is what I came to see you about.'

The boy looked wary. 'To see me? I thought you'd just come to complain about the noise we were making. I haven't done anything.'

'Miss Hardy has been to have a word with my boss.' Janil stared down at his grazed knees without speaking. 'There's a rumour going round school that Robin has a gun. You can imagine how difficult that makes things for him and for his family in the present circumstances. Miss Hardy thinks you began circulating that story.'

This time, Shakila was determined to sit out the boy's silence. After more than a minute, she was rewarded with the story of the forbidden DVD. 'Robin's new dad is a nutter. He's not allowed to watch anything with any fighting, not even cartoons. He'd have thrown a real fit if he'd known we were watching *Stormbreaker*. Robin was really lapping it up. Then he just suddenly pressed the pause button and said he had a gun, a real one.'

'Did you believe him?' The boy shook his head. 'Do you believe him now?'

After another silence, Janil said, 'I'm not sure but I wish I hadn't laughed at him and I wish I hadn't told anybody.'

Five minutes later, as Shakila left the Iqbals' house, it occurred to her that it might be more honest to claim her afternoon's pay from Social Services rather than from the police authority. She closed the gate and had paused to retrieve her car keys from her pocket when she caught sight of Jaswinder Iqbal turning the corner and approaching his house. Unwilling to reveal to Janil's father that his son's rather unkind mockery of a schoolfriend had led to an official police visit, she hoped he would not enquire too closely into her presence. She need not have worried. The man stopped in front of her, gave her a vague smile, then turned away and wandered up the path to his front door.

Robin Ridgeway was sitting by the lake in the park. It felt slightly better to be here than at home. At home, you were expected to be normal. Here you didn't have to be anything, not just now, anyway. That was good because he wasn't sure any more what or who he was.His body was slumped on this bench but he wasn't there, inside it. His eyes saw things but his mind didn't respond to them. He could see the blue tinge in his fingernails but he didn't feel cold. He could see yellow irises growing out of the edge of the water, like they did on a smaller scale in Janil's garden. No! Don't go there!

The flowers didn't seem beautiful – or ugly either. They were just there. Everything was just there – like his mother beside him on the seat with tears running unchecked down her cheeks. Not many, just one now and then. He was afraid that she might speak. He didn't like ignoring her but he didn't dare speak himself, even just to answer her. If words came out of his mouth, he wouldn't have control of them any more.

People walked by. Two of them spoke, probably to him. He didn't answer these people either and neither did his mother. Even she was on the other side of the invisible wall that surrounded him. If he could sit here for always, for ever, safely inside his wall, then, maybe, he'd stay together, still be Robin. If not, when he moved, his body might separate out into all its little atoms and the wind would blow them away.

DC Clement was standing beside a clean, white-painted gate, considering the house in which David Page lived with Margot Ridgeway. It had been – and legally might still be – the property of her late husband. It was substantial, Edwardian and semi-detached, shielded from the road by a long front garden, well planned and well stocked. The plot, both actually and metaphorically, was only a little gone to seed and Clement walked slowly up the path, enjoying the colours and scents of cherry blossom above and hyacinths below.

Invited into the hall by David Page, Clement looked around him. The garden, in its semi-neglect, he decided, had fared better than the house, which had obviously enjoyed the full attention from its current inhabitants. Everything in sight was immaculately cared for but the flowery wallpaper and frilly door curtain were an insult to the entrance hall's proportions. He thought that they would not have been chosen during Paul Ridgeway's occupancy.

David Page welcomed him effusively, leading him into a lamentably adorned sitting room where a tray with a fussy cloth had been prepared as if this were a social occasion. Page himself, Clement thought, would have been handsome, but for his weak mouth. He was slightly built with clear, long-lashed eyes and thick dark hair, severely cut, but his shoulders were rounded and he walked with a slight stoop, as though the world had proved too much for him. Last night, Clement had attributed his manner to shock but now he suspected that the half apologetic, half resentful demeanour was Page as he usually presented himself. He realized that the man's nervous chatter had turned to the topic of his new family and, abandoning his mental inventory, hastily tuned in to his witness again.

It seemed that David Page was in the house alone. Clement was not sure whether he was glad or sorry that Margot Ridgeway was absent. He might have learned more from the smiles and warning glances that the pair exchanged than he was likely to get from the mindless soliloquy he was currently hearing.

He let his mental tape recorder remind him that he'd been invited to sit and explain how he liked his coffee. He liked it best when it was exchanged for tea, but now he merely made sure it would not be sweet. He was glad, at least, that Robin was out of the way.

Apparently, removing the boy whilst the police were in the house had been a deliberate decision. 'Neither of us wanted to cause him any more stress. We're both worried about him. He just won't speak at all – hasn't said a word since the gun was mentioned. It's strange. Margot says he reacted quite normally to the news that Paul was dead.'

'Can you describe this reaction that you thought to be normal?' Clement accepted his cup, not distracting his witness with thanks. 'Did he cry? Did he want to go out and see his father's body for himself? Was he frightened?'

Page lifted his shoulders and let them drop. 'You'll have to ask Margot. She just said he behaved normally until he heard someone say that Paul had been shot. I can't decide whether the boy can't speak or whether he just won't. Either way, he's very distressed. Our GP sedated both Margot and Robin last night. Margot seems to be bearing up. Of course, it's two years since she lived with Paul and she's very happy here with me – but I hope she'll talk to me soon, tell me how she's feeling about Paul's death, especially the manner of it.'

Clement was finding his coffee more palatable than he expected. He drained his cup, raised a hand to prevent his witness from refilling it and decided that this flow of inane chatter was unlikely to produce any fact, suggestion or impression that would please his DCI. It was time to adopt his own tactics. He smiled to himself. With the team, he had a reputation for being good with old ladies. He certainly had an old woman to deal with here, even if she was only in her forties, wearing flannels and sports coat and needing a shave. He'd see if a few questions caused the man's anxiety to leak from a new outlet. 'What my DCI wanted me to ask for is an account of everything that happened last night from your point of view.'

Page sat, still and silent, for a long time. Clement feared that, like Robin, he was going to retreat into a defensive silence. He felt relief when, after a few moments' reflection, the man seemed to have decided only on bluster as his weapon. 'That's precisely what the other two officers asked. There's nothing I can remember now that shouldn't already be in your files. I don't mind your wasting my time but, for Margot's sake, and the boy's, I wish you'd clear up this business more quickly by not wasting your own in duplicating –'

Clement held up a hand. 'The file certainly does contain DC Nazir's notes. I've read them carefully. I know that you've been careful to support Robin's and Margot's acting ambitions even though the theatre wasn't your "first love" – I think that was the expression you used. You said you enjoyed the plays more than you'd expected to. I know that you were worried because Mrs Ridgeway was tired and shocked and several months pregnant.'

Page gave him a faint grin. 'All right. I'm convinced you've done your homework, so why the revision?'

'Because I don't suppose you got a great deal of sleep last night and you might well have remembered more details about what happened as you turned everything around in your head. Besides, even when different officers ask exactly the same questions, they often get different answers, not because the witness lies or deliberately changes his story but because the chemistry between them is different and produces different attitudes and reflections. You must have used similar tactics in your school. You know – "I can't get any sense out of the lad. You get on with him better. He likes your subject. Can you have a go?"'

Page nodded warily. 'Yes, I suppose, several times, I've said something like that.'

'Right, so, can we get on with it now?' Clement took silence for consent. 'Did you, your partner and her son leave for the theatre together?'

'No. They had a sort of pre-performance briefing to attend and their costumes to put on and their make-up to have done. Margot and Robin left in the car at about a quarter to five. I had to get my own meal. Peter Hall's wife had offered to pick me up because she had to pass our house. That would have been about ten past seven. We'd booked our seats so we didn't need to be there much before things got started.'

'What was your row and seat number?'

Page demonstrated his irritation with a sigh and a compression of his lips. 'Row C in the balcony. Seat number twenty-four.'

'Did you choose it yourself?'

Page produced a louder sigh and an aggressive tone. 'Yes, I placed my finger on the plan and showed the girl which one I wanted.'

Clement ignored the provocation and asked amiably, 'And it was at the end of the row?'

Page looked startled. 'Yes, it was.'

'How long had you known Paul Ridgeway? Did you meet him only as your partner's ex-husband?'

Page blinked at the sudden change of subject. He shook his head. 'No. I met Paul first, had a few piano lessons from him.'

'You're a musician?'

Page scowled. 'Paul didn't think so. It was when the new head came to my school, about four years ago. He had a great thing about diversifying. He said you had to try to be the last word in your own subject, but –'

'What's yours?'

'Mathematics. To finish what I was saying.' He punished Clement's interruption with a schoolmasterly glare. 'He thought we should be able to turn our hands to most subjects, at least up to Year 9 level. My subject was one he gave as an illustration. He said mathematicians were often musical and that all subjects could be combined with sport – and that we'd be a fitter staff as a bonus.'

The headmaster was apparently his guru. As Page became more enthusiastic Clement tried harder to look interested. It was, he thought resentfully, all very well for his DCI to tell his men to let witnesses run on until they forgot they were talking to the police. He wasn't the one who had to sit in front of them trying to stay awake.

The voice droned on. 'Paul was the friend of a friend. We agreed to ten trial lessons to see how we got on. After the second, he said I had no sense of rhythm. I asked if more

123

lessons would help. He said no. So, I suggested that I might try another instrument.'

'No again?'

'He said tunes have to have the right rhythm whatever they're played on, so I stopped. I don't think he was a very good teacher. He was very impatient.'

'Isn't it good advice that you should give up something you're not cut out for? He could have gone on taking your money and wasting your time.'

'I suppose so. Anyway, that was how I met Margot.'

Clement managed a smile. 'You've anticipated my next question. Did your relationship with her begin before she and her husband parted?'

'Yes, but not before she had decided that she had to end it.'

'It was his wife who ended it?'

'Yes.' Clement nodded to him to continue but Page shook his head. After a moment, however, he added, self-righteously, 'You need to ask her about the details of the split – but not till I consider that she can cope with your questions.'

Clement ignored this timid defiance. 'When did Mr Ridgeway become aware of the situation between you and his wife?'

'How should I know? He said nothing to either of us until Margot told him they couldn't go on living together.'

'Was he surprised?'

'Margot said he didn't even pretend to be.'

'How long had your relationship been a physical one?'

'What possible bearing can that have on what happened last night?'

Clement was pleased. His witness was beginning to sound rattled. He smiled again. 'You're an intelligent man. I think you can answer that for yourself.'

Page's attempted aggression petered out and he made another gesture towards the cooling coffee pot. Clement put his hand firmly over his cup as he spoke. 'Is there anything you'd like to tell me? Anything I haven't asked you that you think might be relevant?'

For the first time Page gave him a genuine smile. 'You could have asked me how Paul and I got on, or whether he made my life here with Margot difficult, or whether I think there's any chance that she would have eventually gone back to him.'

'And?'

'He and I were uneasy with each other and saw as little of one another as possible. Paul was too proud to stoop to nasty tricks to try to split Margot and me. Lastly, I don't think there's been any chance of a reconciliation between Paul and Margot since she discovered she's pregnant with my child.'

Clement added these answers to his notes, closed his book, thanked his witness for his co-operation and rose to leave. Pausing in the entrance hall, he turned back to Page. 'What would you say if I told you that a Mrs Thelma Gordon, mother of Joanne Gordon, who is a pupil at your school, sat in row C last night in seat number twenty-three?'

The question did not disconcert him and he answered it promptly. 'I'd say that I'm sorry I didn't chat to her more, but since I have never had Joanne in my class I had no reason to recognize her.'

'She isn't worried about not being chatted to. She tells us, though, that Mr Page, whom she recognized from her daughter's school, went to the bar in the interval between the two plays and never returned to his seat.'

Mitchell was surprised to discover that Paul Ridgeway had lived in a rented flat in one of the four tower blocks in the centre of town, collectively known as Sainted City. Between them the towers now housed most of the ex-residents of two notorious council estates which had been razed to the ground after the police and Social Services had given up on them.

The Ridgeway flat was on the corner of the ground floor of St Margaret's. Mitchell felt a now-redundant sympathy for his victim. There was something to be said, perhaps, for the accommodation on the top floors of these buildings – provided the other residents had left the staircases navigable and the lifts in working order. The air was cleaner, the atmosphere quieter and there was a pleasing view over to the steeply rising but modest little hills that surrounded the town. The steepness kept the town from spreading and growing and gave life there an intimacy or an insularity, according to your philosophy.

Living on the ground floor, Ridgeway must have been constantly aware of the fumes and the dust of the passing traffic and the noise of his fellow tenants coming, going and generally causing mayhem. This flat did, however, have one advantage. A row of garages faced its front door, shabby but sturdy, much decorated with sprayed-on slogans but not otherwise vandalized. The door of one was labelled *Flat 3* with Ridgeway's name painted underneath. There appeared to be an aged Ford parked inside it. They would investigate that later.

Using the keys that Margot Ridgeway had given them, Caroline let them into the flat's cramped hall and Mitchell stood for a moment, wondering how this accommodation compared with what his victim had formerly shared with his wife. The scents inside were fresher than those outdoors, a mixture of wax furniture polish, toothpaste and something slightly more exotic, perhaps a scented candle. The paint on the four doors was clean and the runner carpet had been recently vacuum-cleaned. Unless he had a female relative or friend that no one had yet mentioned, then Paul Ridgeway had been a fastidious man.

Apparently thinking along the same lines, Caroline said, 'I wonder if he looks after it himself. He probably did. He wouldn't live here if his wife had left him enough spare cash to afford a cleaning woman. Besides, she'd get mobbed on her way in.' She turned to the first of the doors

126

and saw that it led to a shower room. The walls were neatly painted but scars in the plaster showed that there had once been a bath. Caroline nodded approvingly. 'Good move. A shower not only uses less water – it would give him just about room to bend down and cut his toenails as well!' Two shelves over the sink held shower gel, shampoo, deodorant and shaving equipment but no scents, powders or potions.

The bedroom too was tiny and spartan. On the wall, above a chest of drawers, hung a framed and much enlarged snapshot of Robin. Mitchell recognized the fountain and flower beds in the background. The boy was perched on the climbing frame in the local park. Over the bed was a more intriguing picture. Mitchell blinked at it. Margot Ridgeway, dressed in high-heeled, knee-length boots and a low-necked satin mini-dress, her hair crimped and cascading over her shoulders, was holding a huge silver-filigree picture frame. She bent forward so that her torso and one arm protruded through the frame towards the photographer. Her lips pouted. The son's picture had a cheap, ready-made frame. The wife's was surrounded in plain, matt, dark wood, the whole picture seeming to be the work of a professional.

'So, it looks as though the separation might have been more her idea than his,' Caroline ventured. 'He must have been besotted to have had that monstrosity so expensively mounted.'

Mitchell sniffed. 'Unless it's there to remind him what a lucky escape he had to be shut of such a weirdo. Can you imagine Ginny posturing about like that?'

Caroline paused to imagine the unlikely scene. 'She wouldn't be able to stop laughing and I don't think she knows how to pout. Anyway, it might have been Margot herself who insisted on being so exorbitantly framed.' She set about checking the drawers of the chest and suggested, over her shoulder, 'Better see what he sleeps with under his pillow.' She grinned to herself as she heard her DCI actually cross the room to the bed to follow this advice.

'A handkerchief,' he told her, his voice solemn. 'Do you want to do the kitchen whilst I make a start on the living room?'

'You're the boss. Was it a man's or a woman's hand-kerchief?'

'Look for yourself.' He strode off leaving her to finish running her fingers through the last drawer of the chest, which contained blameless, very clean and rather old-fashioned men's underwear.

Mitchell opened the last door at the end of the hall. He was warming to his victim and highly approved of his housekeeping. This was his main room. In it he had to eat, entertain, give his piano lessons and chill out at the end of the day. It had to contain a dining table, a piano, seating, space for books and hi-fi equipment. He had them all in a space that was no more than about a hundred square feet, yet the room felt peaceful and spacious. The man had the eye. His means, it seemed, were straitened but the eye, Mitchell considered, was always more important than full pockets.

He spent a few moments on a nostalgic mental return to the flat where he had lived before he met Virginia. He too had painted over the wallpaper, bought a table that opened wide but folded small and decided on one large sofa rather than two small ones. He too had decided that bare walls gave a spacious feel and so had hung no pictures. He had not had to make room for a piano. Ridgeway's was small and Mitchell was no judge of pianos but it seemed to him that here was the only object upon which money had not been stinted.

A wide but shallow alcove had been shelved in a work-manlike fashion. Reference books of every kind filled the top row. The four in the middle held a mixed collection of general books, and the wider one, almost at floor level, a number of what appeared to be theatre programmes, music magazines and albums of photographs. All were neatly arranged.

On the narrow wall facing the window, again with a tidy but home-made look, a series of shallow boxes were fastened. They contained CD and tape players, more sheet music and a lap-top computer. The top six boxes were open-fronted but the bottom row of three had doors to conceal their contents. The doors were locked. Mitchell looked hopefully at the second key on the ring he had obtained from Margot Ridgeway but it was obviously far too big to fit the neat keyholes in front of him. He supposed that, having given his estranged wife access to his new home, Paul Ridgeway would want to have certain places in which to keep some things private from her now.

Mitchell winced as a door hinge whined and Caroline came in. 'I've finished the kitchen. It took so little time that I don't feel as though I've done a proper job, but the place is minute and there's absolutely no clutter and nowhere much to search.'

'Come and help me in here then. Do the books tell you anything? They're all Greek to me.'

Caroline laughed. 'Well, the Plato and the Aristotle certainly are, though he seems to have read them in translation.' She wandered over to look more closely. 'There's quite an eclectic collection here – fiction, poetry, philosophy . . .'

'If you mean varied, then say so.'

'That isn't what it means exactly, but never mind.' She took out a couple of volumes at random and riffled through the pages before replacing them. 'They're all mismatched, no sets of anything, and they all seem to have been handled a lot. I get the impression of a keen reader who picked up books that interested him, bought them and read them.'

'Isn't that the usual thing to do with books?'

Caroline grinned. 'Ginny would say so. In my experience more people buy this sort of literature to impress their friends than because they're anxious to study it. These books weren't just part of the furnishings. Can I have a browse through the photographs? They might tell us a lot about his past life and his friends and family.'

Mitchell glanced out of the window at the miserable vista of rough ground, an abandoned and rusty pushchair, a smashed television set that might have been dropped from a balcony above and a fair number of people going about their business and ignoring their depressing surroundings. He waved a hand towards the albums. 'Be my guest. I'm going to mix with the local populace in the guise of a civilian and see if they'll tell me anything they wouldn't tell a copper.'

Caroline laughed. 'I'm not impressed with your civilian guise. You'd need to change your hairstyle. Good luck anyway ... Oh, just a minute.' He turned back to listen and she pointed to the bottom bookshelf. He saw nothing amiss and waited. 'Are you getting the impression that Mr Ridgeway was what my mother calls a "place for everything and everything in its place man"?'

Mitchell nodded, looked harder at the lowest shelf and nodded a second time. 'Right. The albums are all numbered, presumably in date order, but one's been pulled out and left lying across the top of the others. Why didn't he put it back in its place?'

'Could be he was just in a hurry but it would only take a millisecond longer to slide it into position. I think he intended to look at it again.'

'All right. Start with that one but have a look through the others as well. It might be interesting to see how far back David Page quite literally comes into the picture.' He went across to the bookcase and carried the heavy books across to the sofa for her, pausing to look over her shoulder as she began to leaf through the one that had been out of its place.

The first few pages were obviously holiday snaps. Ridgeway featured in about half of them, quite recognizable as the man whose body lay in Dr Holland's lab but with longish curling blond hair in the fashion of the eighties. Caroline picked him out with her finger in several, then tilted the book towards Mitchell. 'I'd put him at early to mid-twenties here. I'm going partly on the women's clothes. He was forty-four, wasn't he? So these would be late eighties.' She turned another page. 'Oh, look, he used to be a scout leader.'

The album had seduced Mitchell away from his plan to talk to the building's residents. He came round to the front of the sofa, sat beside his DC and considered the postcard-sized photograph of the young Ridgeway, in uniform, seemingly inspecting a row of six little boys who were similarly clad. There were other pictures, mostly not featuring Ridgeway, of campfire scenes and sporting activities. 'He probably took most of these himself.' The one at the bottom of the right-hand page showed the same six boys, one of them proudly displaying a small cup. Mitchell slipped it out of its moorings and turned it over. 'Bingo.' He showed Caroline the scrawled *York, June 1989.* 'Now we have a date and a place.'

Caroline grinned. 'I can see why you got to be DCI. How is that going to help us?' Getting the answer she expected, that none of them yet knew what was helpful and what wasn't, she turned another leaf. They both stared at the double-space, then at each other. Corner supports had been stuck on to the pages to hold four photographs which had all been removed. They sat for a moment, considering, before Caroline asked, 'When do you think these were taken out?'

'I'd guess sometime on Friday – otherwise he would have put the book away. Why did he take them?'

'Perhaps he didn't. Maybe someone else did and he's only just missed them. Then he might have left the album on top until he'd tracked them down. Perhaps Margot has them, or Robin. At least they might know where they are. It probably doesn't have anything to do with who killed him or why.'

Mitchell's mind had taken a leap. 'Did you find any bottles in the kitchen?'

'What kind of bottles? There was a bottle of oil on the table, the sort you use for rusty locks, with an applicator instead of a screw cap. All kitchens have bottles.'

'Sorry, yes. Beer or wine bottles – or spirits? Empty ones?'

She shook her head. 'Didn't see any. Should I have done?'

'Dr Holland said his liver was shot. I wonder where he keeps his empties.'

'Well, not in his tiny, tidy flat. Shall we see if that second key opens the garage?'

'We may as well. We'll have to come back and see what's in those locked boxes later. Anything else strike you before we go?'

Caroline crossed the room and lifted the piano lid. 'This is nice. He didn't spare any expense for this.' She sat on the stool and played a few bars of what Mitchell triumphantly recognized as one of Schubert's *Moments Musicaux*. Silently, he gave thanks for his son, aged twelve, who was busy filling in the gaps in his father's education as well as turning into an excellent pianist under the tuition of Caroline's renowned husband.

Caroline made no comment on his unexpected erudition beyond raising her eyebrows. When she had reached a cadence, she stopped playing and told him, 'I asked Cavill about Ridgeway. He doesn't know him well but he played in pubs, jazz mostly and quite brilliantly. Cavill thought he wasn't highly rated as a teacher. The garage now?'

She lowered the lid over the keyboard, left the piano and made for the door, then paused. 'Can I take the photo album with me?'

'Let's take the whole lot. You can go through them all in your copious spare time.' He went back and scooped them up, but, as another thought struck him, dumped them on the piano. He saw Caroline flinch but ignored her. 'Just another minute.'

Caroline followed her DCI into the hall, and saw him disappearing into the kitchen. 'What are you going to do in there?'

He came back, grinning sheepishly and clutching the oil can from the table. 'This poor blighter won't rest easy on his stretcher knowing that he's left a squeaky door unfixed.' He lubricated the offending hinge, carefully wiping away the surplus oil with his handkerchief, then gathering up the photographs again. 'Now Mr Ridgeway and I can both sleep in peace!'

Chapter Seven

Mitchell had called only his regular team to the debriefing on Saturday evening. Clement supposed that the DCI intended to spend the later part of the evening mulling over the reports from all the uniforms before calling the full complement of officers on the case together and deploying them on Sunday. He wondered what his own task would be. Arriving at Mitchell's office early, he found it empty, but the door had been left open, the chief's signal that they could make themselves at home whilst they waited for him. Clement settled into the most comfortable chair – which he would give up to Caroline when she arrived – and looked over his report on his interview with David Page. On reflection, he decided there was more to the man than met the eye. Towards the end of their chat he had taken the initiative to an extent and shown a gleam of humour.

However, Clement considered this was a bit subtle for his DCI. He never talked about what someone might or was likely to do. It was always a matter of opportunity and proof. Mitchell had the sort of mind that tended towards vigorous action and that saw only one side to every question. He succeeded in everything he did because he seldom stopped to split hairs. He had abounding confidence in his own ability – a bit like a successful journalist who simplified every problem and condensed it into an arresting phrase. Clement considered himself in many ways to be Mitchell's intellectual superior, though he could see that this would never be reflected in his own promotion prospects. In the force, people with subtle and cultivated minds sometimes got lost in their maze of fine distinctions. He himself always saw how complicated things really were, and how complex the characters they interviewed, so that his powers of persuasion with his DCI were practically nil. Often he was irritated when Mitchell roundly commended him for something of which he was not proud and which he considered not important.

This was true in the whole of life, Clement concluded. The world was led by people least suited to raising its moral and cultural standards. Although, he had to admit that his chief inspector's integrity was unquestionable.

Mitchell breezed into his office, interrupting his DC's great thoughts. 'You were miles away, Adrian. Thinking about how much better you'd do my job than I do?' Colouring furiously, Clement handed over his report, then, with relief, leapt up to offer the best chair to Caroline as the rest of the team trooped in. Neither he nor Caroline missed the hard looks they received from both Mitchell and Jennifer.

Clement was given first turn to account for his morning. Leaving aside his private and subtle observations on his interviewee, he described their conversation in less than two minutes.

Mitchell grinned at him. 'So, you weren't plotting how to get my job. You were stripping your report down to the essentials to save us time. Even so, since you often see below the surface that witnesses show you, you can give us your assessment of this one."

Clement's blush deepened. 'I started by wondering how any woman would want to exchange a Paul Ridgeway for a David Page. I ended by seeing that, although he has some issues to sort out, Page was sufficiently detached from them to be laughing at me.' He subsided on to a hard-backed chair and made silent apologies for misjudging first his interviewee and then his DCI.

'How did he answer you,' Jennifer asked, 'when you faced him with leaving his theatre seat during the second play?'

'Claimed to have been taken short as the interval ended. Then that he crept in at the back and sat in an empty seat next to a complete stranger. I asked if he'd know the person again. He said, "Yes, but I wouldn't know where to look for him." Then he tried to distract me, as I've already told you, with his opinion that Robin was being abused by his father.'

'Sexually?'

'That's what he says he thinks.'

Mitchell turned to Jennifer. 'Did Margot Ridgeway confirm that?'

'I didn't know to ask about it. I hardly got anything out of her. She only spoke in answer to direct questions. Their GP was there, hovering and threatening to sedate everybody again. I don't think he did it because, as I was leaving, she told him she was going to take Robin for a walk.'

'Right. If she's fit to go out walking then she's fit to answer some questions, doctor or no doctor, but we'll give her until tomorrow morning. We'll send you again, Jen. Ask whatever you like but try to find out why she still had a key to his place, how long he'd been drinking and how it affected family and friends.'

Mitchell turned to Caroline. 'What did we learn that's worth sharing?'

'That he hadn't much money to throw around but he was a wonderful housekeeper. Everything spotless. I wouldn't have believed you could make one of those minute places in Sainted City fit to live in, but he did. His car was in the garage, a very old Cavalier, beautifully cared for – in the same condition as the flat. He was due a visit to the recycling centre. The boot was full of his empties – and there were more in the dustbin. He'd even lined that with heavy duty plastic to keep it clean. I think those locked cupboards probably contain his full bottles.'

'Or, if Page's suspicions are right,' Clement observed, 'there might be some naughty pictures of Robin.'

Caroline shook her head. 'That's not the impression I'm getting – but we need a lot more evidence.' She asked a question of her own. 'How did he get to the theatre if his car was at home?'

'One of the company, Peter Hall, had to pass his door,' Clement volunteered. 'He picked up a couple of the audience as well. I was talking to them in the bar last night. Has the lab got the car?'

Mitchell nodded. 'Well, they're examining it *in situ* at present. Report still to come from the SOCOs. With luck we'll at least have some snippets of information tomorrow. Finally, we have the history of Paul Thomas Ridgeway and family almost from birth to death in several volumes of photographs. We're anxious to find four of these that seem to be missing –'

'No we aren't.' With a smug expression, Caroline produced an envelope from her handbag and handed it to Mitchell. 'This was tucked behind the plastic cover at the end of the relevant album. We still want to know why they were taken out though.' They waited as he examined them before laying them out on the table, being careful to touch only the extreme edges.

For a few moments, the five officers examined the pictures in silence. Each shot featured the same four men. They were obviously the leaders in charge of a scout camp. In two they all wore uniform, in the others, three of them were in sports gear. The fourth, enormously fat, had chosen to keep his flesh covered and to sit watching the antics of his fellows. In all four photographs, younger scouts were to be seen in the background.

Mitchell asked, 'Any of you recognize anybody or anything here?'

Three of his team shook their heads. Shakila frowned. 'The fat one. Just for a moment he seemed familiar but it's gone. He isn't ringing the bell any more.'

137

'Let it go,' Jennifer advised her. 'It'll come back more easily if you don't chase it.' She turned to Caroline. 'You said some of these scout pictures had places and dates. These?'

Caroline got out her notebook and showed the others what she had copied from the back of the snapshots. '1989, the same as the others, but no place name. It certainly isn't anywhere in the Vale of York. Look at those hills behind them. The uniformed pictures have initials. It's likely to be their names because the top set is PTR. Then there's SJTM, DK and CWV.'

Mitchell picked up the relevant two photographs, checking the backs. 'The initials on this one are the same ones in a different order. Paul Ridgeway is standing second from the right and his initials are third this time. The fat man's far left and SJTM comes first. In the other he's second from left and the four initials come second, so it looks as if we can fit their initials to the right people. It might not have the least relevance to the case, of course. We'll see if Margot Ridgeway can shed any light tomorrow.'

There was little to be done tonight until he had read through the reports of the many interviews with last night's players, scene shifters and audience members, which had been conducted today by the uniformed officers he had been allocated. He sent his team home to their families. They would be seeing little enough of them when the case really got under way tomorrow. To Clement, who no longer had any immediate relatives to return to, he raised a hand to keep him behind. He watched the man trying to decide whether his gesture had been an order or an invitation.

'No, not a complaint. Quite the reverse, in fact. Adrian, please don't take this amiss. I have no wish to be rid of you but I happen to know that my father-in-law – a chief super in the Met – is looking for a bright sergeant. You've done the exams and, if you're wanting to go further up the ladder, it's about time for another rung. You've done some good work here and I'm happy to provide a useful reference. Have a think about it – a fairly quick one.' He watched surprise and pleasure succeed one another across the DC's face.

'You'd recommend me rather than one of the girls?'

Mitchell laughed. 'Caroline's going to have extra work on her hands before long without looking for more responsibility at work and I need Shakila around to make me laugh. Seriously, I think you're ready for this if you want to try.'

'Has Caroline told you . . .?'

'No, but you just have. You gave her the coveted green chair. Besides, when you've collected four youngsters yourself, you're experienced in reading the signs, not the least of which is the silly grin Cavill's been wearing recently. Think about it – the job, I mean, not Caroline's future plans.' He nodded a dismissal to the young constable, gathered up the file, already growing thick, and scribbled a quick list of questions to be answered before he went to bed. Where else could he look for the gun? Why was Ridgeway shot in the middle of the play? Who was the fat man that Shakila might have recognized? What would the PM report have to tell them and how long would the news from the ballistics team take to arrive? That would do for now. He's better leave at least a few minutes spare to enquire about Ginny's day.

When Mitchell arrived home the demand for his attention was not from his wife but his son. 'Did you remember the DVD, Dad? The one about how the gun works.' Since he had slipped the disc into his pocket earlier in the day, he decided to fulfil his promise now.

Virginia was disapproving. 'You'll be the one to get up to him,' she warned, 'when he's yelling in the middle of the night.'

'He's seen the newsreels and read the gory headlines. It should help to have some of the mystery dispelled. For Pete's sake, there are enough disadvantages in being a copper's son. Let me at least give him a bit of inside information to impress his friends with. This disc is about how a piece of machinery works, not instructions on how to order one on the internet.'

Declan had appeared in the doorway looking distinctly interested. 'I didn't know you could do that.'

'You can't in this country,' his mother told him, her tone repressive. Mitchell opted out of the conversation and fiddled with the DVD player. When he had set the disc playing and turned, he saw that Michael had settled himself beside his brother, claiming his right to participate in this male activity. Mitchell waited for his wife's explosion, but she merely remarked that their younger son would not understand enough to do him any harm.

The commentary began. 'The Glock 00 is a high-velocity, rifled pistol . . .'

Declan looked up. 'That's a German word. It means bell.'

'It's also the name of the man who invented this type of gun.'

'Was he a German?' Mitchell nodded. 'So "glockenspiel" means the playing of bells and playing with guns as well.'

This obviously amused both boys until Declan settled to listen again. 'Pistols, with their short barrels, are intended for shooting at close range. Bullets carry only four hundred to six hundred yards . . .'

Declan frowned. 'But that's a long way, isn't it? That's about the length of one lap of our running track at school, if you unwound it . . .'

His father hushed him. '. . . and a low-muzzle velocity of up to a thousand feet a second . . .'

'How fast is a thousand feet a second?'

Mitchell scratched his head, failed to find any point of comparison and replied feebly, 'Pretty fast.'

'. . . bullets fired from rifled weapons spin from two to three thousand revolutions a second . . .'

Declan shook his head. 'However did they manage to count them?'

Mitchell began to wish he had left the DVD in his office. He strongly suspected that his firstborn was hugely enjoying his father's discomfiture.

'Over the first few yards of trajectory, the flight is slightly unstable. The end of the projectile wobbles before it picks up a smooth flight path. This is known as "tailwag" and is of significant importance in evaluating gunshot wounds.'

Mitchell opened his mouth to explain but saw that Declan had understood the concept as what he saw complemented what he heard. At the mention of tailwag, Michael nodded and offered helpfully, 'Like a dog.' Declan and his father exchanged indulgent smiles.

The short film ran on to its end without any further embarrassing questions. It finished with a diagrammatic form of the gun being fired, each stage of the process being shown in slow motion till the final thunderous explosion in glorious Technicolor settled to a rosy orange against which the credits appeared in black. Michael blinked. 'That's magic.'

'No, Michael. It's not magic, it's physics.'

For a few seconds the child's face crinkled into uncharacteristic furrows as he considered this new concept. Then it cleared, to be replaced by the usual beatific smile, which he bestowed on his father. 'Yes – but you see, I don't believe in physics.'

Early on Sunday, Jennifer rang her DCI to excuse herself from the morning briefing. 'Margot Ridgeway has agreed to see me but wants to have our discussion over by nine o'clock. Her GP has made an appointment for Robin to see a paediatric shrink at half past and she naturally wants to go with him. It was a very polite request for our co-operation.'

'As yours is to me. Granted. The consultant must be more than a bit concerned about the boy to see him on a Sunday morning. If you keep your foot down on the way back here when you're done, we might still be gathered to hear what the lady had to tell you.'

Jennifer delivered her own two daughters to her mother-in-law, knowing that the arrangement pleased all three of them, and set off cheerfully to the Ridgeway house. Having heard such varying opinions of this lady she was curious to know what she would have to say on her own account and how she would conduct herself in a challenging interview. Today she was allowing no semi-comatose evasions.

Remembering Mrs Ridgeway's crisp delivery of her telephoned request, she hoped that today there would be a change of attitude. Jennifer parked outside the white gate in the appropriately labelled Ridgeway Road and walked up the drive towards the house. Last night's rain was being quickly evaporated by a sun that was strong even at this early hour. The steamy mist rose to wrap Jennifer in an almost tangible scent of hyacinths. She rang the bell quickly before it could seduce her from the hard line she intended to take with this witness. She had met her twice already since her ex-husband's death. She was still not sure, though, whether Margot Ridgeway was grieving for a man she had – maybe still – loved or whether she had play-acted her way out of straight answers. Today, Jennifer was going to find out what was really going on, both in her head – and in her family.

The woman who opened the door to her was a different Margot Ridgeway. She wore a high-necked cotton shirt over maternity jeans. Her face was bare except for a touch of mascara and the tawny hair was pulled away from her face into a bunch, half bun, half pony tail. There had been nothing she could do about the narrow, pouting mouth. She greeted Jennifer with just a nod but, as she led the way into the sitting room, said, 'There's coffee – or have you just finished breakfast?' Jennifer was nonplussed. Had the woman read her mind or was she also ready to strip away the pretence and begin to try to sort things out?

She had expected David Page to be hovering in the background, lending his support, but there was no sign of him. Best to seize the moment. She said, 'Let's just get on with our business, shall we? I don't want you to be late for your appointment.' They sat facing each other in two armchairs and Jennifer tried not to stare at the frills, flounces and flowers.

Margot warned, but with no trace of aggression, 'I can't let you talk to Robin. You wouldn't get anything out of him anyway. He won't eat, he won't speak and he only slept when he'd been drugged.' She sat quietly, waiting to be questioned. Jennifer remained silent, willing her to make more revelations, and, in a few moments, she was rewarded. After a deep breath, during which she seemed finally to make up her mind to be frank, Margot confessed, 'I'm in every sort of trouble. What happened on Friday night is only a part of it – the worst part, of course, but there's Robin, and the school and what they suspect and David and what he suspects . . .'

Now Jennifer was prepared to help. 'I won't pretend to misunderstand you. Your partner thinks your ex-husband was sexually abusing his own son. The school has recognized signs of abuse but thinks your partner might be the guilty one.'

'That's it in a nutshell. The school even thinks he was given his black eye at home. Robin was never like other boys. He's a dreamer and I think he might be a talented actor, seriously talented. He has a right to be who he is – but how he is just now is wrong.'

'Has anyone made any open accusations?'

Margot shook her head. 'The school's made it pretty obvious what they're thinking. David and I went to Miss Hardy. She rang the next morning and asked to speak to me privately. She said Robin was generally nervous, picked at himself, his fingernails and any little scratches, until he made them bleed. They asked me if he was having nightmares. Then they got round to checking the dates when

David and I became – well, an item and when he moved in. They weren't very subtle but they weren't direct either. They said I should take him to our GP.'

'Do you think Mr Page has sensed these suspicions? Could he be accusing Mr Ridgeway as a way of defending himself?'

She held up her hands in a despairing gesture. 'I don't know what to believe. It's unthinkable that either David or Paul could be . . .' She was weeping now, but not for the sergeant's benefit. Jennifer thought she was hardly aware of the tears. 'I can't even say it. Not in connection with either of them.'

'Did your ex-husband have any idea of what Mr Page suspected?'

'Not as far as I know.'

'Did he try to interfere with Mr Ridgeway's access to his son? What were the access arrangements ordinarily?'

Margot seemed taken aback. 'There were no "arrangements". There was absolutely no restriction. Robin went to the flat whenever he wanted and Paul took him out whenever he asked to. He wasn't asking permission – just checking that we hadn't made other arrangements. David wasn't sure enough to interfere. He realized he'd have to prove what he thought and he couldn't. Neither of us wanted to question Robin about it.'

'So, you were not certain yourself that your partner was wrong?' There was no answer and Jennifer asked, 'You had a key to the Sainted City flat, didn't you?'

She flinched. 'Don't remind me where it was. I don't like to think of him being there . . . Yes, I had a key. Your inspector has it now. I only use it when he gives permission, asks me to collect something when he's not in, that sort of thing.' Jennifer nodded, noting the return to the present tense.

She tried an abrupt change of subject. 'What do you know about the story that Robin had a gun?'

Margot blinked away the tears. 'How could Robin have

a gun? I can see why he made the claim. David's a bit obsessed with non-aggression. He won't let Robin watch the sort of TV his friends see. They laugh at him and he can't enter into their discussions on what they see. He'd be keeping his end up, trying to go one better.'

'If it's any comfort to you, that's how it seems to me – though he chose an extremely unfortunate time and an even more unfortunate story. Perhaps we can discuss this further after you've heard what the consultant thinks. If you feel able, I'd really like to talk to you now about your ex-husband. Incidentally, is he ex? Are you divorced?'

Margot nodded. 'I should never really have married him, or indeed married anybody – I don't even think I'll marry David now. Robin was on the way and it seemed the right thing to do, but what went wrong between us is very simple. Paul was a one-woman man. I'm not a one-man woman. He tried much harder and much longer than I did to make it work. He kept forgiving me for my affairs, which was very difficult for him because I wasn't sorry. We both knew that, sooner or later, I'd go off with someone else.'

'So, you didn't care when he left you?'

'Oh, I did. He was a safe place to run back to. I won't be able to use David like that. I don't need to at present. He still attracts me and he can shut his eyes to who and what I am and make himself believe the split was Paul's fault.'

'He's told us it was you who made the final break.'

'That doesn't surprise me – but he's persuaded himself that Paul deserved it. You're shocked, aren't you?'

Jennifer thought about the question, tried to answer it honestly. 'It's not the worst confession I've heard. I think you're to be pitied, though.'

'Why?'

'You lose your men and you'll probably lose your children.'

'That's nonsense. Robin has the best of everything. He's considered in everything I do.'

145

'Is he? How secure do you think he feels, having to live by someone else's strict principles that cut him off from his friends and schoolmates? It's not even much use his getting used to it, or trying, as he gets older, to reason with Mr Page if he thinks you won't stay with him.' Jennifer was surprised that the boy had not been taken screaming into the nearest mental hospital long since.

Margot was indignant now. 'David never made any secret of his views and it was Robin himself who opted to come and live here with us. Paul was gutted about that. I was quite sorry for him and a bit surprised at Robin's decision . . . Oh no!' Suddenly, her features froze and her body slumped against the back of her chair. Jennifer saw that this was the first time Margot had thought about her son's choice of home in any terms other than a smug satisfaction at being the chosen carer.

There was more to be asked, but she could see that her witness had had enough for the present. She glanced at her watch. 'Nearly time for your appointment. Perhaps we'd better leave things there for the moment.'

Reluctantly Margot nodded. 'You're right. I'll have to go. Can we talk again tomorrow?'

Surprised, Jennifer agreed that, subject to her DCI's approval, she would return at the same time next day. She gathered her belongings, then, on impulse, gave the troubled woman's arm a squeeze. 'I hope your consultant is reassuring. I'll see myself out.' Her mind was too busy for her to notice the scent of the hyacinths as she returned to her car.

By the time Jennifer reached the DCI's office, Mitchell was the only officer still in it. Pen in hand, he sat at his desk, a sheet of pink paper in front of him. She grinned at him. 'I've never caught you filling in a form, have I? Don't worry, I won't tell anybody.'

He swivelled his chair to face her and waved her to the

seat Clement had vacated for Caroline. 'Did you manage to spend half an hour with the lady without committing another murder?'

Jennifer shook her head. 'It wasn't like that. She was quite alert and refreshingly honest, though I still didn't like her very much.' Briefly she gave him such new information as her interview had brought to light. In return, he summarized the briefing she had missed. 'We had a long look at David Page since the general opinion was that he had more motivation than anyone else. What they came up with was a bit flimsy though. We know that Page says he suspects Ridgeway of buggering his partner's son. That doesn't necessarily mean that he believes it himself.

'Margot Ridgeway had a key to Paul's flat and some of the team think there was still something going on between them. Someone said Page had been humiliated over his piano lessons with Ridgeway. That's hardly serious enough to make him murderous, especially in view of his anti-violence views. Adrian, though, thinks he booked his own ticket at the end of a row so that he could get out unobtrusively. He discovered that most of the spouses just get complimentaries from the company.'

Jennifer frowned. 'Page would have done better, if he was guilty, not to sit there in the first place. Then the person next to him wouldn't have missed him. I don't think he could have known exactly when Ridgeway was on and off stage. He could have asked someone but that wouldn't have been very clever either.'

'We had yet another longish discussion on what might possibly have tempted the man to go outside when he was only off stage for six minutes. He loved his acting. He was revelling in the better parts he was being offered. Stephen Thompson seems to have what it takes as a producer and as an entrepreneur to get the company some good publicity. Why would he risk it?'

'Maybe,' Jennifer said slowly, 'somebody had the gun in his back when he suggested they took a walk outside.'

147

Mitchell blinked. 'Right We'd considered everything but the obvious. You should be leading this investigation. Seriously, Jen, when are you going to apply for an inspector's post?'

'I'm waiting for yours when you move on.'

'I said I'm serious.'

'So am I. How could I manage the girls and work as well without Jane? And I couldn't uproot her at her time of life.'

He nodded, knowing that, without her late husband's mother, he would not have his sergeant. 'Yours is the only sensible reason anyone's suggested for Ridgeway's leaving the stage at that point – and, in that case, we could confine our search to the company.'

'Well, that and its following of scene shifters, dressers, make-up people and so on. What about the audience?'

'It's unlikely that any of them could send a message that would get him outside.'

'And even less likely that someone other than staff and players would risk wandering about backstage in the middle of a performance. So what now?'

'We think about it a lot more today. Was there any point you'd have raised if you'd got back in time?'

Jennifer nodded. 'You thought the boy's teacher wasn't telling you all she knew. You said she left abruptly because, you thought, she was scared of confiding too much. Any further thoughts on that?'

'Only that it was their suspicion that the boy was being abused. Anything else?'

'It struck me that the new producer was taking his disappointment very calmly.'

Mitchell shrugged. 'He doesn't have much choice. They're all disappointed. Besides, he's got much more publicity now than he'd have had from a half-inch in the *Clarion*'s review column. Caroline's with him now.'

'OK. What about the file? How much did you manage to plough through last night?'

He scowled. 'Not enough. In fact, let's go through it

together now. It'd be as useful as my sending you chasing off to ask questions of someone who should have been ruled out of the enquiry by a constable's scribbles in that folder.'

'Where have you sent the others?' Jennifer asked enviously.

'Back to Sainted City, searching for booze and porn. On the knocker in the flats overlooking the scene. Oh, and York to try to trace a probably defunct scout company.'

'I bet it's Shakila that you've sent there.'

'Yes. She left at the crack of dawn. I let her off the briefing. How did you know?'

'Because she'd gatecrash the Archbishop's morning prayers if that's what it took to find her man!'

With the file open between them, the two officers read silently, making occasional written comments on a fresh page in their notebooks. Jennifer was the first to speak. 'The SOCOs mention a small patch in the far back corner of the waste ground where someone had been digging.'

Mitchell nodded. 'It wasn't extensive and it was only very shallow. We investigated it, of course, but found nothing. We thought someone might have seen a small shrub there that they fancied for their garden . . .'

'Or buried a gun?'

'We considered that, yes. It's certainly possible but there's no confirming evidence . . .' Suddenly, he froze. 'Yes there is! Not physical evidence in the soil but . . . Have you got the notes on Miss Hardy's visit?'

Jennifer scrabbled through the pile of papers that she had allocated to herself, found the required sheet and passed it across the desk. Mitchell reread it carefully. 'Last Friday, Robin Ridgeway was late for school and gave his form tutor a bogus dental appointment as his excuse. Miss Hardy says he claimed to have lost his mother's explanatory letter and his fingernails were filthy.'

Jennifer said, slowly, 'And we're pretty certain he'd had the gun in his possession. I don't like where this is leading.'

149

Both officers considered the new line of thinking in silence. Again, after almost a minute, Jennifer was the one to break it. 'It adds support to the theory that his father was his abuser.'

Mitchell added, unwillingly, 'And it accounts for the state the boy is in now. Didn't David Page say that Robin had asked to have his name changed to Page when he and Margot are married?'

'He won't need to bother. Margot says now that she's changed her mind. There isn't going to be a wedding.' Jennifer's expression was rueful. 'I might have let you down here. I wonder how much Margot knows that she's not told me. Do you want someone else to go and talk to her?'

'No way!' Mitchell shook his head vigorously. 'But I do want you to go back to her again. Challenge her with this theory. Tell her that if she knows Robin has committed a crime and covers up for him, then she'll be preventing him from getting the help he really needs.'

Jennifer nodded soberly, then, disconcerted by the odd expression on his face, asked, 'What are you thinking?'

He gave her a half-smile. 'I'm thanking the God I've spent my life trying to avoid for my exhausting, infuriating but relatively wholesome and uncomplicated children. If we can't interview Robin – and I don't think at this point that we should – then we have to speak to the consultant who's treating him. We also have to check with the whole cast of both plays. We need someone who can alibi Robin for the whole of the relevant time.'

They turned back to their file-reading until a sharply indrawn breath indicated that Mitchell had discovered another significant piece of information. 'One of the uniforms has interviewed a stagehand who was called in on Friday to repair a piece of scenery. It was damaged after a bit of horseplay after the dress rehearsal of *Harlequin*. He – the joiner that is – overheard an argument between Paul Ridgeway and another person. This report is too brief

to be useful and the incident is almost certainly relevant.'
He picked up the phone. 'Magic, can you get Jamieson up
here pronto? Good man.' Mitchell replaced the receiver.
'He'd better be able to give me more than he's bothered to
write here!' He drummed his fingers impatiently on the
desk. 'If Smithson, or young Beardsmore, had talked to
this joiner, he would not only have produced a fuller report
but he'd have realized its significance and brought it to
me personally.'

Sergeant Mark Powers proved he was indeed the good
man Mitchell had dubbed him. The hapless PC presented
himself in less than five minutes. Mitchell never delivered
a serious reprimand in the hearing of another officer so
that Jennifer was not offended by being dispatched to find
coffee. As the door closed, Mitchell assumed the icy tones
he reserved for careless work. Incompetence was excusable
but Jamieson's ability was not in question, merely his
commitment. 'I suppose Magic found you so quickly by
looking in the canteen.'

'On my scheduled coffee break, sir.'

'On a murder case we don't have them.'

Jamieson was not easily cowed. He glanced towards the
door through which Jennifer had just departed. Mitchell
swallowed and tried again. 'If you want my sergeant to
witness the censure you deserve, I'll bear that in mind for
the future. I didn't have you down as a masochist.' He
picked up and waved the offending piece of paper that
Jamieson had put in the file. 'This is not a report. Sit down
and describe this significant incident – which you have
kindly mentioned though not reported – in all the detail
you can remember.'

Under fire, Jamieson's account was exemplary, concise
but with the detail the DCI required. 'The ladder and frame
had to be repaired *in situ*. It was part of a bigger structure,
so Mr Goddard was working on stage. He was interested
in the quarrel he was hearing but the work was urgent and
he had to keep hammering. He could see Paul Ridgeway

on the far side of the stage but the other person was just backstage, behind the big flat with the trees painted on. At the start they were hissing at each other, fairly quietly until Paul really lost it. The other person didn't raise his voice – or hers. Paul had evidently recognized somebody that he had a grudge against. Goddard heard disjointed phrases, "Knew I'd seen you before somewhere" and "I was foxed because you've changed so much, but I knew the vibes weren't right." The last thing he heard was that if the other person was up to his old tricks with Paul's boy then he'd swing for him.'

Jamieson obviously thought his report was now finished. Mitchell punished him with fifteen seconds' silence, then waved the paper again. 'And you considered this was adequate as a record of what the witness had just told you?'

'I thought, if you wanted more, that you'd speak to me at the briefing, sir. I didn't realize it would be so long before you consulted the file. I'm sorry about that.' Jamieson followed his back-handed apology with a dignified exit. Mitchell grinned to himself. This man would go far. He was pleased. Now they had a possible reason for the shooting having taken place on Friday evening. Presumably, Robin's abuser had offended before. Now he had been recognized, Paul Ridgeway needed dispatching quickly before he exposed him. Until the first performance was over, Paul would be concentrating on that, but in the socializing, after the play was over, he would be dangerous.

The door opened again and Mitchell resigned himself to drinking coffee made by Jennifer. At least it would be better than Ginny's!

Dr Ewart Grainger was sprawling in an easy chair in a room that, apart from the smell, didn't seem like part of a hospital. Nor did the man himself look like a doctor.

'I understand that you don't want to talk, Robin. Well, that's fine because there's a lot I want to say. I want to tell you how sorry I am to have missed your first night. A lot of people had told me how good it would be.

'I wasn't familiar with the play you were in. Since my chess match prevented my being at the first night I bought tickets for a later performance. Then, when it looked as if there wasn't going to be another, I asked Adam Lessing, who lives in my street, if I could borrow his copy. It didn't take long to read but I was very impressed and even sorrier to have missed seeing it performed. I'm assuming you played John Taplow.'

The boy remained mute and still, not raising his eyes. Undismayed, Dr Grainger continued to speak in the same level tone, working through the one act of the play, scene by scene.

'Did the chocolate box you had to steal from before the dialogue began have real chocolates in it? I do hope so. I've never met a young lad who didn't like chocolate.'

There was still no response. Dr Grainger was unconcerned. He had not yet planted his mistake. He thought he detected an increase in the boy's tension as he approached the crucial scene where Crocker-Harris was finally reached and touched by his pupil's kindness.

'I'm sure your father played that episode with great sensitivity. I've heard so. I suppose that Terence Rattigan was a Greek scholar. That was a very appropriate quotation from Agamemnon's speech to Clytaemnestra. *God, from afar, looks gently upon a gracious master.*'

'*God from afar looks graciously upon a gentle master.*' The voice was sepulchral but the words were clearly enunciated.

Dr Grainger moved on cautiously. After a few moments of silence, he asked, 'You know I misquoted the line deliberately, don't you?'

'Yes.'

'Do you think I tricked you?'

'No. You knew that I knew.'

'That's good. I think that's all for now.'

'You're not going to ask me questions? About . . .?'

They were on precarious ground. Dr Grainger said, 'That's not my job. It is my job, though, to recognize that someone's been abusing you. Am I right?'

'Yes.'

'I won't be asking who it is. That isn't my job either. I will ask you if you'd like to talk about it. Would you?'

'Yes, but not now.'

Dr Grainger nodded. 'Fine. You'll have to tell me when you're ready. Will you?'

'Yes.'

'If you're willing, I'd like you to stay here for a few days, away from people who are – shall we say, a little more impatient than I am. Will you stay?'

'Yes.'

DC Caroline Jackson was questioning her witness slightly less sympathetically but he was bearing up well. 'You had just six minutes to decide what to do. You were almost suspiciously quick-thinking.'

Stephen Thompson took no offence and showed no concern, at least on his own account. 'I had a lot less than six minutes.'

'Take me through the three or four minutes before that – before you realized that Paul Ridgeway wasn't where he should have been.'

Thompson arranged his long legs more comfortably and leaned back on his expensive leather sofa before beginning his account. 'I usually sit at the side of the stage, towards the back, next to the prompt, during an actual performance. I can see most of what's happening on the stage from there and it's where they cast their agonized glances if everything's not going smoothly. From the same place looking the other way, I could see right across the back of the flats. If I'd stayed there I would have seen Paul make his exit and where he went – but *The Browning Version* had gone so well and was so nearly over that I walked behind the backdrop to the other side, in carpet slippers, of course. They're obligatory footwear for all stagehands, dressers and people like me. The *Harlequinade* people, on my orders, were in the women's dressing room and I wanted to have a word with them.'

'Why did they have to be there?'

'It's the only space backstage for the essential people to be. The place was designed as a church, not a theatre. So, I had my word, congratulated them and started wandering back to my usual place. Then I noticed Mary James, the BV prompt, frantically beckoning me. I hurried over and she hissed at me that Paul was not at the door. There were six more lines to go and he wasn't there for his entry. There was no time to think or to guess where he was. I grabbed the academic gown that Paul had left on the hook in the back wall – just by instinct, and put it on. Later, when I'd thought about it, I claimed to Adam that I'd done it deliberately as a sign to the two on stage. I grabbed Mary's book off her, though I never looked at it. I usually know the script off by heart by the time we get to the dress rehearsal. Tony shoved the medicine bottle into my hand. Somehow he'd worked out what I was going to do . . .'

Caroline held up a hand. 'Just a minute. Wasn't he in the other play?' He nodded. 'So why wasn't he in the same room as the others?'

Thompson's expression was half grin, half grimace. 'Because he always does his own thing, doesn't take direction.'

'Not even on the stage?'

'Fortunately, that's a place where we almost always agree so it's never been an issue. It worried me at first. I thought the others would see that Tony was a stronger character than I am and would see him getting away with pleasing himself. They seem to understand though that you can't tame him.'

'Are you telling me that he was prowling around back-stage all the time, right through the evening?'

'I don't know so I can't say. I am telling you that no one would have thought anything about it if he was.'

Chapter Eight

It had been just before six in the morning when Shakila had set out for York. After a moment's consideration, she had decided that to take the shortest route through the middle of Leeds at this hour on a Sunday was unlikely to hold her up and duly proceeded directly east from Cloughton towards Bradford. She enjoyed driving on what felt like a secret road, knowing that, under the translucent mist that the sun would soon clear, colours were still bright and the little hills were still steep, at least until she was through Bradford.

On the narrow road out of Cloughton her car had been brushed by several varieties of tall-stemmed, lacy white flowers that she had often tried but failed to differentiate. Hawthorn blossom that had been fat buds only yesterday was now fully opened. The branches overhead no longer carried buds but their leaves were still a fresh, young green. She passed her brother's house and noticed that the fragile blossom had disappeared from his cherry tree. As the sun penetrated the mist, she could see that a cheerful summer was establishing itself with dapples of broom and dandelions.

She was sorry when she began to approach the big cities but pleased to find Leeds as empty of traffic as she had hoped. She continued her journey across the plain of York enjoying the flat scenery less. Everything was now under bright daylight and she drove the rest of her way as quickly as was safe.

Shakila had promised herself two treats before she began her day's work. Her DCI could not reasonably expect her to disturb any witness before nine on what was officially a day of rest. First, therefore, she would take a walk round at least part of the old city wall and then she would have a second breakfast at a small pub, just outside the old city on the bank of the Ouse. She had discovered, on a trip she had taken last year, that it served a mammoth breakfast to the crews of passing craft, with coffee as good as the DCI's. She would call on Colin Vernon at nine o'clock. Margot Ridgeway had told her that he had been a keen church-man, and a telephone call the previous evening had confirmed that he wished to be free by ten o'clock so as to be at the Minster in time for Morning Prayer.

When her interview was finished, she would have earned her lunch which she planned to have at the King's Arms. She paused now, halfway across the river, looking down on it from the bridge. She was glad to see its sunny terraces, peopled with early drinkers braving the cool breeze. She remembered watching the television news and seeing that all the wooden decking was invisible below slimy water during the last floods. It would be a fraction warmer by lunchtime. She would eat out here, waving, along with her fellow diners, to steamer-loads of tourists chugging through the water and fracturing the surface so that the sun sparkled on it.

Feeling full of virtue, on account of her early start to the day, and of eggs and vegetarian sausages from the Ring o' Bells, Shakila presented herself at Colin Vernon's modest, semi-detached house at the appointed time. When the front door opened, she compared the 1980s picture of her witness with this later version. She estimated him to be a touch younger than Paul Ridgeway. The well-muscled legs had probably weathered the years better than the rest of him, but his Sunday, church-going suit revealed less of them than had the khaki shorts in the photographs. The man was still slim. His hair was still not grey, though the flaming red had faded and its owner now preferred a Number 3 to curls that just touched his shoulders. The striped blue and white shirt set off his light tan. He would look unexceptionable in the Minster congregation in a couple of hours' time. Shakila smiled to herself as she remembered the unseen pair of tattooed dragons that Margot had described, wrestling with each other across his shoulder blades.

She allowed herself to be ushered into a pleasantly cluttered front room and placed in an armchair with a clean and practical loose cover. She smiled at Vernon as the muted sounds of a lively children's game floated up the hall. 'How many?' she asked.

'Two of ours and two cousins for the weekend – hence the excitement. They won't disturb us. Thanks for putting me in the picture last night. I haven't kept in close touch with Paul but he was a good bloke, cared about the lads and worked hard for them. I heard he was living somewhere in West Yorkshire and teaching piano. Then I heard that he'd married some actress woman that he'd got in the family way. I wasn't surprised that he did the decent thing by her. I actually quite liked her once I'd got used to her. I hope you get whoever did this and make him pay for it. Can I see the photographs?'

Shakila handed over copies of the four pictures and he sat for over a minute, examining them. He nodded as he gathered them up and handed them back. 'They are the ones I thought you meant. I'm still recognizable and so is Paul. DK is Denis Kingsley. He's living over in Bradford now so you could catch him on your way back if he's at home. I'm afraid we don't keep up with him either but Julie will have an address for him in her Christmas card list. He's a social worker. He's a good bloke too. We had some rare old times with those lads, especially when we went camping. I still give a hand with teaching for some of the badges but job and kids mean I don't put in the hours with them that I used to.'

Shakila waited but Vernon seemed to have nothing to add. 'And the fourth man?' she asked quietly.

His voice hardened. 'That's James Mostyn.'

'Did you keep up with him?'

Vernon grimaced. 'He mucked about with the lads. Two of them. Nasty. Derek and I reported it. He got put away for quite a long stretch but he's out again now. Not back to scouting, of course – and he didn't dare to show his face round here.'

Shakila said carefully, 'I'm very interested in Mr Mostyn. Would you tell me all you know about him?'

He shrugged. 'I already have, just about. We all used to wonder why he'd volunteered to help us. A bit slow off the mark, I suppose. He was too fat and unfit to take part in the sporting activities that the lads enjoyed and he didn't offer to do any craft or practical skills either. Eventually we tumbled to it, got rid of him sharpish.' He smiled at Shakila's disappointed expression. 'Don't worry. My Christian charity didn't – doesn't – stretch to sympathy with a paedo but Derek's did. He visited James in Armley and wrote countless letters. James responded whilst he was inside but, when he came out, he gave Derek the wrong release date and left him waiting outside the prison the day after he'd gone. He's disappeared. Derek says it wasn't a waste of his time. I'll leave you to decide for yourself.'

Shakila prolonged the interview for a few more minutes but felt that Colin Vernon had given all that he could tell her. When he had produced the promised address for Derek Kingsley, together with the bonus of his telephone number, she thanked him and left. Back in her car, she fished in her purse and produced a two pence piece. She grinned to herself. Heads she rang the DCI and asked for further instructions. Tails, she tried, on her own initiative, to arrange to speak both to someone at Armley who had known Mostyn inside and to Mr Kingsley, the social worker. Tails it was! Splendid!

* * *

160

Using the telephone number that Colin Vernon had given her, Shakila was abashed to realize that she had woken Derek Kingsley. Too late, she remembered what *un*sociable hours social workers had to keep. However, he was gracious – until she mentioned Mostyn's name. 'If you're wanting to hound James, then I'm very pleased to tell you that I don't know anything that might help you. You're wasting your own time and my precious sleep time.'

Shakila apologized and hurried into an explanation before he could hang up on her. 'We're dealing with a thirteen-year-old who has unquestionably been abused. The boy is the son of someone you used to know, Paul Ridgeway, who was murdered in Cloughton.'

'Yes, I know about that. I can't think of any comment to make about it that comes anywhere near to expressing what I felt when I read about it. I didn't realize he was living so close to Bradford or I'd have been in touch with him.'

'Look, can I come over and talk to you? We want to find both Mr Ridgeway's killer and the boy, Robin's, abuser. They're possibly the same person. If it's Mr Mostyn, you can't possibly want to protect him. If it's nothing to do with him, you might be able to help us to prove it and we can stop looking for him.'

Shakila heard a heavy sigh, but eventually Kingsley said, 'All right. You'd better come. Where are you parked?' Having decided to help, he gave her efficient instructions on how to find his house. Shakila decided not to forfeit his goodwill by telling him she had already fed his postcode into her Satnav.

By the time she arrived, Kingsley was shaved and dressed in tracksters and a sweatshirt and the house was pervaded by the smell of ground coffee. She observed that the decorations were stark but the house was neat and clean. The walls were bare, but for framed evidence that Kingsley had achieved respectable times in the sixty-one-mile Fellsman Hike and in the Durham Dales hundred-mile race in 1991.

They exchanged apologies, he for his bad manners on the telephone and she for disturbing his lie-in. 'I'll keep this short,' Shakila promised, 'so that at least you'll have time for your pre-lunch run.' She listened patiently to the story she had already heard of his letters and visits to Mostyn in Armley and the ungrateful trick played on him at the end of Mostyn's sentence.

'I don't blame him,' he assured her earnestly. 'I know he trusted me not to try to make trouble for him, but maybe he thought I'd keep obs on him, that I'd be breathing down his neck. And possibly I would have been, trying to keep him on the straight and narrow. Then again, he might have been scared that, in the course of my work, I might forget myself if his case ever came up in conversation and inadvertently let something slip. I've no regrets. Doing the right thing makes you feel satisfied – though not *self*-satisfied, I hope.'

He paused to gulp at his coffee and Shakila hastily slipped in a question. 'Colin Vernon said there were two scouts who were abused. What happened to them?

'Young Anthony had counselling and then made a good career for himself. He seemed none the worse, but who knows? Ian went wrong. Not drugs or crime – so far as I know – just aimless, under-achieving and bitter. Colin told me he went to watch James come out, on the *right* day, though I don't know who told him which it was. He spoke to James, told him that, wherever he settled, he would make sure that everyone there knew him for what he was. The lad wasn't clever enough to keep track though. He lost him and I did. I don't know anyone to suggest to you who might be able to help. All this has stirred my conscience. I must look Ian up again, see how he's doing . . .'

When Shakila managed to interrupt again and asked for contact details for the two young men, Kingsley refused her. She realized that none of the information he had given her was sufficiently specific to be useful and doubted whether even the two forenames he had mentioned were the real ones. As she returned to her car, she could think of nothing Derek Kingsley had said that had helped the case along in any way. At the same time, she had a strange feeling that her time had not been wasted.

A morning's stewing over the file justified an afternoon out of the office, Mitchell decided, as he cleared the crumbs from his desk after his sandwich lunch. He would go and talk to someone who had not yet told all he knew. Young Adam Lessing had so far escaped with only the briefest of questioning. Along with Margot Ridgeway, he could be eliminated from the search for whoever had actually fired the gun. Being relatively new to the company he might well be reasonably objective about them. He'd see what he had to say for himself.

A telephone call ascertained that Mr Lessing was both at home and at the DCI's service. A four-minute drive brought Mitchell to his door. The house was small but Cousin Lane was a pleasant cul-de-sac in a respectable area. Mitchell was surprised that a semi-professional actor could afford it. Even if he was the tenant rather than the owner, the rent would be high. He was surprised too to find Lessing dressed in a formal suit with a white shirt and sober tie.

It was through PC Beardsmore, so far, that they had learned something of this witness's philosophy of life and his opinion of his fellow actors. To Mitchell, Lessing had so far been a shadowy figure at the back of a crowded dressing room plus two sheets of concise notes from a promising constable. Now, as they settled themselves in comfortable chairs in a tidy room, half old-fashioned parlour, half office, he studied the man's features. It was a young face, the contours soft like a child's and the mouth relaxed, almost slack. The fair hair, trendily tousled and blond-streaked, contrasted with the dark suit and made him look like a boy actor not quite succeeding in his role as a businessman.

He sat now with his head bent forward, looking up at his visitor from under delicate brows, the hairs fine and fair. Mitchell wondered if it was an unconscious defensive mannerism or a deliberate pose. Giving him the benefit of the doubt, he began the interview with general questions about the victim. Did the company always consider Paul to be a good actor or had it taken Mr Thompson's direction to develop his talent?

Lessing replied unhesitatingly. 'If he's a good actor now, he must always have been so.'

'Do you think that in future productions he would automatically have been given the lead?'

Now there was a hesitation. 'There was no doubt about his versatility. I don't like to speak ill of the dead ... but there was a bit of a drink problem. Sometimes at rehearsals he'd be very loud and hearty and you could smell the whisky on his breath. Mind you, he always did turn up – and on time. He always knew his lines and when he was up on the stage and the rehearsal was under way he was completely into his part as usual.'

'Did he drink when he was living with his wife or did it start afterwards?'

Lessing shrugged. 'I wasn't here then.'

Mitchell nodded. 'Had you come across Paul, or any of the other players, before you joined the company?'

He shook his head. 'It would have been possible. I only come from the far side of Huddersfield – but no. They were all strangers to me when I first arrived.'

'Did you work as an actor in Huddersfield?'

'No, but I did belong to an amateur group. They weren't very good. They did the same stuff that this company used to do before Stephen came, but not so well. I earned my crust as an accountant.'

Mitchell was surprised. The man must be older than he looked. 'Did you enjoy that?'

'Not really. This is much more fun. I don't regret the training, though, because now I can do freelance account-ing when funds run low. I had a client here earlier this morning.' So that explained the man's sober dress. 'We all have to have a sideline to make ends meet.'

'So I've heard.' It was time, Mitchell decided, to get to grips with this witness. 'You were sent to look for Mr Ridgeway, weren't you? Why didn't the director go himself?'

'Why ask me? Since you did, I'd say he knew he was the only one who could keep control over everyone left inside and stop them panicking.'

'What did you expect to find out there?'

'Nothing. We didn't realize till Stephen tried the door that it wasn't locked.'

'It usually is?'

'Yes, it's safer and there's nothing out there to go out for.'

'So why is it there?'

Mitchell had asked the question of himself but Lessing gave him an answer. 'You've lived here longer than me. You should know that the area where the flats were built used to be the churchyard. I've talked to people who remember the gardens and seats for the old folk – and the church garden parties.'

Mitchell grinned. 'You're right. I should have known. Was the key usually left in the door?'

Lessing thought about this with his eyes closed. Mitchell decided to be magnanimous and take this as a genuine attempt to answer the question rather than a piece of melo-drama. 'I don't think so. My mind isn't picturing the door now with a key.'

'Was Mr Thompson surprised that the door was unlocked?'

'How should I know? He obviously thought it might be or he wouldn't have tried it – although we'd looked at all the likely possibilities and we were beginning to try silly places. A few people were getting quite worried but the general feeling was puzzlement. I went outside because Stephen told me to but I didn't have a premonition of disaster. I thought it was a waste of time. The door was first mentioned because the general opinion was that the furthest Paul could have gone was to the cloakroom at the bottom of those few stairs.' Mitchell nodded, remembering his exploration of the cramped arrangements backstage. The door to the outside was immediately next to the cloakroom.

Lessing was happily continuing his story. 'When Stephen asked if the door was locked, no one spoke. We all looked at each other so he went to try it . . .' He stopped and blinked. 'As far as I know it hadn't been used for months but it opened without a sound, no squeaking or sticking. Someone had prepared it!'

'Yes, the hinges and the lock too had been oiled. Go on with your very clear account, please.'

Lessing seemed pleased with the approval. 'Stephen said just to go as far as the wall that goes round the flats because there were lots of folk already in the car park. He sent Tony after me. I was glad to have company and glad it was Tony. There was a bit of light from the flats but the wall blocked most of it and not all the windows were lit but we'd left our door open. I saw a hand sticking out from a laurel bush. Paul's clothes were a dinner suit he was wearing for the play and black shoes so the rest of him didn't show. I'd come out first but Tony went in front of me. He was going to sit Paul up or help him or whatever – then I heard him gasp and swear under his breath.

'I'm not sure how I knew he was dead, but I did. We pushed branches aside for more light. It was only a little hole and not much blood but his face . . . Anyway, I took my jacket off and Tony covered him with it. Not his face. That would have somehow suggested there was no hope. I went back in to tell the others. Tony stayed there. He was crying.'

Mitchell gave Lessing a moment or two to recover himself before asking, 'What did you personally think had happened? Before you found him?'

'I thought it might have something to do with his drinking and I was very sorry about that. It was something we could ignore up to a point but if it ruined an important performance then Paul would be finished. I didn't want that. We needed Paul for the things we were beginning to tackle and, anyway, I liked him. I thought he might have covered up well for a while and then suddenly passed out – or maybe he'd gone out for a quick nip and it had been the last straw.'

'And, you say, you liked Mr Ridgeway?'

'As far as I knew him, I did. I keep telling you, I've not been here long and the rest have known each other for years. If the general conversation wasn't about the current play – and it usually was – I tended to talk to Stephen.'

'What about?'

'It varied. Sometimes it was about plays that we might tackle in the future. Once we had a long conversation about whether Robin Ridgeway might become a seriously great actor.'

'And what conclusion did you come to?'

'Yes. He will.'

'Can I take you back on stage now, to when Paul had had his cue and should have entered? What did you think?'

Lessing smiled. 'Well, certainly my first thoughts were not about what might have happened to him. I wondered what to do, how we should cope. I wondered if we could manage a bit of stage business or whether to make up a line or two that fitted in. I decided not to because I knew that Margot wouldn't catch on and play up to me. She'd have stared at me as though I'd lost the plot.' He smiled at this apt simile.

'And what did you think when Mr Thompson came on instead?'

'I realized what he was trying to do. I nodded to Margot. She carried on as if it was Paul but it felt very wooden. The audience didn't seem to be breathing. It's funny but, when there's a dramatic moment on stage, and there's silence, you can hear them all breathing, but on Friday they seemed to be holding their breath. I said my lines and made my movements, but, in my head, I was wondering why Stephen had put the academic gown on. We were supposed to be having a miniature dinner party. I asked him about it later. He said it was a signal to us that he'd entered in Crocker-Harris's character and not just as himself to make an announcement and bring the play completely down on the floor. That was smart thinking because that's exactly how the gown did work. It said, "I'm Crocker-Harris. Carry on to the end of the scene.'"

When Mitchell left the house a few minutes later, he felt that he had been presented with a fresh aspect of both the situation and the characters involved in it. He had not wasted his time.

Chapter Nine

The telephone in the Mitchell house was in great demand on Sunday evening. Soon after their evening meal, Janil Iqbal was deep in conversation with Declan. They happily interrupted one another. 'I've just had my piano lesson with Mr Jackson –'

'I didn't know you learnt the piano. You've got the same teacher as me –'

'I know. He's been telling me about the senior citizens' concert and the piece you're playing for them. He's taking me to hear it. I've never seen a glock.'

'You can come and see mine, if you like.'

'Can I? When? Actually, I rang to say that the first round draw for the lower school chess tournament was put up after last lesson this afternoon. We're drawn against one another. I'm not very good.'

'Neither am I. My cousin was teaching me but – well, he had to go away. You'll be sure to beat me.'

'I don't care who wins. Are you free to do it tomorrow lunchtime – then we'll have it done with. One of us'll lose then and the other'll lose in the next round. Er . . . Dec, would you let me have a go with it?'

'A go with what?'

'The glock. I'd be really careful with it.'

Declan considered. 'Yes. You're not likely to damage it unless you're trying to . . .'

The Mitchells' living-room door opened and both boys heard Virginia ask, 'Will you be long, Declan? I need to speak to the *Guardian*.' Declan excused himself to his friend, cancelled the call and handed over the handset.

'Who was that?' his mother asked.

'It was Janil. I said he could ring me. He's a bit unpopular at school just now because he laughed at Robin Ridgeway's story about having a gun. They laughed as well but then Robin's dad was shot. Everyone was sorry for him and now they're treating Janil as if he's the only one who teased.'

Virginia frowned. 'I didn't know you knew either of those boys.'

'I talk to Robin over the wall when he comes to visit his gran. Mrs Gledhill sometimes asks me over for lemonade and to play. Both of them go to my school.'

His mother nodded and dispatched him to do his homework. When he had gone it was not the *Guardian* that she rang.

She waited, hoping not to hear a message on the answering machine. 'Shakila?' Good. She was in. 'It's Ginny. Just a quickie. Declan seems to be striking up a friendship with a boy, Janil, who has a connection with Robin Ridgeway and your case. I'm don't want to ask out-of-order questions about the case, but Benny said you knew the family. Do you know any reason why I should discourage it? I don't like interfering with my children's choice of friends – especially Declan's as he doesn't mix very easily anyway. On the other hand I . . .'

'You don't want him taken hostage while he's mixing with people who might be connected to a current case. Well, all young Janil has done is tease the Ridgeway child about telling porkies . . .'

Virginia listened gratefully to Shakila's reassurances. 'Thanks for that. Don't worry. I know there are no guarantees. I'm only asking for guidance. Janil doesn't seem to be involved in anything illegal. I'll leave well alone. Enjoy your evening.' Her mind at rest, she smiled at the way

Shakila had learned as much schoolboy slang as Queen's English. She had a good grasp of which was which too.

Before she could make the call to her features editor, the phone rang again. She called Mitchell. 'It's for you.'

'I'm out.'

'It's my father.'

'I'm in.' He came through from the kitchen where he had been loading the dishwasher and took the handset to a comfortable chair. 'I'm sitting comfortably. You can begin.'

He could hear Browne was grinning. 'You're showing your age, Benny. How's your case?'

'At the stage where there are plenty of jigsaw pieces but they may not all belong to the same puzzle. We might be searching for one gun or two. We've an unbalanced school-boy who might hold the key to everything or might just be on his way to raving lunacy. The poor kid's certainly had enough to send him there. We think he's being abused. The abuser could have been the victim himself, who's the kid's father. That's the story of the ex-wife's new partner who may be the perpetrator himself.'

Mitchell sighed. 'Or else it could be someone who has nothing to do with the shooting. The victim was a bit of an alcoholic, divorced, father of the aforementioned disturbed boy and the lead actor in our semi-professional repertory company.'

'Aforementioned indeed! You're catching Ginny's dis-ease. Otherwise, very neatly summed up.'

'I've had practice. I've done it for the benefit of the assembled team, the super and the local rag.'

'The last was a waste of time. They'll write what they like.'

'No. That's unfair. There's a lot worse local rags than the *Clarion*.'

'It's also an old argument so we'll leave it.'

'Right. The victim's star role in the rep is fairly new – came with a new director who's doing more highbrow productions for which Ridgeway was suited. It's put a few noses out of joint.'

'Sounds like excellent progress.'

'We're moving on, I suppose. I have great hopes for some photographs we've found in the victim's flat. Not sure quite how they'll help yet. Anyway, what about Hoodie? That's what you really rang to tell me.'

'We're quite a lot further forward. He has a name now. The problem is, it doesn't seem to be the only one he uses. You remember the student who worked with Hoodie as a brickie for a few weeks last year? Irish youngster, Patrick O'Reilly – another Irish name to save up for when you produce your next set of twins.'

'I should hang up on you for that, but, in case you're really worrying, I'll set your mind at rest. Your daughter believes in birth control even if her Irish mother-in-law has her doubts about it. Now tell me about Patrick O'Reilly.'

'He has now recalled a drinking session he and Hoodie had one Friday which was payday. We took what he said with a pinch of salt because he only remembered it under the stimulation of a reward offered by Timothy Ellis's boss for information leading to his employee's killer. O'Reilly says not to take too much notice of the information anyway – admits he told Hoodie lies about himself that night, boasting about things he had never actually done and he expects his mate did the same.'

'Tom, you're stretching this out to annoy me!'

Browne hurried on. 'All right. Only when he's drunk. He always tells the truth, he assured me, when he's sober. Hoodie's story was that, just over two years ago, his father was beaten senseless by a gang of white youths. The incident was in Blackheath, "where the bloody nobs live", though Hoodie's family lived in Whitechapel, only a stone's throw from Brick Lane. One of the white lads, the ringleader in fact, was the son of the local super and there were no prosecutions. His father was expected never to be more than a vegetable and couldn't be consulted. The mother accepted fairly handsome compensation.'

'Don't suppose that Blackheath were too anxious to dig out the records on that for you.'

'You suppose right, but we have our ways and means – and our narks. Most of it links up and so Hoodie is almost certainly the son of the Qreshi who was the victim there. It's not an unusual name but we're going round the relevant local schools. Someone will certainly be able to tell us more when we get the right one.

'Meanwhile, Hoodie/Qreshi hates whites, especially coppers and particularly when they appear to be spying on Asians. They might as well have killed his father, they corrupted his mother with their filthy money and they're a load of Fascist bastards.'

'Sounds like a nice bloke. You'll be anxious to make his acquaintance.'

'Actually, I can see where he's coming from.'

'And where he's going to will give you an exciting time.'

'The next step will be tedious, digging out all the evidence for this. It might get exciting when we've found enough to nail him and start to track him down, learn what he's up to at the moment. If we've got it right, I must admit I do have some sympathy with him.'

Mitchell was indignant. 'Don't go soft on him now! He tried to kill a cop who had nothing to do with his father and he mowed down an innocent unarmed civilian who had the guts to try to help . . .'

Once again, it was Virginia who put an end to a long call. She came into the room with Mitchell's cellphone in her hand. 'I thought, if I fielded this for you, I could put off whoever it was till you'd finished with Dad – but it's Superintendent Carroll. He says he's fed up with listening to our engaged signal.'

Hastily, Mitchell excused himself to his father-in-law and took the mobile from his wife. 'Yes, sir?'

'Sorry to spoil your gossip, Benny. It's just an early warning before you deploy your troops for the rest of the week. About Tuesday.'

'Nothing to spoil, sir. I deploy them on a daily basis. Until the morning arrives you don't know what situations you'll be dealing with and what your priorities will be –'

'Right. I don't need a time and motion study. DC Nazir – Shakila – has asked for a day's leave for personal family business. You probably know more about it than I do. I gave permission. We probably owe her some time off and she's not a skiver. She wouldn't ask in the middle of a murder enquiry if it wasn't important. You can have someone else for the day if things get hairy.'

Mitchell opened his mouth to say they'd be no use compared with Shakila but he shut it again. He didn't want to jeopardize the granting of the day and if he could give Beardsmore detective duties for a day he might cover himself with glory and further his chances of a permanent transfer to the team. He thanked the superintendent for the prior warning and rang off, smarting a little to find he was not as far into his DC's confidence as the superintendent expected him to be.

Sinead came into the room and saw that at last the handset was back in place on the charger. She stood with legs apart, hands on hips, ready to bring the force of her six-year-old's displeasure to bear against her father. 'I suppose, now that no one else needs the phone, that you'll say it's my bedtime and too late to ring Megan.'

Mitchell hid a smile. 'You suppose wrong. I'm going to say that you can have five minutes exactly to talk to Megan, so you'd better get on straightaway with whatever you need to tell her.' He saw that she would have preferred to win a drawn-out argument that included a polite and reasonable request for a mobile phone like Declan's so that family use of the house phone didn't inconvenience her.

174

She was prepared, however, to consider his concession a victory. He passed her the handset and gave her ten minutes before sending her upstairs.

When Janil Iqbal had replaced his receiver, after his conversation with Declan, he noticed that Youssef had come into the room. Mindful of the advice that Shakila had given him, he grinned at his brother. 'Dec Mitchell and I are playing a chess match at school tomorrow. You're good. You couldn't give me a few tips, could you?'

He was impressed by his own social skills when Youssef immediately responded. 'I don't know this Dec. You can tell me about him whilst I decide the best tricks to teach you.' The restored amity lasted easily until bedtime. Janil had high hopes by then of giving Declan Mitchell a surprise trouncing.

Darkness fell and the townsfolk of Cloughton settled down for the night. One or two of them found that sleep was eluding them.

The man born Omar Qreshi had learned very early in his existence that there was no justice in this world. No one would defend him or his family. He had done his best to defend his own kind and to get his revenge for what had been done to himself and his family. He wondered how soon his intelligent mother would realize that the family money he 'managed' for her had been spent ages ago. Could she not see that inflation had made the one-off compensation payment derisory? Maybe she could. She was an intelligent woman. Perhaps she had known about his other life soon after it began and accepted it because it was inevitable. He was of age. In their culture, though she had influence, she had no power. He was pleased with what he had achieved and what he had acquired. He served his masters well and they rewarded him, if not generously, at least sufficiently for him to soften the blows that had fallen on his family. Today he had laboured for them physically so that, at this point in his reflections, sleep intervened. He dreamed, though, that this brief respite from physical danger was over. He had to watch out for himself again. It was not a restful night.

Superintendent Carroll's sleeplessness was partly due to the good supper which he had prepared for a colleague from the neighbouring North Yorkshire force, and in which he had over-indulged. They had commiserated with each other about a superintendent's responsibilities, not least of which was keeping within their allocated budget. He lay back on his pillows, reviewing his station's finances. He knew his discussion on the subject with Benny, earlier in the day, would have little effect. He was unrepentant at having sent out the pulsar team on the strength of a squashed bullet and a collapsed wall. Now he was demanding saliva tests on a theatreful of people because the SOCOs had discovered a small pellet of chewing gum.

He wanted evidence from the lab to support or to rule out every hare-brained theory he came up with. Doubtless, one of them would prove to be right, but not before the West Yorkshire budget had been blown out of the window, across the moors and all over the M62!

Shakila Nazir, unusually for her, was also wakeful and worrying. She was hatching two plans which would astonish her colleagues and break up the tightly knit and efficient team of detectives at Cloughton HQ. She really should have advised her DCI of both, but, if either of them failed, things would remain as they were – so, why bother him with what might never happen? But she was not comfortable with her secrets.

* * *

Nigel Turner, known to the Cloughton Players as Props, reached up to stow his now-empty suitcase on top of his wardrobe. The clothes it had contained, which he had worn on holiday, were now swirling around in the washing machine. The other miscellaneous possessions he had taken with him were cluttering his bed, together with the gifts he had brought back for friends.

He tutted with annoyance as he realized that the protective towel he had wrapped round the whisky he had chosen for Paul was still doing its job and had been omitted from the washing load. He decided to nip round to Paul's flat when he had had his supper. He had not bought anything so expensive for anyone else in the company so the bottle needed to be handed over in private.

Supper would be just a sandwich that he had picked up in a service station whilst refuelling with diesel. He would have to do a supermarket trip early tomorrow. He made instant coffee since the unimaginative sandwich didn't deserve wine, or even Douwe Egberts. Then, being a methodical soul, he fetched his 'to-do' book and a pen to the table and listed his Monday tasks as he ate and drank. First the shopping, then sort out the bags of props that his son would have filled for him and left in the empty half of his double garage, which had been their home since the roomy old theatre had been sold. Then he would ask around, catch up on the news, find out how the Rattigan double bill had been received.

He had been very sorry to miss their first night, but when his mother's sixtieth birthday had coincided with his cousin's offer of a free two weeks in her cottage in Argèles sur Mer, he could hardly have refused, and was glad he had not. His mother had had a ball and he had found the two weeks mostly tolerable and sometimes interesting. He would look forward now, though, to seeing what the limited vocabulary of the *Cloughton Clarion*'s drama critic had made of 'Harl and BV' as the two one-acts had been dubbed by Stephen.

* * *

Arriving at the Ridgeway Road house early on Monday, Jennifer wondered which of the two versions of Margot would greet her. She soon saw that here was yet another – the angry one. After the most cursory of greetings and whilst they were still in the airy, high-ceilinged hallway, Margot was unleashing a torrent of annoyance and frustration. Leading Jennifer into the same room as before, she shouted her complaints over her shoulder. She had been quite unreserved with Dr Grainger. 'For Robin's sake, so that he knew what the child had been through, I told him all about how I behaved with Paul – and with David – all about David's principles, everything, right down to your opinion of me that you gave me yesterday! Then he took Robin into another room and shut me out. Made me wait in the general waiting room –'

Jennifer took a deep breath before interrupting. 'Maybe that's what Robin needs, a chance to talk to someone with no axe to grind, who isn't questioning him to get information which, once he's told it, will be out of his control.'

Margot sat in silence for some seconds, then she asked, 'What information does he have? What can he know that matters if someone else knows it too? Do you think it's David that he's afraid . . .?'

Suddenly, Jennifer had a complete change of heart about Robin's importance in the case. She could think of no immediate logical reason for it but she knew that her subconscious mind would reveal the evidence for it in due course. This had happened to her before. She said, quietly, 'I think he might know who killed his father. I think he certainly knows where the gun came from and possibly where it is now.'

She held up a hand as Margot made to speak again. 'I'm going out on a limb with this. I'm not at all sure that my DCI would approve of my having told you that and I'm sure that the superintendent would go hairless. I must make it clear that it's only my opinion. I'm sharing it with you because I believe you really want to do what is best for Robin. I don't know anything about the therapist he's been referred to but I'd guess he knows a better way than we do of treating the dreadful anxiety he must be suffering. Our well-meant efforts to find out what's particularly worrying him might just send him over the edge into a permanent psychotic state.

'There's his physical safety to be considered too. With the knowledge that he might have, someone wants him where he can't share it – and that someone may still have a gun. Robin's safer in hospital than he would be at home, as well as getting the treatment he needs. I have to speak to my superiors before I say any more on that particular topic but he'll have all the protection he needs before the day is out. In fact, if you'll excuse me for a minute, I'll ring the chief with the ideas that have just occurred to me and we'll get measures taken immediately. Stay free, please. We've more to talk about.'

When she returned she shook her head at Margot's panic-stricken questions. 'I don't know who my boss has sent to the hospital or what whoever it is will do there so don't ask me. I trust him and you can. If you want to help, explain to me what you meant when you spoke to Mr Page. You told him that Robin's reaction to the news of his father's death was normal but when you told him that Mr Ridgeway had been shot, his behaviour was abnormal.'

Margot shot Jennifer an anguished glance and parried her question. 'For pity's sake call them Paul and David. We aren't making police statements yet – or am I?'

'When you do, you'll have it clearly explained to you. Now answer the question.'

'I need to go back a bit and you need to talk to Lucille. She's in charge of costumes, making them, storing them, repairing them.'

'Let's stick with Robin, shall we?'

'I am. She was with Robin when the explosion was heard. I was onstage. We know now it was the gun being fired. She told me that Robin's reaction was extraordinary.

He almost leapt up in the air and he looked round at everyone quite wildly. She pointed it out to Tony but he said the lad was still strung up with the success of his bit of the play. He knew he'd done well and the tension we all feel on stage was difficult to cope with for a child who wasn't used to it – but Robin was used to it.

'I'm not sure I was right when I said his reaction to knowing Paul was dead was normal. What I should have said was that it was calm. We all had a sort of certainty that ... well, I think we thought he was dead, or at least seriously harmed. It was easier to believe that than that he would walk out on a performance. That's what Robin thought too. He cried and I bathed his eye. Then he overheard Adam saying there was a hole in Paul's head. The people standing around pointed out that Robin was within earshot and told him to shut up. After that Robin got like he is now, staring and saying nothing and not even crying.'

Jennifer decided it was time to change the subject and asked, 'Why did you ask to see me again this morning?'

'Because you cut through everything that's not plain common sense. Yesterday you helped me to see myself and everyone else as we are. The thing is, this baby could just possibly be Paul's. I can't marry David. I can't mess up life for another good man, or change things again for Robin and make him even less secure than he is. I can't put this coming child through what Robin's had to bear. I sorted all this stuff out in my head overnight. First, we've got to find out who did this to Paul and I have to help.'

'Good. I've brought some photographs to show you.'

Margot managed a half-smile. 'I think I've already seen them.'

'You mean, Paul showed them to you?' Jennifer was excited. 'Did he tell you why he'd taken them out of the album?'

'I didn't know he had. I thought you people must have.'

'So how did you know we had them?'

Margot shook her head. 'Don't you people talk to each other? A DC Nazir popped in yesterday and showed me. She had to go to York and find the place and the people. She'd got phone numbers for the scouting headquarters but she thought I'd be a better bet. I only recognized one of the men besides Paul. I'll look at them again but I'm sure I don't know where the place is. The DC, Shakila, thought she would be able to find Colin Vernon from what I told her.'

Jennifer felt the wind had dropped out of her sails. She smiled to herself as she remembered the days when Benny and she were DCs together and had interpreted DCI Browne's instructions as freely as Shakila now treated those of the son-in-law who had succeeded him. 'Let's look again then, though, if Shakila found this Colin Vernon yesterday, he's probably identified all the rest.'

Margot reached for the pictures and began to study them. 'You couldn't forget Colin with that flaming red hair and he's got a huge tattoo right across his back and arms. That's not clear in the photos. I'm not surprised no one noticed it.' She stared hard, willing herself to remember. 'I don't think I've forgotten the other two. I'm pretty sure I didn't meet them. I never went to York with Paul but Colin came across to Cloughton a few times after Paul moved here to be with me. I think both Paul and Colin really disliked the fat one but I never found out why.'

Suddenly dispirited, she dropped the photographs on to a coffee table. 'Well, you'll get all you want from Shakila now and I won't have helped.'

'You've probably saved her a whole day of rushing around looking for Mr Vernon and time is the best thing you can give us. Cases cool whilst we sit thinking about them and, when they're cold, they're dead.'

'Right. Can I ask you one more thing? This psychiatrist man had the nerve to say I shouldn't visit my son just now. I'm still angry with him but he has got Robin to say a few words when I couldn't. It's just that, if I could go and tell

181

him about not marrying David, it might help him a bit. He'll know things aren't going to be different.'

'But they are. He'll have a new brother or sister before long, when he's had thirteen years of not sharing you. I'd co-operate with this doctor for the short term. Let him make all the improvement in Robin's condition that he can. Children are very resilient. Mine have survived their father being killed. Besides, before you tell anyone else that you're not getting married, hadn't you better tell David?'

Jennifer sighed as she pulled away from the house. What had Shakila said about feeling she was Janil Iqbal's social worker? Wasn't that what she had become to Margot Ridgeway?

It was the same room that Robin had been taken to on the previous day. The furniture was the same, and the decorations, but a less sunny day made it all seem more dismal. Dr Grainger looked quite comfortable there, sprawling in the same position in the same chair.

Robin sat upright on the edge of his own, gazing at his hands that were resting on his knees. Today, though, the hands were still rather than picking threads from the fabric of his jeans.

Dr Grainger shifted slightly forward and began talking as before. 'Good morning, Robin. It's miserable in here without the sun. Let's talk about something positive and cheerful. I've been told that you seriously intend to make acting your career. I don't imagine that will be an easy path to tread, but then, neither is medicine. You're very fortunate to be clear about what you want to make of yourself. It means that you can take hard knocks without assuming that they're a sign that you should give up.

'I wonder if there is a part that you've made it your aim to play – one that would give you the scope to prove what you can do or can be?'

'Not Tubby Wadlow.' Robin bit his lip. He had responded involuntarily.

'I don't think I'm acquainted with Tubby Wadlow.' Robin refused to be drawn into speaking again but he raised his eyes to Dr Grainger's face. 'Perhaps you don't know enough plays yet. I promise you there are plenty that will set your juices running. You could borrow copies of them from the library.'

'Yes. I'll do that.' A considered response this time.

'Are you ready to talk about the abuse today?'

'It won't happen again.'

'Are you certain about that?'

'Yes.'

'Are you ready to leave here now? To go home?'

'Not yet.'

Half an hour later, Dr Grainger was called to the telephone to speak to Margot Ridgeway. 'Yes. I think we are making headway . . . No, not chattering exactly. He probably said less than two dozen words . . . He looked at me, though, when I was speaking to him and he did take up a positive suggestion I made. That pleased me very much . . . No, nothing like that. I merely suggested that he should go to the library and take out some texts of serious plays that he might one day aspire to . . . '

He made his report brief. He knew that it had disappointed her.

On Monday evening, as he was driving home, a theory was forming in Mitchell's mind. He had been irritated beyond measure at hearing that the results from the ballistics team might take three weeks to arrive. He wondered what could be holding them up, or which cases were taking precedence over their own. The kind of work he had requested

183

could be done overnight. He could quote occasions when it had been.

Even as he was still taking off his coat, he began regaling Virginia with his complaints. She was less than delighted but had learned not to take such greetings personally. Having let him mention the cases that had been better served than his own, she pointed out that they had all been of overriding urgency. 'Your case doesn't compare.'

'You mean they won't hurry themselves over an actor in a poncy, two-star drama company who's been killed by somebody who wants his leading parts? Or over an abusing father whose son has killed him to escape his attentions?'

'Yes, I suppose I do mean that. Now the poor man's dead, although his killer has to be found, it's unlikely that anyone else is in imminent danger and it isn't a matter of national security.'

'Ah, but what if . . .'

'Go on.' Virginia's tone was resigned.

'What if the gun that killed Tim Ellis and wounded PC Buchan is the same one that shot down Shakila's neighbour's wall and killed Paul Ridgeway?'

'And how likely is that?'

'It's extremely unusual to have gun-related crime in Cloughton – and this Hoodie chap is said to have relations "up north", which your blinkered father and his friends translate as Leicester. Why not Cloughton?'

'Why not Edinburgh – or John o'Groats? Are you serious?'

'You sound like John McEnroe.'

'Well, what you're saying isn't evidence.'

'I'll just say we have reason to believe –'

'You mean you personally have the temerity to propound . . .'

He grinned. 'Ooh yes! I'll say that. That'll catch their attention. That should convince them.'

She grinned too. 'I'd stick to having reason to believe. At least that's true, so long as they bear in mind that the only reason you need to be able to believe something is that that's how you want it to be.'

Mitchell said, wistfully, 'It's a long time since I went out on a limb.'

'That's true. It must be all of six weeks.' Virginia's expression was solemn. Then, grinning again, she said, 'Do it if you like. Why break the habit of a lifetime? Just one piece of advice though. Wait until tomorrow. They're unlikely to humour someone who's made them miss half of their favourite game show.'

There had been more than one occasion when Ginny's note of caution had prevented a demand for his resignation. He'd sleep on the idea – just to humour her.

Chapter Ten

Shakila's first port of call on the day's leave that she had been granted was a house in Luton, where, for the sixth time, she was to meet her future husband. She quite realized how astonished her Cloughton colleagues would be when they learned that she had agreed to an arranged marriage. She firmly believed, however, in the Muslim custom concerned with finding a life partner. It supplied plain girls, who would make excellent wives, with men who would appreciate and learn to love them.

She was aware that she herself was not plain and that neither was Resham. She had met him on five occasions now and they had talked together about most of the issues that were important to them. On this sixth occasion, she had come to tell him that she would accept his offer of marriage. She considered that the fleeting feelings which came early in a relationship, and on which most Western women based their choice of partner, were a far less reliable way to make sure of a happy marriage.

Anyway, didn't the Christian Bible contain stories of partnerships where love developed after marriage, nourished by shared experiences and consideration for each other? She'd read the story of Isaac and Rebekah and she'd like to bet that most English brides had not!

Shakila stayed an hour in Resham's house, chaperoned by his family – which did amuse her a little – and departed from it as a betrothed woman. Now to find the south

London police station where her DCI's father-in-law, who was the chief superintendent, had invited her to visit.

In his office, in Cloughton Royal Hospital, Dr Grainger nodded to his PA. Yes, he would accept a call from DCI Mitchell at the Cloughton station. He took the receiver from her and listened carefully to what he was being told. He then considered for a moment before telling him, 'No, I'm not willing for Robin Ridgeway to be interviewed ... Yes, at a convenient time, I am willing to be questioned myself, though I reserve the right to withhold information about my patient ... I'm surprised that you accept my edict without protest – or maybe Robin's answers, if the questions were in opposition to my advice, would be inadmissible as evidence? ... I thought so.'

The appointment for the consultant to meet the policeman was eventually made 'to suit to our mutual availability'. (Dr Grainger's rather than Mitchell's terminology.) The doctor smiled as he replaced the receiver. Chief Inspector Mitchell had inadvertently given him an excuse to probe into Robin's recent experiences a little without forfeiting his confidence.

He went immediately to the boy's cubicle. 'Robin, I've just had a call from a police officer. He wants to talk to me both about your condition and about anything you might have told me regarding your father's death.' Robin refused to look up. 'I've come to ask whether there is any particular thing you would rather I didn't mention.'

'I haven't told you anything about it.'

'Even so?'

Now Robin raised his eyes. 'I can't tell you what it's right for you to say.'

Dr Grainger nodded and left, well pleased with his patient's progress.

* * *

On the whole, Shakila had been fascinated by her tour of Chief Superintendent Browne's station, though the custody suite had depressed her a little. It was not so much the place itself. In fact, the charge room and cells here were marginally more attractively decorated than those in Cloughton. Even some of the prisoners managed to be jokey and cheerful, the prostitutes and petty thieves obviously being old acquaintances and familiar with their surroundings.

For the others, though, being here was a once in a life-time degradation. She had noticed in particular a checkout girl, wearing the uniform laid down by Tesco. The young woman had seemed to be trying to sink through the floor, face down, eyes veiled, job lost. Meanwhile, all her secret, personal and private possessions were being first dis-played and then bagged in plastic by a glum-looking officer who knew that it would all be returned to her in a couple of hours when her humiliation was complete.

Shakila cheered up considerably as she and Browne moved down the flight of stairs to the huge, bare incident room in the basement. Browne sketched out for her the main facts of his current enquiry. She knew that the more sensitive aspects were being withheld and would have expected nothing else. She concentrated therefore on the wall-sized whiteboard, on which proven facts had been entered and which gave an instant picture of the state of the case. She read quickly. The names of the victims meant nothing to her beyond a fleeting memory of the death and wounding which had been nationally reported about two weeks before. Not so the suspect. Three names were listed which at various times he was believed to have assumed. One of these she recognized.

Just before lunch on Tuesday, Magic announced, to Mitchell's surprise, a call for him from his father-in-law. In working hours, this was unprecedented. He pushed his papers aside and prepared to enjoy this respite from them that had been thrust upon him. 'Got the day off, Tom?'

'I should be so lucky.'

Mitchell was alarmed. 'So, what's up?'

'Nothing, so far as I know. I've just been showing your protégée DC round my shop –'

'You can't have. I've just sent him –'

Browne went on, unheeding, 'Since you think she's so good I did it personally so as to get a good look at her.'

Mitchell had got his breath back. 'Tom, who on earth have you got there, impersonating . . . Oh, no . . .' Taking another deep breath, he tried, fearfully, to clarify the situation. 'I have just written the first draft of a glowing reference for DC Adrian Clement to include in his application for your vacancy for a sergeant. I gather that Shakila has, independently, found out that you're looking for somebody and presented herself to you.'

'If that's so, her initiative is a virtue rather than a fault. We aren't on first-name terms yet, but I certainly have a DC Nazir who is presently being entertained in my canteen. From what I've seen so far, I think I shall be taking steps to persuade her to stay.'

Mitchell was silent. The deep sadness he felt was partly caused by the thought of his team being deprived of the services of this irrepressible, cheerful and hard-working member, but more by that member's duplicity. He tried to make his tone light. 'Then I'd better tell you two things. One, I can't spare her and two, she's a devious monkey. She asked for a day's leave for personal, family reasons.'

'That's right. She's just got herself engaged, apparently – one of these family-arranged affairs.'

Mitchell's head was spinning. 'Stop right there. The idea of Shakila Nazir letting someone else tell her who she can marry is more than my system can deal with. I'm going back to bed.'

'Not for a couple of hours, though. I've got work for you to do.'

After listening for a few seconds more, Mitchell grabbed his notebook and began to scribble down the details Browne was dictating. After a couple of minutes, he replaced the receiver and emailed his wife. *Shakila has claimed today's scoop. If I hadn't listened to you last night, it would have been mine! I still love you. Not sure about Shakila though.*

Next, he rang the desk again. 'Magic, can you get Ray Hopper in for me. If the best photograper on the team is the one with the ponciest camera, he's the one I need.' He sat at his own desk as he waited, trying to decide whether to fill in the pink form first or the yellow one, and willing the phone to ring, excusing him from either.

It did. 'Jamieson, sir. I've written a report, but I thought I'd just mention this personally. It might be urgent.' Creep, Mitchell thought.Quick learner but still a creep.

'And the vital information is?'

'Deaf chap, living in the flats overlooking the waste ground behind the theatre. Was at the window, Friday a.m. Remembers seeing a young lad there, digging in a corner. Someone came round the side of the building – a man – and watched him. When the boy turned round the man ducked back, then the boy went on his way. The man came out again, went over to the corner, either to see what the lad had been doing or to look at what he'd discovered.'

'Did he recognize either of them?'

'Afraid not, sir.'

Mitchell thanked the PC, took details of his witness's name and flat number. Next, he called Clement on his cell-phone. 'Adrian, does Sheena McDonald still live in Fenton Road?' Pleased with the reply, Mitchell explained what he wanted. 'Can you fix it pronto?'

Whilst waiting for a reply, he returned to glaring at the two garish forms but he had written nothing on either when Clement's confirming call came back. He was in high good humour when a tap at the door was followed by Ray Hopper's head, peering round it. The man came in, his clothes hung about with an elaborate array of photographic equipment. Mitchell pushed all his paperwork out of the way and began giving Hopper his instructions. ' . . . Take as many shots as you can but everything through your tele-photo lens. Don't let him see you. I've found a chatty old lady living opposite who's lending you her front bedroom to work from. Correction. Clement found her for you. He recommends her fruit cake but says to tell you to ask for tea if she offers coffee. I've no idea what matey's plans are for the day so you may be in for a long wait. If he uses the back door all the time you might have a fruitless day.'

'Except for what's in the cake.'

Mitchell managed a weak smile. 'Come and show me what you get. I shall want some of the shots faxed to the Met so they'll need to be sharp.' He handed over a sheet scribbled with details of Hopper's hostess for the day and various numbers where he himself could be contacted.

When the door opened to let the photographer out, Jennifer came in. She settled, notebook out, to listen to his recital of the morning's developments. Mitchell omitted to mention Shakila's defection which he was not yet ready to discuss with anyone.

Jennifer asked, 'Do you want me to speak again to Jamieson's old man?'

'I thought Adrian would be best for that.'

'You'll send him off into another neurosis!'

'Can't be helped. He'll get more out of the old chap than any of the rest of us. I've got another job for you. Our resident computer whizz has deserted us but you're quite . . . er . . . with technology . . .' He paused to search for a polite word that meant 'half as good as Shakila'.

'I think competent is the word you're searching for. I'm Holmes trained and all. What's the job?'

'I need you to find me some details from Egypt.'

She grinned. 'Oh, good. I did that last night. Lucy's doing a school project on the pyramids. I'll go home and get it. I can't see what possible bearing it could have on the case, but mine not to reason why . . .'

'No levity this morning. I'm not feeling strong enough.'

Her grin disappeared. 'Are you all right, Benny? I thought you seemed a bit subdued when I came in.'

'Fine. I've just had some very surprising and not very welcome news.'

No more details seemed to be forthcoming. Jennifer did not press. She was pretty sure to hear them later from Ginny. Mitchell grabbed the pink form and began to write on the back. She waited silently until he handed it to her. 'That's the information I need, including all the phone numbers. ASAP please. If Adrian's in the general office, could you send him in to me? The least I can do is inform him of his despised mission personally.'

As the door closed, his spirits sank lower. If Shakila was determined to work for Tom and Tom was determined to have her, Clement would soon be receiving news that he would like even less than being sent to yet another geriatric witness. Oh well, since Jennifer now had possession of the pink form, he would fill in the yellow one.

Half an hour later, looking round for further distractions, Mitchell checked his emails again. He found an indignant reply from Ginny. She had checked with Jennifer what his cryptic message to her might mean. Then, having made her complaint, she suggested that her request that he should delay his harassment of the ballistics people had done him a favour. Now he was not going out on a limb. He had not antagonized the experts and he had good reason for asking them, 'Can you now *confirm* that the bullets taken from the bodies of PC Buchan and Paul Ridgeway were fired from the same gun?'

Well, of course he could phrase it like that. It was exactly what he had intended to do and he would do it now – or, at least, as soon as he had deleted his wife's message. He knew perfectly well what ballistics' answer would be but the court would want their say-so rather than his, so he had better file their reply. What they wouldn't tell him, and what he really needed to know, was where the gun was now.

* * *

Immediately after lunch, Mitchell rang the desk in the foyer with a request that no one be sent up to him for the next thirty minutes. Next, he rang Jennifer's cellphone and asked her to steer all the men on the case away from his office for the same length of time. Then he sent for Clement.

He had allowed his DC to enjoy whatever delicacies the canteen was offering for lunch, but before he began on the afternoon's work, Adrian must be told what Shakila had done and what Browne's reaction to it had been. The poor bloke might well be forfeiting his favourite TV programme or cancelling a trip with friends to his local in the later part of the evening in favour of completing and polishing his application to the Met. After all, his own intention had been to give the same treatment to the reference that he had already written in rough.

Clement took longer to appear than he had expected. Mitchell realized why when he heard raised voices along the corridor. Jennifer was shouting. Jennifer? he asked himself. Shouting? 'Well, at least tell him that I tried to stop you!'

His DC was equally irate. 'The bloody boss sent for me, I tell you!'

He rushed out to deal with the misunderstanding that he had caused himself, hoping that the end of the encounter would be more successful than the beginning. He winked at his DC and told Jennifer solemnly, 'Adrian and I are eloping together. You'll understand we need some privacy to make our plans.'

Jennifer smothered a grin and departed. Clement had flushed scarlet and was looking askance at him. Things were going from bad to worse. All he could do now was to deliver his news to Adrian, apologize, then send him off, in a rage, to tear a strip off a poor old deaf flat tenant who had already suffered an interrogation from Jamieson. He indicated that Clement should sit in what had become 'Caro's chair' and poured out the coffee he had made himself. Decent coffee, respectfully treated, would smooth the way for both of them. Unable to think of any further delaying tactics, he explained his embarrassing problem.

To his amazement, Clement beamed at him, drank more coffee, then remarked, sunnily, 'Oh, good, though I shall miss Shakila. She makes this place buzz a bit.'

Mitchell blinked. 'Which are we having first, my apology or your explanation?'

Still smiling, Clement said, 'Skip the apology, sir. None of it was your fault. The explanation's simple. I was thrilled to hear that you thought I'd make a good enough sergeant for you to risk sending me to your father-in-law. The problem was that I could hardly tell you that there was nowhere I'd less like to work than in London. I like Yorkshire. If you'll keep that reference handy, I'll start looking for something fairly local.'

Mitchell nodded. 'And what will happen to this new-found cheerfulness if I send you to Sainted City to reinterview a deaf man who's probably eighty and proud of it?'

'Well, at least I'll do it better than the rest of the tribe.'

'True. By the way, did you find anything interesting in Paul Ridgeway's flat that's worth reporting?'

Clement shrugged. 'Some books I'd like to borrow, some wine I'd like to drink. No porn and nothing incriminating in any of the little cupboards I unlocked. Of course, Mrs R might have been there before tipping up the keys to us. I do have a theory about the weird picture above the bed. It was the last spiteful act by his ex. She probably had it specially done to spoil all his new decorations.'

After several days of pleasant late-spring weather, the sky was overcast and the air like breathing in bath water as Clement made his way to St Crispin's Court. He studied the plan in the foyer and worked out that George Jessop lived on the seventh floor. He felt angry at the town council's lack of consideration. He could see the point of putting young families on the ground level. They had babies in buggies to contend with. Surely, though, they could have put a deaf old man lower than the seventh. Half the time the lifts in these places were either out of order or in the sort of condition that made using them too unpleasant to contemplate. The old man would be a prisoner in his little flat. No wonder he'd been gazing out of his window.

He found, however, that the lift was surprisingly clean and sweet-smelling. A small white card was blu-tacked to the wall just above the panel of buttons that operated the cage. Reading it gave Clement his second surprise of the afternoon. In black ink and in a firm hand was written, *Having seen this lift cage left in the condition in which you would wish to find it, I now request that you leave it in a condition in which I and other decent people would wish to use it. George Jessop.*

Clement chuckled to himself. At least the old chap wasn't gaga and it seemed that he had by no means given up on either life or people. He had never been in this particular block before but it suddenly struck him that the whole building was considerably cleaner and more graffiti-free than the rest of Sainted City. The lift behaved well and bore him with a minimum of creaking and clattering up to Floor 7 and a freshly washed white door bearing Mr Jessop's name was opened to him.

A young man, wearing a discreet hearing aid, invited him inside. His son, maybe? Perhaps the disability was hereditary. Enunciating clearly, he asked to speak to the flat's tenant and was told, 'I am he.' Clement was puzzled, but also worried that the interview would be continually interrupted by the correction of his own grammar mistakes.

Mr Jessop said, 'You look puzzled, constable.'

Raising his voice, Clement explained, 'I've been misinformed, sir. I was expecting an older man.' This one looked good for a run up the nearest mountain and could not have been older than forty-something.

'There's no need to shout at me. In fact you upset my aids when you do, which was the cause of the difficulties when your bumptious young colleague came to see me. Just speak as clearly as you did when you made your first request. Constable Jamieson is of an age and temperament to dismiss a disability as a sign of age and low intelligence.'

Clement wondered how long it would be before he had a chance to ask for the information he had come for. A headlong plunge seemed his best option. 'I've never met Jamieson but I'm sorry that a colleague offended you. I'm probably ten years older than him – than he is,' he amended, hastily. 'Can you tell me what you saw out of your window last Friday morning?'

'Was I not sufficiently precise?'

Clement was getting bolder. 'Please, just answer my question.'

A little offended, Mr Jessop complied. 'I saw a movement down on the waste ground. I keep an eye on the theatre as well as this building.' He moved over to his window and Clement followed him. It afforded an excellent view of almost every square inch of the area. 'I saw a boy, wearing the uniform of Heath Lees School, with a satchel on his back, come round the side of the theatre building. He took two objects out of the satchel. I think they were both made of metal because the sun glinted on them. I think the shinier object was a trowel and he bent down and I think he began to dig. The wall obscured him a little when he stooped.'

'You can see almost vertically down from this height.' Clement hoped this comment had not diverted the man from his story.

'You want details? The boy's blazer seemed a size too large for him. He wore what I believe is called a baseball cap so I don't know if he was dark or fair. He was quite tall. He was engrossed in his task so that, when another person came round the far side of the theatre building, he did not turn round. It was a man, also tall, taller than the

196

boy by some inches I would imagine, but the angle was quite . . . is acute the right word?'

'I'm not sure, but I can see that you couldn't judge comparative heights from up here.'

'The man stood back when he saw the boy, but only so far. He was still watching him. When the boy finished digging and stood up, the man disappeared back the way he had come. He must have done it quietly because the lad never turned round. He just wiped his hands on his blazer. He only had the trowel in his hands. I think he'd buried the other object.'

'What did you think it was?'

'At the time I had no idea. Now, of course, having read the papers and heard the news, I believe, as you do, that it was the gun that shot the actor, Mr Ridgeway.'

'Mr Jessop, we know who the boy was. Is there any other detail about the man that would help us to identify him?'

There was a long silence, during which Clement felt that Jessop was making a genuine attempt to recreate what he had seen. Then he spoke slowly as he described what he had called up. 'I don't remember the hair colour, which I think probably means it was nondescript. I think I'd have remembered red or blond or really black. Thin face. His stance was odd.'

'You mean he had an injury or some kind of deformity?'

Jessop shook his head. 'No, it was just the way he was standing, rocking on his heels, hands, not on his hips exactly but on his waist, thumbs behind and four fingers spread in front as though he was holding his stomach in. He stood like that all the time the boy was digging – perhaps three minutes or so, so it was probably his habit. Is that too ephemeral?'

Clement shook his head. 'No, I think it is a very valuable piece of evidence. Please don't mention it to anyone else.'

'Or he'll stop doing it. I see. I won't even say I saw him.'

*   *   *

The impatiently awaited report on the two bullets, taken from Chris Buchan's chest and Paul Ridgeway's head, reached Mitchell before eleven on Wednesday morning. He was less than grateful. 'They haven't offered any thanks for the enormous clue we sent them yesterday – just this great heap of extraneous material to show off. We aren't going to wrap the case up any sooner from knowing that the Austrian and Norwegian armies and the German police use the same guns as the Met.'

Jennifer had been reading the information, extraneous or not, with some interest. 'Quite a bit of it's relevant for us. I, for one, didn't know that PC Buchan's gun had a magazine capacity of seventeen rounds. We know that three of them have been used. Four, if Robin Ridgeway shot one.'

'We haven't proved he's even touched the gun yet,' Mitchell snapped.

'Whatever – there could be a dozen more bullets left in it.'

'It doesn't get us much further forward to know the history of the gun that was used. We just need to find it.'

This was nonsense. Jennifer tutted impatiently and turned a page. 'Listen to this! *A criticism of the Glock action is that the trigger must be depressed prior to disassembly or insertion into the storage case, which can lead to unintentional discharge if the operator is careless.* Young Robin was very fortunate to be let off with nothing worse than a sore eye.'

'He didn't have a storage case to put it in. Only the gun itself was stolen from Buchan.' His tone was sulky and childish.

Jennifer had had enough. He might have become her DCI but they had begun police training college together and she always spoke her mind to him. Now she marched to the door. 'If you're cheesed off with someone else, don't take it out on me.' The heels of her elegant shoes clicked down the corridor. Mitchell got up and closed the door.

* * *

198

Robin's nurse looked into Dr Grainger's room from the doorway. Seeing him sprawled in his usual manner, in his usual chair, she left Robin to go in alone and went off for a cup of coffee.

'Good morning, Robin.'

'Good morning, Dr Grainger.'

The consultant showed no surprise at his patient's greeting but merely waited to see if he had more to say. Robin remained silent but he went across to his chair and sat well back in it, looking more relaxed and alert than on the previous day. After perhaps fifteen seconds, Dr Grainger asked casually, 'Shall we talk about the weather?'

Robin blinked as though wondering if this was a joke. 'If you like.' After a further few seconds, he added, 'I haven't got anything to say about it.'

'Nor have I. There are things I would rather discuss with you but only if you're ready.' By raising his eyebrows Dr Grainger made the remark a question. Robin was watching and gave him a single nod. 'Did you really have a gun?' Another nod. 'Where did you get it from?' Robin's eyes dropped. 'All right. What did you do with it?'

'I shot a garden wall down.'

'Deliberately?' This time the boy's head was shaken. 'And the recoil of the gun caused your eye injury?'

'Yes.'

'So, you invented a boy who hit you?' Another nod. 'Then what?'

When the silence had lasted twenty seconds, Dr Grainger asked, 'Do you find specific questions easier to answer?'

'Yes.'

'So, did you take the gun home?'

'Yes.'

'And hid it perhaps.'

Robin nodded. 'In my bedroom.'

'Then you said you didn't want to go to rehearsal with your father. Were you afraid of him?'

199

'No.' Robin drew a deep breath and added, 'I thought David might find the gun if I was out.'

'Does David go into your room? Interfere in it?'

This produced a shrug and another silence, then, 'He's always asking questions – about whether I'm keeping his rules. Sometimes I won't answer him.'

'So, you think he might keep a check when you aren't in?'

'Yes.'

'Do you resent that?'

'Yes.'

'Is the gun still in your room?' The boy shook his head. 'What did you do with it?'

'Buried it behind the theatre.'

'Is it still there?'

Robin ignored this question and asked one of his own. 'Did someone shoot my dad with it? Was it the same gun?'

'Yes, I think it was.'

'So, it was my fault . . .?'

'I don't think it would help you if I answered that with a straight no. You're too intelligent not to see that it made things a bit easier for whoever wanted to kill your father to find a gun to hand. Do you think it's unkind of me to tell you that?'

'No. I wouldn't have believed you if you'd said I had no part in it.'

'Does it help to have that out in the open?'

Slowly, the boy nodded, then, in a firmer tone than he had used so far, said, 'Yes. It does.'

'Shall we stop there for today?'

'Yes.'

When Robin had been taken back to his cubicle, Dr Grainger sat on in his chair. He had cancelled his next patient's non-urgent appointment in favour of getting his session with DCI Mitchell out of the way and had asked his PA to hold back coffee until his visitor arrived. He had ten minutes to make a final decision on what he would say and what he would keep back.

It was too late now to wonder whether he should have pushed the boy more. He supposed his moral decision was made already, since everything that Robin had admitted to was commonly being assumed. No harm could be done by answering all the police's questions to the best of his knowledge. Did he think the boy had shot his father? No, he did not – and, therefore, from the patient's point of view as well as the public's, the sooner the whole matter was cleared up the better.

Mitchell's arrival interrupted these mental meanderings. He was early, but only by two minutes. Involuntarily, Dr Grainger did a professional assessment of him as the two of them introduced themselves and settled to their business. The policeman was short, probably about five feet nine, but big-boned with wide shoulders. He suspected that a not-yet-serious layer of fat covered what had been, until recently, solid muscle. Probably his promotion and his family responsibilities had curtailed his sport. A sportsman he surely would be – rugby certainly, and maybe cricket, a Graham Gooch kind of batsman with a good eye who flailed accurately and powerfully with his bat.

He took up considerably more of the capacity of Robin's chair than was comfortable for him but he sat serenely, probably still choosing the opening words of his assault. His eyes were alert and bright. This man would not be an academic but he would be fearless in verbal battle, sure of himself and unlikely to be shaken. He would be good in court. Mitchell refused coffee. Well, that showed intelligence – or maybe he had tasted this hospital's coffee before.

Looking him in the eye, Dr Grainger saw that the detective inspector had made an equally thorough and professional assessment of himself. He decided that his best plan would be to take the initiative. 'Robin and I talked about the gun for the first time this morning. He was frank on some points but refused to answer others.'

'Was the refusal aggressive?'

201

'No, he just punished unwelcome questions with silence. Mostly, I asked what you would call leading questions, leaving the boy just to admit or deny what I had suggested. Anything open-ended he parried.'

'What's the significance of that?'

'Medically, it told me that, although he had certainly been traumatized, he had not been at any point divorced from reality. Everything that he's been saying has been deliberate. He's still making his own decisions and keeping to them. Therefore there is not a great deal that I need to do for him, beyond using my authority to ensure that he gets the time-out that he needs to restabilize himself.'

'Leave him alone and he'll get better anyway.'

'Precisely. But that doesn't mean there's nothing wrong. The leaving alone was very necessary.' He saw that Mitchell had noted his use of the past tense.

'All right. I accept what you say, but I don't see the connection. I don't see how what you've described tells you what you've diagnosed.'

Dr Grainger made an effort. This man was no fool and it was part of his own job to be able to explain his findings to a sane sensible person. 'What I'm saying is that Robin has never lost control of his normal thought processes. His silence is studied, deliberate.'

'Attention-seeking?'

'Not at all. Attention is what he wants to avoid at present.'

'So, what is he gaining by refusing to speak to people?'

The consultant hoped he was not patronizing Mitchell. 'You know what we both mean by a leading question. You put a proposition to someone and that someone can either accept or reject it, agree or disagree. The whole matter is contained in the question. It can be examined before you respond.' Mitchell nodded. That was not quite what he meant by the term but he was beginning to see the doctor's point.

'An open question,' the consultant continued, 'can lead anywhere. You give free rein to your thought processes in considering and answering it. You might easily say things you meant to keep to yourself. I think there are things Robin knows which he is determined not to tell. He's not going to be tricked into revealing them. When he comes up against a question that might lead him to mention what he's protecting, he won't speak at all.'

'I see. Wouldn't it be psychologically better for Robin if he talked about what he knows?'

'You're sharp.' Dr Grainger pulled himself up. Now he was being patronizing. 'That's just the danger I'm going to point out to the lad when I see him tomorrow – the unfortunate consequences for his mental health if his dilemma is not resolved.'

Mitchell was becoming tired of psychological philosophy. He said, 'We neither of us think that the boy shot his father. Do you think Robin knows who did?'

'Yes – or at least he has strong grounds for his suspicion of someone.'

'Any idea why he's protecting whoever it is?'

'I intend to find out – or else to persuade him to tell some other person who can help him deal with it. Would you like me to summarize what he's already told me?'

'Would I learn anything new?'

'Only his confirmation of it. And, remember it all came from leading questions.' Dr Grainger watched as Mitchell silently assessed the situation.

After some time, their eyes met and Mitchell smiled. 'I think our best bet is to let you finish your work on the boy. My sergeant told me that and I didn't believe her.'

Dr Grainger returned the smile. 'I think we're well on the way.' He was not sure himself whether his final remark concerned his patient's treatment or his rapport with the police.

Chapter Eleven

When Shakila came into the foyer early on Thursday morning, Magic beckoned her to the desk and pushed an envelope into her hand. It had a Bradford postmark and was addressed to her using her correct rank but in the top left corner of the envelope was written PERSONAL, in the same ink as the address.

Intrigued, she retired to the cloakroom before tearing it open. It contained two closely written sheets and she deliberately began reading the first without checking the signature at the end. When, she wondered, would she stop playing childish guessing games with herself?

Dear Constable Nazir, I have had a great struggle with my conscience before writing to you but dishonesty never pays and sins of omission are as culpable as stealing or killing.

(So, it was someone whose moral code differed from her own and who had more spare time than she had to turn a short letter into a work of literature.)

As I told you I intended, I visited Ian, one of James Mostyn's victims, and found him, as I expected, depressed and full of self-pity, but still refusing my professional help.

(Ah, now she had her man.)

Since I am now being completely honest, I will tell you that 'Ian's' real name is Jason Kelley and that he currently lives within the jurisdiction of your Cloughton force. I told you that he had gone along to the prison to harry and hassle James upon his release . . .

Shakila sighed and skim-read the next few paragraphs, then concentrated again.

I am grateful to you for helping me to remember my respons-ibility towards this young man who suffered so much psycho-logical damage when he was in the care of our company.

Shakila sent up a prayer that Jason would manage to escape this enthusiastic and almost certainly unwelcome help. She began to understand why James Mostyn had decided to give him the slip.

She read further, then stopped and felt in the envelope for the enclosure which Mr Kingsley referred to and which she had failed to notice. She went over to the window to examine it closely in daylight, then stuffing it back, together with the accompanying letter, into the envelope, she ran upstairs to Mitchell's office. She knew who Robin Ridgeway's abuser was.

Shakila had not yet mentioned to anyone her self-appointed interview with Derek Kingsley. Why confess a peccadillo when it had achieved nothing useful? When she left Bradford, she had had a good feeling about it but no point raised in the conversation had surfaced in her mind as significant. Here though was her reward for going the extra mile. She supposed diverting to Bradford had liter-ally been not much more than that. For Mitchell, she sum-marized in a couple of sentences what had taken Kingsley half an hour and a two-page letter to tell her. 'The young chap took a picture of Mostyn as he came out through the gates – wanted to taunt him with it, possibly blackmail him once he got settled where he wasn't known. Mr K didn't like the idea of him staring at it to stoke up his anger so he took it from him.'

'Who can blame the lad? He should have had dozens of copies made and posted them all over the country. No, I take that back. Then we'd have had the job of stopping him. So why has he sent it to you?'

'Because Mostyn changed physically so much during his time in prison that even Paul Ridgeway didn't recognize him for a while. Colin Vernon said he weighed twenty-three stone when he went into Armley. Now he weighs less than eleven which, at his height, makes him emaciated. His face is a different shape, his hair's long and straggly instead of almost shaved to his head –'

'So, hand over the picture and stop playing games.'

Reluctantly, Shakila did so. Mitchell looked at it, whistled softly, then passed it to Caroline who had just come in. 'Who's that?'

Caroline looked. 'It's Stephen Thompson. Why?'

Because Jennifer had an early court appearance, the morning briefing that day had been called for a later time than usual.

Since she had walked out on her DCI the day before, Jennifer had heard, first from Clement and later, again, from Shakila, the news that she would be leaving the team. She understood Mitchell's empathy with the young DC. Like himself in past times, she usually, with a cheeky grin in the direction of protocol, did whatever she thought was necessary to crack the case they were currently working on. This news was what had caused his ill temper. Should she apologize for her own bad manners?

No, she would not. Benny was old enough and senior enough to be in better control. However, she would not sink to his level by sulking. She greeted him, therefore, with her usual grin when he came into his own office where she had preceded him. She was almost disappointed when he immediately apologized for his boorish way of addressing her, depriving her of the chance to feel superior.

She told herself not to be childish and concentrated on the details she was being given of Shakila's letter and their virtual certainty that James Mostyn and Stephen Thompson were the same man. She nodded and reflected for a moment. 'Both names use up the four initials. If he had two forenames and a double-barrelled surname, he could start again with a new identity but no need for all the palaver of forging new documents to match.' She offered her own news in exchange. 'I made all the Egypt calls. Cairo has several universities. None of them has a current undergraduate with any of the three names that CS Browne's given us.'

Mitchell was pleased. 'It's all working out. Splendid!'

Jennifer scowled. 'It's not very splendid for Robin Ridgeway – or for his little friend Janil –'

They were interrupted by the simultaneous entry of the other three members of the regular team and the Scene of Crime photographer. Mitchell fixed Hopper with a steely glare. 'I expected these last night.'

Unabashed, the man handed over the first of the two folders he carried. 'You could have had these last night, sir, but it was so overcast yesterday afternoon that I couldn't bring any of them up any better than those. He only showed his face a couple of times. Early this morning, though, he was out in the sun, tidying the front garden, sweeping the paving stones, cutting the grass, weeding. I took these shots to the lab straight away. I think you'll find they were worth waiting for.' He passed over the second folder.

Mitchell opened his mouth to speak, caught Jennifer's warning glance and closed it. He examined the contents of the second folder, then turned to Hopper. 'They're good. Clear views from all sides and two full-face ones. Thanks for getting up early.'

Hopper removed the rejected folder, then paused at the door on his way out. 'Could you give a message to Clement, whoever he is?' Clement indicated that he was present to receive his message personally. 'Mrs Mc-Donald's's full English is even better than the fruit cake.'

Mitchell spread the pictures out on his desk and they gathered round to examine them, unanimously deciding which three were to be sent to the Met.

Shakila asked, 'What does the Ridgeway boy say about –'

Mitchell smiled sweetly as he interrupted her. 'Robin isn't allowed to say anything to us. Doctor's orders. You've been in the station two hours this morning. The first job for a detective, after an absence, should be to acquaint herself with what's new in the file. You'd better go and do it before you set off with your action sheet. By the way, I believe congratulations are in order.'

She accepted them shyly before being sent off to fax the pictures to Browne.

As Dr Grainger bent over his filing cabinet to extract the file on Robin Ridgeway, the boy appeared in the doorway and greeted him cheerfully. 'Good morning, Dr Grainger.'

'Good morning to you too. Where's your minder?'

'Down at the nursing station but she did watch me all the way up the corridor.' He wandered over to the consultant's own chair. 'Can I sit here for a change?'

Grainger blinked. Was the boy deliberately putting him in the patient's chair, signalling that he intended to dictate the proceedings this session?

It seemed so. 'I need to speak to the police, don't I? And I ought to be in touch with my mother again – not the two together, though.'

The doctor lifted his eyebrows. 'What brought this on?'

'I'm not exactly sure. I thought you'd know that. You're the one who's supposed to tell us what makes us do things, or not do them.'

'I am, but we psychotherapists do like to have our theories confirmed.'

Robin smiled. 'Well, I've had time to decide what it's right to tell – and to let the wrong person be blamed for something isn't right.'

'So, who is being wrongly blamed?'

'My father.'

'And who was he shielding?'

'Shielding? No one. I think someone might have killed my dad to stop my dad killing him.'

'Do you know who that someone is?'

'That's a policeman's question, not a doctor's. You said the first time I came in here that all those things weren't your business.'

'I think I might have finished my business with you.'

Now Robin looked worried. 'I didn't mean to be rude.'

'And I didn't mean to reprimand you. I meant, merely, that we have completed our business. You don't need me any more.'

When Robin left him, Dr Grainger rang the number Mitchell had left with him and gave him some welcome news. 'I've just been well and truly put in my place by young Ridgeway. I'm lifting my ban on his being interviewed but I would like you to come and do it here.'

'We'd insist on that ourselves. Until the boy's told us all he knows and our villain knows he has, I don't want our supervision arrangements changed. Can someone come over now?'

'Today, yes, but I'd rather Robin had a rest after my session with him. Shall we say after lunch?'

'Fine – and could you be his chaperone? His mother might inhibit him and I don't trust her not to interrupt.'

'That's Robin's proviso.'

'He wants her there?'

'On the contrary, he insists that she isn't to be there.'

'Shall I send my female sergeant?'

'I don't think so, Chief Inspector. Robin thinks he deserves the attention of the man in charge.'

Mitchell grinned as he turned back to his team and began to distribute their action sheets. Shakila, having finished her faxing and reading up the file, reappeared in time to back the team's suggested amendments to their orders.

Robin's abuser was in custody and they needed to turn their attention to their next villain. They had three names for him and one of them they recognized. Clement was especially keen to take immediate action. 'We've got a name. Do we really have to wait for confirmation on film? Can't we bring him in on suspicion? Not an arrest but just to help with enquiries.'

'Not very bright –' Shakila stopped speaking suddenly. Yesterday she had virtually stolen Adrian's promotion and now she was calling him an idiot.

Clement rescued her himself. 'OK, yes. We'd put him on his guard, we couldn't compel him to stay unless we did arrest him and, if we didn't, he'd scarper as soon as we let him out. As you said, not very bright. We ought to keep tabs on him though. Hopper got two full-face pictures. He might have been spotted through the window.'

Mitchell was both pleased to have escaped a squabble and willing to allow some changes. The case had progressed since the sheets had been filled a good couple of hours previously. 'Good point, Adrian. You two have got yourselves a job for the rest of the day – you at the front door in a car and you, Shakila, at the back on foot.'

'What's my cover for hanging around?'

'I'm sure you'll have thought of one before you arrive there. If Adrian gives you a lift, get out at least two streets away.'

Jennifer settled back in her chair. 'If two of us are tailing the chief suspect, and Beardsmore and Smithson are inviting Stephen Thompson to have lunch at the station's expense, the rest of us can start knitting little jackets whilst we discuss the connection between killing PC Buchan and killing Paul Ridgeway.' Caroline blushed so that the scars on her cheek stood out white and raised. Jennifer continued, placatingly, 'We all know about it separately, Caro, so it might as well be out in the open.'

Caroline bit her lip, then grinned. 'All right, but he or she is not going to wear anything that the CI has knitted.'

'I haven't got time to learn. You've got action sheets. I have an appointment with Master Ridgeway.'

In his south London station, Browne received the faxed photographs with some of the excitement he'd felt when working on his very first murder investigation. It looked as though his final case was coming to a successful conclusion. Far from resenting the assistance of his son-in-law and his borrowed DC, he was glad that the case had become a family affair.

He summoned a PC to find Patrick O'Reilly and to show him copies of the pictures. Then he drove himself to the London Hospital where, though making good progress, PC Buchan was still detained. He found him in the day room, watching an old Morse film and obviously reluctant to switch it off. Browne had little sympathy. He would have thought the man would jump at the chance to take part in some real work. However, he controlled his eagerness, told Buchan, truthfully, how well he was looking and enquired about his progress before producing his pictures.

Buchan stared at them for a long time and then shook his head. 'I know that last time you were here I assured you that I'd know the fellow again – but I don't. It all seems far away and ages ago from here. It could be him but I can't swear to it. I know you'll be disappointed, but . . .'

Disappointed wasn't the word. Browne felt like a child who had broken his Christmas toy before he had even eaten his Christmas lunch. He managed to thank the invalid for his honesty before diving back to his car and reaching for his cellphone. He had to find out whether his PC had had any better luck with his Irishman and waited impatiently for him to pick up. O'Reilly, it seemed, was 'pretty sure' that the photograph he had been shown was of Hoodie. How far, Browne wondered, as he offered less than heartfelt thanks, could he proceed with a 'could be' and a 'pretty sure'? Legally, he couldn't even proceed with a witness's 'Yes, I'm certain,' unless it was someone picked out from a line-up. Still, this was his last case and the photographs were very sharp.

Suddenly, he was inspired. He grabbed the phone again and jabbed at the numbers that would reach Terry Fletcher. Having identified himself, he asked, 'Can you bring in the Bird lads again. Just the younger one will do. Kyle, was it? I'll meet both of you in my office in half an hour.'

It took three times as long for the boy to be traced to the arcade that he currently preferred to his school desk but Browne considered that Kyle was worth waiting for. Presented with a photograph, and before anyone had had a chance to ask a question, he exclaimed, 'Bang on, mate! That's the bugger!' He was disappointed that so little was required of him. His disappointment turned to disgust when Mr Fletcher insisted on driving him back to school.

In Cloughton, Mitchell drove towards the Royal Hospital, wondering why he felt some trepidation about his coming interview. Since rising to the rank of detective chief inspector, he had jumped at every chance to be out of his office and playing an active part in the investigations he was directing. He enjoyed encounters with co-operative witnesses and aggressive offenders alike.

He had no problem either with the fact that Robin Ridgeway was a minor or even that he was vulnerable and psychologically damaged. He had four children of his own with widely differing temperaments and a sixteen-year-old nephew in a young offenders' unit, convicted of a serious offence. He related well to all of them, although the last had caused him some professional embarrassment.

He thought the problem might be that, although his Cloughton case could well hinge on Robin's evidence, he was still not sure of what exactly he wanted the boy to tell him, nor of how much he actually knew. At least he and

212

Robin were not complete strangers. They had spoken over Mrs Gledhill's garden wall.

When Mitchell arrived at Dr Grainger's office, he found Robin seated there, looking perfectly at home. He considered the boy gravely, then told him, 'That shiner's fading nicely.'

Robin ignored the observation and demanded sternly, 'Do you want me to answer the same questions you were asking me before?'

'Pretty much, yes.'

'Right then. I found a gun and stole it. I shot a wall down with it accidentally. Then I took it home and hid it in my bedroom. Later on, I took it to the theatre and buried it in a corner of the waste ground at the back. I don't know where it is now but I've heard that it isn't still there.'

Mitchell raised an eyebrow. 'I can see that you'll never have to answer a charge of wasting police time. Can I ask a few questions about the details?'

Robin dropped his eyes and Mitchell saw that he had not anticipated this request. The details were, therefore, not rehearsed. 'Where did you find the gun?' Robin remained still and silent.

Mitchell accepted the boy's refusal and moved on. 'Did you realize when you picked it up that the gun wasn't a toy?' There was no answer.

'Did you have any idea who it belonged to?' Mitchell glanced at Dr Grainger and saw that his mouth was turned up at the corners. If the consultant was amused, then he was not concerned about the boy's state of mind. He would take a leaf out of the expert's book. If the court muttered about leading questions he'd plead that they were on medical advice.

He got up and walked to the window, looking out and speaking with his back turned towards his witness. 'All right. Let's come to it another way. I'll tell the story. You stop me if I get it wrong.'

Dr Grainger, who was still within Mitchell's line of vision, gave an encouraging nod. Mitchell took it as conveying the boy's agreement. 'I think you found the gun in the extension to the Iqbals' garden. You found it by accident when you were good-naturedly digging a patch of ground because Janil's family was called away to deal with his grandmother's accident. You hadn't been allowed to play any kind of fighting games since David Page came into your life and here was a real gun for the taking, although you knew you wouldn't be able to play with it. You cleaned the tools and put them away whilst you thought about what to do. Just knowing you had a real gun would put you one up on both David and the boys at school. You could hug the thought of it to yourself.

'I don't think you shot the wall by accident. I think you couldn't resist the temptation to try it out. You didn't know it was loaded but you hoped that it was.' Now Mitchell thought it would be safe to make eye contact with the boy. 'Tell me what it was like.'

Robin was staring in his direction but Mitchell knew he was seeing the scene that he had just described. 'The wall fell to bits and the gun kicked me in my face. It seemed to have come alive and attacked me. I can't remember running but I must have because I ended up at the corner of the park. I was shaking. Half of me wanted to keep on and on, shooting things till the bullets ran out, and the other half wanted to drop it and go and hide somewhere.'

Mitchell said, half to himself, 'I don't think it would have been buried with the safety catch off but it probably got caught by the spade. You were very lucky not to kill yourself. Let's go on with the story. You got it home, and then you began to worry that it wouldn't be easy to keep it hidden in your room. Your mother cleaned in there, maybe even tidied your drawers and changed the bedclothes for you. So you took it to the theatre and buried it again until you could think of a better hiding place –'

214

'No, I didn't!' Mitchell blinked. The words had been less an interruption than an explosion. When Robin continued speaking it was in almost a whisper. 'I put it there till I could shoot Mr Thompson with it, so that I wouldn't have to . . . so that he couldn't make me . . .'

'It's all right. I can imagine what he's been doing. I can promise you he won't do it again. Two of my officers will have arrested him by now. He'll go from a police cell to a different kind of cell.'

'A prison one? What about me? Will I be arrested?'

'For stealing the gun? No, I don't think so.'

'For making a plan to kill Mr Thompson.'

'Not if you didn't carry out your plan. Why didn't you tell somebody what Mr Thompson was doing to you?'

'Then he wouldn't have let me be in his productions and later, when I leave school, he promised he'd write to all his London theatre friends about me. He doesn't have any, does he?' At last, Robin began to cry.

Mitchell was aware of Dr Grainger's quiet sigh of relief. Since the boy's medical adviser made no move either to console his patient or to postpone the rest of the interview, he decided to continue his questions, though with some misgivings. He was a policeman but a father too, of four children. How could he balance the relative importance of the mental health of a vulnerable and much-wronged adolescent and the potential danger of a perverted maniac in possession of a Glock?

'Don't worry. From what I hear, you might well get to the RSC without anybody's help.' Mitchell was proud of that reply. He'd heard Ginny speak reverently of the RSC, though he wasn't exactly sure what the initials stood for. The lad seemed comforted by this thought but he had to move on. 'Robin, we need to know who else besides you knew where the gun was. It was Friday morning when you buried it, right? At about nine o'clock?'

Robin scrubbed his face with the back of his hand and Dr Grainger passed him a box of tissues. 'No. A bit later.

My mum and Lucille were coming down at nine. Mum needed her skirt letting out a bit. The baby was getting squashed in it and Luce was going to fix it. I waited in the grounds of the library and watched until I'd seen them go.'

'So you knew you had the place to yourself?'

The boy's lip quivered. 'I think so. Mr Thompson was likely to be about later on but not usually so early. I always try to watch out so I can keep out of his way but I didn't see him on Friday morning. No one else would be there unless they'd been called.'

That didn't mean Thompson had not seen Robin. Now that they had him safely in a cell on a charge that they could prove, though, they could put him in a line-up and let Clement's Mr Jessop pick him out. Mitchell thought the boy had now told as much as he knew. Certainly, he had answered as many questions as he could cope with for the time being. He would go back to the station and see whether his father-in-law's witnesses had recognized Hopper's pictures and identified Tim Ellis's killer.

Re-entering the station, Mitchell had no need to ask his question. As he approached the desk in the foyer, Magic gave him a shake of the head and a 'Nothing yet'. It was possible, of course, that Superintendent Carroll would have some information that had bypassed Magic but news, good or bad, seemed to reach the laconic sergeant by osmosis and Mitchell had little hope that a trip up to his office would offer anything further.

He did, however, find Jennifer in his office, her action sheet completed, smugly drinking his coffee. She reached for a cup and poured for him as he came in. She wanted to know, 'How long before we have a go at Thompson? Or do we call him Mostyn now?'

Mitchell disposed of half the contents of his cup in a gulp, then answered the questions in order. 'He's safely stowed. I think we'll leave him for as long as the rules allow. The angrier and more worried he is when we talk to him, the better.'

'We can get on with the sex abuse charge, can't we? There's no way he can wriggle out of that.'

'Isn't there? We've Robin's word and that's about it. The defence can point out how he loves melodrama and how unsettled his family life has been. I'm not sure what medical evidence there'll be. I don't know exactly what form the abuse has taken or how much evidence a physical examination will reveal. It's a week since the bugger had a chance to touch him – and I'm not swearing. I speak advisedly whether I can prove it or not.'

'I don't see what we gain by waiting. The evidence is just getting older.'

'I didn't say we aren't collecting evidence yet – but we're convinced of his guilt because of his previous convictions. The jury won't be. I don't suppose any of the members will have heard of something that happened in York twenty years ago under another name . . .'

'Can he insist on his new choice of name being used this time?'

Mitchell beamed. 'I'm glad you've found yourself something to do this afternoon. I was wondering how to amuse you. To be serious, he might get angry enough to accuse us of raking up his past that he's already paid for. Then it would become part of the evidence for this case. I think the CPS might accept the abuse case, but I'm not sure we have much that will pin the shooting on him to a judge's satisfaction.'

'What about the handyman who heard Paul Ridgeway threaten him?'

'It's only supposition that it was Thompson he was talking to. We've got to try to prove it was him who found the buried gun. Can you set up an ID parade for Adrian's old chap in the flats? You can manage two jobs in one afternoon?'

Jennifer cast up her eyes, then helped herself to more coffee.

When lessons at Heath Lees School finished for the day, there was the usual hurly-burly as its pupils made their getaway. Declan Mitchell and his friend Janil Iqbal were overtaken by almost all of them since the weight, and the considerable bulk, of a glockenspiel in its case hampered Declan's usual stride. He had brought the instrument to school against his parents' advice, though not without their reluctant permission. They had warned him that neither of them would be free to give him a lift home at four o'clock. Declan's arms were aching by the time he and Janil reached the end of the school drive and, though the remaining distance he had to walk to his home was short, he was wishing already that wiser counsel had prevailed. He was delighted, therefore, when the driver of the silver grey car parked by the kerb tooted at them and they recognized Janil's brother Youssef.

Janil, astonished, demanded, 'Have you bought it?'

Declan, hopeful now that his problem looked like being solved, grinned to himself as he noticed the car's registration plate. Its letters, appropriately, were GLO though without a CK after the numbers.

Youssef answered his brother. 'What with, for goodness' sake? I'm a student, in case you'd forgotten. I'm just doing a job for a mate because he's got an interview for a job. He's not back till late tonight so until tomorrow morning I've got wheels. Get a move on, the pair of you. Declan, give that thing to me. Whatever it is it'd better go in the front seat and you two in the back. The boot's full.'

Declan opened his mouth to give a polite explanation but Youssef, unusually chatty, didn't wait for it. 'I'll take you and your baggage home as my apology.'

'What for?'

'Teaching Jan the tricks he tried on you in the chess match.'

'So that's how he beat me so quickly.' He frowned as the car turned right at a T-junction. 'We should have turned left there for my house.'

'I'm taking Janil first. Mum's wanting him. Something about your piano lesson being changed to tonight.'

Janil was dismayed. 'I've not got my piece ready yet. I should have had all weekend for it.'

Declan understood his friend's agitation. He would never have dared to go to Mr Jackson unprepared for his own lesson. As the car drew up at the Iqbals' house, Janil scrambled out hastily and Youssef drove away with equal haste. His chatty mood seemed suddenly to have passed. Declan knew that it was good manners for a passenger to make polite conversation with his driver. Timidly, he began trying to explain the coincidence of the car's registration and the instrument that was being transported on its front seat. As Youssef understood the significance of what he was saying, he swore furiously and drove faster.

Declan, who was a policeman's son, realized the futility of saying, 'This is not the way to my house.'

Chapter Twelve

It was well past mid-afternoon when Mitchell arrived back from the hospital to the station. As he crossed the foyer, Magic, at reception, raised a beckoning finger. Mitchell made a detour towards him and was rewarded with four words, 'Note on your desk.' A request for more details produced three more words. 'From Sergeant Taylor.'

Giving up on Magic, Mitchell ran up the stairs to his office where he found his hopes confirmed. Jennifer's scribbled message was less terse than Magic's verbal one. *Cautious man, your father-in-law. He says, on the strength of a 'Could be,' an 'Almost sure,' and a triumphant, 'That's the bugger,' he's now asking us to bring Youssef Iqbal in, on his authority, as a favour. We're to hold him till someone from the Met arrives to remove him. He says we're to remember, when we go in, that Iqbal senior – the father – has the mentality of a six-year-old in most respects. Page me when you're back.* Mitchell smiled to himself. He supposed Jennifer had a right to be in at the kill. She answered his call at the first ring and presented herself only a minute later.

She had more news that he had been hoping for. Clement's Mr Jessop had picked out Thompson from a line-up they had collected. 'It wasn't easy finding people tall enough. We borrowed the long skinny librarian that Lucy always insists on going to – to have her books stamped. He was her suggestion, so she's waiting for your fulsome thanks for helping your investigation.'

'Maybe she'd like to go and bring Iqbal in for us too.'

'Doubtless she would, but let's get back to reality. Which of us are going?'

Knowing that she would be disappointed, he told her, 'Clement and Beardsmore. Adrian needs me to make him feel valued, at least until he's got a few sergeant's applications off . . .'

'You don't feel you should include me, to encourage me to apply for DI?'

Mitchell shook his head. 'Too selfish. I want to keep you. Anyway, it's neither lack of confidence nor lack of experience that's holding you back – and you've passed the exams. I can't change your family circumstances for you.'

'I know. So, what am I going to do for the rest of the day?'

'You can take tea to Interview 4 where you'll find Thompson being guarded by Jamieson.' Seeing Jennifer's face, he added, 'I mean it. He knows you're my sergeant. He'll expect a going-over and he'll get a smile and a cuppa. When we've got him angry, puzzled and wondering what further evidence we're waiting for before we attack, we'll see what he has to say.'

'We haven't got any evidence to wait for.'

'You can make it a very nice smile but you can't comfort him with our lack of evidence. When I've been upstairs to get our Great White Chief's permission, we'll –'

'You mean when you issue a five minute warning of what you intend to do!'

'Whatever. Itemizer can find explosives as well as narcotics so we're hoping his clothes are going to help us, including the academic gown that he grabbed to cover any visible traces of cordite on the strange garment he wore last Friday night. We've no reason to believe he has any drug connection but we might even find we can add that charge against him as well if the magic machine comes up with something unexpected.'

'Right. So, what do I do when I've finished being a waitress?'

221

'Then you'll be very gracious and invite Adrian and Bob Beardsmore to my office – in fact, do that first. After that you can do your own thing but don't leave the building without telling me and don't switch your phone off. We don't know how things are going to turn out tonight so we've got to be ready for anything. By the way, if Thompson gives you a tip, you can keep it.'

'You're too kind.' Jennifer gave him a sweet smile and left him.

Clement arrived in short time at the DCI's office followed by a smug-looking PC Beardsmore who was obviously aware of the purpose of the summons. Mitchell repeated the warning against alarming Youssef's handicapped father. 'Go easy on the mother too. She might believe the whole story about Cairo university – could have embroidered it in her imagination and made him student of the year. Watch out for the young lad. He's only thirteen and, according to Shakila, he thinks the sun shines out of his big brother.'

The telephone rang. Since Mitchell was scrabbling in a drawer, and continued to do so, Clement picked it up and gave his name. He looked startled when he heard the voice. 'It's your wife, sir.'

Mitchell was alarmed. Ginny never ever rang him at work. He grabbed the handset from Clement and barked into it. 'What's up?'

'Benny! Declan hasn't come home from school. It's an hour and a half past his usual time. I rang his headmaster and then round his friends, though I know he'd have rung if he wanted to go off with one of them. When I tried Janil, the boy answered. He said Declan should have been home ages ago. Youssef gave him a lift because he saw him struggling with the glock. They're worried too. They haven't seen Youssef since he tipped Janil out of the car with some story about an altered music lesson. His mother's rung the hospital, just the local one, but they haven't got either of them. I suppose the car's stolen. Apparently Youssef doesn't have one. Never mind that. I'll clear the line. You find Declan.'

At first, Declan had tried to keep track of where Youssef was heading but the car changed direction so suddenly and so often that he had soon given up. His watch told him that the time was approaching six but the gathering cloud cover made it seem later and the combination of speed and bad light made it impossible for him to read signposts.

Through the window, he could see that the road they were on now was narrow, winding its way across moorland. They had passed no particular landmark that he recognized, but he thought this might be the same area they crossed when the family visited his Aunt Siobhan in Manchester.

Suddenly the car swerved left, taking a dive on to a grassy lay-by that had appeared out of nowhere. Youssef jumped on the brakes, stopping just before the grass petered out and the wheels got wedged in tangled clumps of heather roots. The car threw both its occupants forward and rocked for some moments before it was still. Declan steeled himself as Youssef swivelled round to speak to him. 'Right, Declan. Give me the gun and then I'll take you on to the station in Manchester where you can catch a bus home.'

Youssef sounded calm and reasonable. How was he to keep him like that? Trying to seem equally practical and cool, Declan said, 'I haven't any money for the fare, not here with me now, anyway.'

Youssef had a smile on his face but it was not friendly. 'I'm sure, if you explain your circumstances, someone will help you out and your parents can settle up later.'

'I haven't got a gun either.'

223

The smile disappeared. 'The longer you mess me about, the darker it will be when you're travelling home. I know perfectly well that you have it with you. You and Janil spoke on the phone on Sunday. I don't know where it's been since then. Maybe you shot Robin's father with it, but it's not my job to give clues to the police – at least not if you're co-operative.'

'But it's not –'

'Janil told me you were taking the Glock to school today . . .' Youssef's eyes narrowed. 'You're not telling me one of the teachers saw it and took it? No, they wouldn't have let you out of school without sending for your parents or the police if they thought you were mixed up in . . .'

An idea had struck Declan, and, before he could stop himself, he said, accusingly, 'You're the man my grandad in London's looking for, aren't you?'

'What!'

Declan closed his eyes. What had he done? 'It doesn't matter.'

Youssef seemed impatient rather than angry. 'Just give me the gun. Where is it? It's too big to be in your pocket.'

Light dawned on Declan. He wanted to laugh but knew he mustn't. 'The glock? It's in there. It's a musical instrument. That's what Janil and me were talking about. I know it's the name of a gun as well because my dad brought a film about it home from the police station.'

'Your dad's a copper?'

'Yes. So's my grandad in London.'

There was a silence. Declan knew Youssef was assimilating this information, revising his plans. He wondered if his family were going to be his salvation or the reason that his captor was now planning to kill him. Both occupants of the car were thinking furiously. Declan knew the doors were locked. He wasn't sure of the make of the car but it was new and upmarket and would certainly have central locking. He had tried to open the door already when the car stopped in a queue of traffic on the outskirts of the town. Youssef had made no protest, obviously knowing that he couldn't escape.

Youssef came to a conclusion first. He released the locks and, without turning, ordered, 'Get out!'

Declan hesitated. Did Youssef have any other guns? Was he going to be shot? Or abandoned here? That would be better, but it was not a welcome thought. A glance out of the window showed him a line of pylons marching across the moor, still discernible across the sky, but they wouldn't be for much longer. His phone was in his pocket but there was no point in getting it out, only to have it taken from him. He knew it was forty-eight hours since he had charged it. Would it still have enough juice to ring home? He tried to remember how many calls he had made with it in the last two days. It used up the battery just being on.

He realized that he had thought about things for too long. Youssef leapt out of the car, leaving his door open, and came round to open his own. Grasping him by the nearest arm and the scruff of his neck, he flung him to the ground. Amazed at his own cool reasoning, Declan decided that there probably was no other gun. A kicking, then. Youssef however had gone round the front of the car again. Had he gone for some other weapon? The roar of the engine made him start up. Exhaust fumes choked him, then the rear lights of the car grew smaller and disappeared into the distance. With a roar of rage rather than fear, Declan realized that the glockenspiel had gone with him.

Mitchell sat at the desk in his office, glowering at the skin that had formed over the coffee Jennifer had brought him but seeing only the frightened face of his son.

When the telephone rang, he snatched up the receiver. Let this be one of his searching officers with the news that Declan was safely found and on his way home. Let it even be Youssef Iqbal, ready to do a deal that would satisfy him sufficiently to let Declan go . . .

What he heard was, 'Dad?'

For a moment, he felt the room spin round him. His son said no more, waiting for an acknowledgement. He managed, 'Yes, it's me. Where are –'

'Dad, I know you're angry because I got into a car with somebody I didn't really know . . .'

Angry? How could he ever be angry with Declan again? 'Never mind that now. Is Youssef with you? Did he make you ring? Did he tell you what to say? Where are you? Is he listening?'

'No. Calm down.'

It occurred to Mitchell that the two of them had had this conversation before but their roles had been reversed. He began to pull himself together. 'Declan, tell me –'

'Dad, my phone hasn't got much juice. Let me talk. When Youssef found out that you and Grandad were policemen, he pulled me out of the car and drove off fast. He thought I had his gun because he'd heard me talking about the glock. His tyres squealed. I was hoping he'd have a puncture –'

'Where are you?'

'I don't know exactly, but it looks like the moor we cross when we go to Manchester. I'm by the side of the road and there are pylons and lots of heather.'

The boy's tone changed from efficient to rueful. 'That doesn't help much, does it?'

'Look all around you. Can you see a building, a TV mast, anything we could look for? Have you got anything to wave if we put a helicopter up?'

'I've nothing to wave. My blazer's too dark to see. The light's going so that the pylons look like buildings . . . Dad! I can't see a building but there's lights, where the road reaches the top of the hill. Cars look as if they're coming, then they turn off, quite a few of them all in the same place. I think it might be a pub.'

'Good thinking, Declan. Anything else?'

'In the car lights, I keep seeing something red, sort of blowing about . . .'

Mitchell felt a stab of excitement, almost hope. 'Declan, could it possibly be a big flag?'

'Yes! Yes, I think that's what it is.'

'I've got it. Go there and wait . . .'

'Dad!' Now Declan's voice was a wail as a disastrous aspect of his predicament came to mind. 'Youssef's taken Mr Jackson's glock with him . . .' The boy's phone cut out.

Atmospherics? Battery? Mitchell rang Declan's number with no result. Quickly working out the order of urgency, he dialled first a number he had previously used on much pleasanter occasions. He was glad that it was the landlord himself who announced, 'The Moorlands Hotel.' He identified himself and cut through effusive greetings. 'Sorry to cut you off but I need your help. My lad – he's twelve, name's Declan – is stranded, I'd guess about half a mile down the road towards Cloughton. Dressed in school uniform, tall for twelve, dark hair. Could you –?'

'Say no more. I'll go get him myself this minute.'

'No, wait. He'll be walking towards you. Give him a message from me so that he'll know you're kosher. Tell him I'll fix things with Mr Jackson about the glock. Thanks. I owe you.'

Keeping the handset in his hand, he continued to make calls that were necessary before he could leave the station.

'Ginny? We've located him – or rather, he's contacted us. He's stranded on the roadside near the Moorlands pub. Ben Miller, bless him, has gone out to collect. I'll go myself in a few minutes. I'm sending Jen to stay with you.'

Ignoring protests that this was unnecessary, he cut the call and dialled again. 'Jen, we've found him. I'm leaving to pick him up in a minute.' He had no need to make his request. 'Yes, of course. I told her you'd be coming.'

'Magic, can you get me a car with driver outside on the road in four minutes . . . Good man.'

'Shakila? Where the hell are you? And, what's more to the point, where's Youssef Iqbal? . . . Well, you might be interested to know that for his harmless joyride, he took Declan for company . . . Yes, we know where he is now and I'm almost sure he's safe, no thanks to you. Where's Adrian? . . . All right, I can see how it happened. When I've got Declan back I'll hear all about it. Keep your phone on.'

'Adrian? . . . Yes, Shakila's explained. Pick up Beardsmore and Caroline and get yourselves to the Iqbal house. Take it to bits, but remember the fragile father – and that Janil's only thirteen. Stay in touch.'

Mitchell glanced at his watch, then dived down the stairs to the foyer and into the waiting car. Having instructed his driver to put his foot down but not to use his siren, he settled to more invective and instructions to his various subordinates. After a few moments, he decided he had been rather hard on Shakila. He punched her number again and, this time, listened to her side of the story. Then they spoke simultaneously. 'I think you'd better . . .'/ 'Would it be useful if I . . .?'

He saw that their vehicle was entering the Moorlands' car park. It had been spotted. Mr Miller and Declan appeared in the doorway, lit from behind. Relief at the sight of his son made him light-headed. 'I've things to do, and, as your best efforts always go into the plans you've initiated yourself, I'll let you tell me what you think might be useful.' Declan was running towards the car. 'No, don't tell me. Just get on with it. If it doesn't work . . .'

'Understood, sir.' He could hear her grinning.

Nigel Turner could not bring himself to settle to any of his planned activities. His mind whirled around the facts that had met him on his return to Cloughton – Paul's dreadful death, the idea that that precocious but likeable child was being horrifically abused by the best producer the company had ever engaged, that somewhere a youth

228

was running loose who had killed a computer salesman and shot a policeman.

Was this the sleepy, shabby-but-pretty, hill-encircled Cloughton that he'd left just over two weeks ago? He sold PCs himself, but, before thinking about that, he had another week of his annual leave to use up. He had planned to repaint the walls of his downstairs rooms but choosing and buying the paint and prettying up the house seemed irrelevant to the situation he had come back to. Since, for several of the actors, the drama company provided their main, though inadequate, income, it would be more fitting to do something for them. He would go into the garage and sort the props that Liam had collected for him at some point since that fateful Friday performance.

Still methodical, despite the shocks he had suffered, he grabbed his to-do book. There were lists to make of broken things to be mended, lost things to look for – if they were allowed back into the building yet – and objects borrowed from individuals for this particular production to be returned. Liam couldn't have done that, not being familiar with which properties the company owned, and only Stephen knew who had lent what. He certainly wasn't going to speak to Stephen, but he could put separately all the things that he didn't recognize.

Liam had done a good job, nicely filling the big canvas bags but not to the point where something might fall out. A bit slow he might be, but the last person in the company to call Liam 'daft' had felt Nigel's hand on his cheek and, for a time, it had left the marks to prove it.

He worked for half an hour, putting cloths and drapes to be washed, wrapping crockery, glassware and ornaments in newspaper and placing them in labelled drawers. The 1940s telephone was looking a bit the worse for wear and he put it aside to consider. It wouldn't be easy to spruce that up. A chocolate box nestled invitingly at the bottom of the first bag. He went to look inside, but not hopefully. The cast would have shared them or Liam might have thought them a fair reward for his labours. To his surprise, only two or three chocolates were missing. Nigel chewed happily for a minute, then he remembered what had distracted the others from them and was chastened.

He turned to delve into the second bag and his hand closed on something he didn't recognize. He lifted it out carefully and his heart began to beat faster. He placed the object carefully on a small table and felt in his pocket for his phone.

Mitchell had called his team together at an unprecedented seven o'clock. Understanding the reason, no one complained. His exhaustion too was unprecedented and he knew he would have to concentrate hard on talking sense. His heart had always gone out to the parents of missing children but he would understand them better in future – and some of them had far more to bear. His own son was now safely at home, uninjured. Incredibly, considering his sensitive nature and his history of nightmares, he seemed not to be traumatized and had dealt with his ordeal with cool practicality. Perhaps the counter-irritation of having lost his beloved glock had protected him from fears for his own safety.

He tuned in to his surroundings and discovered that, without his leading, his team was trying to assess the weight of evidence against Stephen Thompson. Jennifer had the floor. '... and the IT forensics folk seem to have found enough stuff on his computer to get him convicted of child abuse. Some nasty pictures featuring Robin, so we might be able to spare him a court appearance. Margot is looking for any clothes of Robin's that might have useful traces. Robin, incidentally, is at home helping her. He says he got through his ordeals by pretending it was all in a play.'

'Hm, pretty nasty play,' Caroline commented. She glanced at Mitchell. 'Report came in whilst you were getting drunk at the Moorlands.'

Mitchell managed a grin. 'I feel drunk but no alcohol was asked for or offered.'

Jennifer continued her peroration. 'We're on thin ice with a murder charge, though –'

Clement interrupted. 'What are we doing now to find the gun?'

Mitchell held up his hands. 'What's left to do besides search again where we've looked already and pray?'

'That'll look good on our action sheets.'

Jennifer silenced Clement with a glare and asked, 'How much use is Mr Jessop's recognition of Thompson from the line-up? He saw him watching Robin bury the gun but it was from a steep angle.'

'Can an angle be steep?' This time Clement took cover from Jennifer's expression.'

Caroline suggested, 'We could run a parallel experiment. Get him to look at someone else from the same positions.'

The door had opened to admit Superintendent Carroll. 'Spending my money again?'

For once, Mitchell could not find the energy to rise to the challenge. The greater part of his day had not been more demanding than usual. The trouble had been in the eternity that had passed between being told that his son was being driven by a mad gunman and then that he was safe at the Moorlands hotel.

Caroline came to his assistance, her tone quite tart. 'We'll volunteer, as we have done before.'

Remembering what she had volunteered for in the past and seeing the scarred face that was her only reward, the superintendent was abashed. 'I'll search my pockets for you,' he promised. He turned to Mitchell. 'I presume we've put out a call for the car Iqbal stole, with the details Declan's given us.' Mitchell nodded. 'What have we found in Thompson's flat?'

'Nothing yet. We can't do our search till the SOCOs have finished – that includes the IT people. They've apparently struck gold, but as I've been otherwise occupied for the last few hours, my team are the only ones who're up to date with the file.'

'What if we do find cordite on Thompson's clothes?' Clement suddenly demanded. 'Will it be proof, or will he be able to say he brushed against the gun backstage, after it was used?'

'It would be difficult then to stick to his story that he never saw it.'

'Maybe he didn't see it. The light backstage was feeble.'

The telephone interrupted and prevented a pointless argument. Mitchell identified himself, listened and suddenly became his usual perky self. 'Someone called Nigel Turner,' he announced portentously. There followed a pregnant silence worthy of Robin Ridgeway before he continued, 'Seems he's found a gun.' When the exclamations had died, he added, 'Afraid it leaves us with egg on our faces. We never thought about the props man and all his gubbins.'

Nigel Turner was waiting in his house for Mitchell to arrive and be shown the weapon. Maybe he should have brought it into the house with him but he had decided that the less he handled it the better.

He had been quite anxious to do his part and help the police until the idea had occurred to him. Now he wished that he'd thought longer before making his call. Could Liam possibly – not deliberately, of course – but might he have . . . not knowing that Paul was outside . . . not knowing that the gun was real? He couldn't form the question, even to ask it of himself. Why ever hadn't he waited, spoken to the lad when he got home from his day centre? Now, he'd probably arrive in the middle of this policeman's visit and be frightened.

Through the window, a movement caught his attention. A car – not a squad car, but he was sure this man was a copper – of the old type too, though he looked a bit young for his short back and sides. He was a beefy bloke, looked like a rugby player. Tackling him would be like running into a brick wall. As he went to the door to let DCI Mitchell in, he panicked. Could he explain things without mentioning Liam? No. If he didn't, someone else would. Stephen Thompson might even try to put all the blame on him because that would reflect least badly on the company. He could say that he didn't know what he was doing, couldn't help it. As if!

The killing must have been an accident on someone's part. Surely no one wanted to harm Paul. And what was a real gun doing in a theatre anyway? He opened the door and his heart sank. Liam was, right now, lumbering towards the gate in Mitchell's wake. He let both of them in and made a sudden decision. Mitchell looked like a family man and someone who'd get to the bottom of things. He would explain to him exactly what he was afraid of and let the professionals sort everything out.

The three of them sat in the front room and Mitchell listened without interrupting until Nigel had finished his story. Then he smiled and introduced himself to Liam – not as a DCI but as Benny Mitchell who had four children at home. Nigel was not surprised and felt confident that Liam was in safe hands.

'What I suggest, Mr Turner, as Liam was the one who was there and who dealt with the props, that we let him tell us what happened. I'm sure he's of age, but, in view of his problems, I'm going to treat him as a minor and ask you to sit in with us and tell me if you think he's getting upset.' By now, Mitchell was Nigel's man. Why weren't all coppers like this? He confined himself, however, to just a nod of agreement. The police had no time to waste.

Liam eyed Mitchell with curiosity but no alarm. Mitchell looked back at him solemnly, then dropped his left eyelid. Liam, delighted, did the same. He was proud of his winking. Having caught the young man's attention, Mitchell told him, 'Your dad and me need your help, Liam. It's about the props. You offered to collect them so that your dad could take your gran to France. If you hadn't helped, your gran would have missed her holiday, wouldn't she?' Liam acknowledged his own generosity. 'Now there's been a slip-up though. There's something in one of the bags that shouldn't be there. It shouldn't have been in the theatre at all. We're pleased that you put it in the bag because we didn't know where it had got to.

'We don't know who the owner is, so we can't give it back. Could you answer some questions to help us find him?' Another nod. 'Right. First question. When did you start collecting all the things and putting them in the bags?'

'Same as Dad. Soon as curtains come down, before all things get moved and lost.'

'Good answer. Next one's a bit harder. Ready?' Liam smirked and nodded again. 'Was the gun onstage when you went to clear up?'

'Yes.'

'Can you remember where?'

'Is it question three or is it still two?'

'It's still two. You get an extra mark for it.'

'Well, it was on table – big table with pots on for teatime.'

'Just lying on top? – er, still question two.'

'Hiding under a pinny.'

'Covered up with the pinafore that Mrs Ridgeway had been wearing?'

'Yes.'

'Did anyone come and watch you working onstage?'

'Not all the time.'

'Who came for a little while?'

'Mr Thompson. He said to be sure to pack everything. I knew that already because Dad said.'

'How did Mr Thompson look?'

'Same as always.'

'Was there anything at all that was different about him? What was he doing?'

'He'd got funny see-through gloves. He were busy taking 'em off. Told me to put them in outside bin.'

'And did you?'

For the first time, Liam looked defiant. 'I might not have done.'

'OK. You don't have to do what he says.'

'I didn't because I'm scared of dark.'

'So is my boy. Did you tell Mr Thompson you were scared to do as he said?'

Liam shook his head. 'I only tell kind people. Others laugh. What question are we on?'

'That was the last one and you got full marks. Oh, no, I've just thought of one more. What *did* you do with the see-through gloves?'

'Put 'em in my coat pocket.'

'Are they still there?' He nodded. 'Could I take them with me?'

'I don't think he wants 'em.'

'No, but I do.'

The next morning, Mitchell was at his desk early, alert and refreshed. Both he and Virginia had expected their elder son to cause them a very disturbed night but the whole family had slept soundly until their usual time. He was undismayed by the litter of papers on his desk. It represented a mass of evidence pointing to Youssef Iqbal's responsibility for Timothy Ellis's death, PC Buchan's injuries and Declan's abduction. A nationwide alert was being kept for the villain and the car he had stolen.

Late the previous night, the Iqbal family had been questioned both separately and together, first by Shakila whom they knew and then by Mitchell himself. Both officers were convinced that the family's astonishment at Youssef's duplicity was not assumed and that their dismay and bewilderment were genuine. The Egyptian authorities had provided evidence of killings in the Middle East in which Youssef had been involved.

The search of the Iqbals' house had revealed a torch which had almost certainly been the one that featured in the Brick Lane videos. Minute traces of blood had caused momentary excitement but had proved not to be Buchan's. A broken hair, however, caught in the switch, was the right colour and texture and would hopefully prove to be of use to them.

A box of photographs, found in a sideboard, poignantly illustrated what had motivated Youssef's metamorphosis from model school pupil to murdering terrorist. Some showed his father attending formal dinners of the company in which hard work had brought him a prominent position. The handsome man to whom other men were obviously deferring had little connection with the bemused shambling creature, still aged only forty-nine but looking seventy, whom they had tried to question last night.

With two arrests in sight, Mitchell hoped that Superintendent Carroll would not jib at the cost of the forensic tests which his DCI had authorized without his permission. If not, he would have two superintendents after his blood. His father-in-law was by no means pleased that, after being on the point of handing him his killer, Mitchell's team had lost him.

He shared all this information with his team and for some minutes the five detectives discussed their options and tried to decide what the best next move should be. Two telephone calls were to interrupt them before the briefing finished. The first brought more news from the forensic lab. The rubber gloves recovered from Liam Turner's coat pocket had had a usefully abrasive outer surface which still held traces of cordite. The smooth inner side had revealed a smear of blood in the left-hand thumb. The left glove also had a right-hand thumbprint, obviously made when the wearer pulled it off. Faint traces of cordite had also been found on the cuffs of the smock top that

Thompson had been wearing on the night of the shooting, even though it had been washed.

Mitchell beamed and felt as though Christmas had come early. When the phone rang again a minute later, he reached for it, remarking to whoever was listening, 'The stocking's not empty yet.' After a minute, his team read in his face that he was not listening to yet more clinching evidence. After identifying himself, he was silent for several minutes, eyes narrowed, mouth tight. When he had offered thanks and replaced the receiver, his body slumped and he shook his head. 'I reckon the case is closed,' he told them as they stared at him.

'Which one?' The demand was, of course, Shakila's.

'The London one. That was a detective superintendent from Charles Street in Leicester. They've found the car, and young Iqbal's body. He drove into Abbey Park, across the grass, and, presumably deliberately, straight into a tree. The weather was awful there last night so no one was loitering and no one noticed it till this morning. Apparently, they can't extricate the body from bits of the bloody glockenspiel. It's probably literally bloody . . . Don't anyone tell Declan that!'

He closed his eyes suddenly and stopped speaking. His team watched him realize that Declan could so easily have still been in the car and waited for him to pull himself together.

After a few moments, Shakila asked, 'Could I do the ID? I've known Youssef a good while and it would be better than someone from the family having to do it.'

Mitchell nodded. 'If they're agreeable, I'll support that suggestion – but his mother might feel she should do it herself. Before we make any more plans, I'd better make sure that the super's in the picture. Then I'll have to steel myself to tell Tom that he won't be able to bring his last villain to justice. I'm not sure that I can take an ear-bashing right now.'

237

Ear-bashing was not what he received. Browne was too thankful for his elder grandson's escape to be very concerned with anything else. He had had some sympathy with his villain throughout the case. 'He was born not to be happy, Benny. In his place, I'd have been just as angry as he was. If I was only nineteen or twenty, I might have expressed that anger in just as wild a fashion. I hope, in his Muslim heaven, there'll be some allowance made for his justified outrage on his father's account. I wouldn't like to think of him rotting mentally and physically in prison. And, this way, there's more sympathy and less shame for his family.'

Mitchell thought about all this, was nearly convinced. He opened his mouth to say so, but what came out was, 'Tom, he killed a brave civilian and shot a copper.'

Epilogue

Declan Mitchell was worried when Cavill's insurance company was less than prompt in replacing the shattered glockenspiel. However another instrument had been loaned by one of Cavill's friends in the Hallé orchestra and Declan had found it suitable. With a week to spare before the concert, he had practised assiduously and was now ready to perform.

He was not in the least nervous, except about the short lecture he had secretly prepared to introduce his piece. As he launched himself into it, it came less as a surprise, more as a shock. His parents in the audience were aghast. They never doubted that he would get his facts right. They suspected rightly, though, that no one in the audience, including themselves, would understand it and that their son's 'little introduction' would be longer than the piece of music he was to play.

Declan continued unabashed. 'Glockenspiels are still quite popular and appear in almost all genres of music, ranging from hip-hop to jazz ...' He looked up, slightly worried. 'I'm afraid I don't know exactly what hip-hop is.'

There was a ripple of laughter. In desperation, Mitchell began to applaud as though his son had meant to finish with this little joke. Cavill used the interruption to play the first chords of his piano accompaniment and Declan was obliged to pick up his hammers and begin to play.

His parents heaved a sigh of relief. They were well pleased with their eldest. After his ordeal in the stolen car with Youssef Iqbal, they had expected a major recurrence of his earlier nervous troubles. There had been none. Declan had explained. 'I thought I was the sort of person who wouldn't know what to do in a crisis, so everything worried me. Then one happened to me and I did know what to do – and you said you were proud of me.'

He had slain his own demons and they were very proud of him indeed.

David Page was trying hard to convince himself that Margot's defection had overwhelmed him with grief. He refused to listen to the small voice in his head that told him to be thankful for his release from a hasty and careless commitment. Margot had hinted recently that her soon-to-be-born child could possibly be Paul's. He would not admit to himself yet his hope that this baby girl would resemble Paul closely so that he could be free from the whole situation.

Chief Superintendent Browne wondered how long the detailed arrangement of his new flat would keep him busy once he was free from his police responsibilities. He must search hard, he told himself, to find some pastime that would keep him from interfering in his son-in-law's cases.

Janil Iqbal was making plans to talk to Shakila about how to become the man of the house in his brother's place.

Derek Kingsley began again his faithful weekly trips to Armley jail. No one, he had decided, was irredeemable.